A HUNGA

DEATH
OF A
FOREST FAIRY

JULIA BUCKLEY

"I myself am a little scared
of the old women. I am convinced
they can see into my soul."

--Theodora Goss, "Old Hungarian Women"

For Lauren and Lisa
Readers, friends, and family

Chapter One

Entering the Fairy Wood

It had been a warm winter, and now it was a cold spring. I sat huddled inside my fleece, leaning on the warmth of Erik Wolf, who sat stoically beside me, looking not cold at all. We were perched on stone bleachers that curved into a crescent around an outdoor "stage" of flattened grass that led to a wide path into the woods. Riverwood nurtured the Arts, and we had seen various Shakespeare-in-the-park productions out here, along with some musicals and ambitious dramas.

My brother Domo, on the bleacher in front of me with his fiancée Margie, turned an impatient face toward me. "When does it start, Hana? I'm getting hungry."

Even knowing that my brother was a bottomless food pit, I was surprised. "Grandma just fed you a ton of food."

He shrugged and waved a hand that rendered me irrelevant. "Anyway. I should have brought some of her kiflis with me."

I sighed and looked to my left, where my grandmother had disappeared inside a parka and a wide pink scarf. Her eyes flicked to me, and she said something unintelligible into the wool. It could have been Hungarian or English—either way it was gobbledygook. "What, Grandma?" I leaned toward her.

She lifted a gloved hand and pulled down an inch of scarf. "Tell your brother I have food in my purse, and Pálinka to warm us."

"Of course you do." Grandma never went far without a bottle of Pálinka, a Hungarian fruit brandy that could sear the throats of the uninitiated, but which she believed could cure all ills, including cold. I relayed her message, and in moments Domo's mouth was full of an apricot kifli (I had snagged the last two raspberry ones for Erik and me) and he was pouring shots of Pálinka into tiny paper containers that looked like dentists' rinse cups.

Erik whispered in my ear, distracting me from my brother's greed. "When in Hungary," he murmured, and took a sip of the Pálinka that Domo handed him.

"We're not in Hungary. We're just at a Hungarian show, produced by Hungarians." In fact, the event we waited to observe had been put together by my friend Henrik, from the Riverwood Chamber of Commerce, and his Hungarian-American group. The concept had been captivating enough to draw my grandma out into the raw March air. Titled "Enter the Fairy Wood," it was billed as "a celebration of Hungarian culture and history via its legends and fairy tales." Essentially, Henrik had told me when he handed me the pamphlet at the grocery store (where I'd found him buying extra-strong paprika and, unrelatedly, Hostess cupcakes), the event would present a series of tableaus, splendid visuals that would celebrate well-known fairy tales.

I'd liked this idea, as had my family, and now here we were, cold and huddled and sipping smuggled Pálinka while we waited for the start time, which had been listed in the program as "dusk." It occurred to me that we would see the visuals better in bright sun, but when twilight came, and the show finally began, I understood: they would provide a different sort of illumination.

The actors began lining up at the edge of the woods, and we clapped in anticipation. I snuggled against Erik, already slightly tipsy, and his arm tightened around me. I lifted my face to his, demanding a kiss without speaking, and he obliged. His mouth was warm . . . .

"The show's down here," said Domo with his mouth full, smirking at us.

"Then why are you turned around?" I whispered. But it did seem the show was about to begin. The crowd rustled with anticipation. Some children ran back from a visit to the public bathroom. A blonde woman on the first bleacher got up and began walking toward the parking lot.

"Was it something we said?" Domo asked, smirking again. I needed to talk with him about his smirking and its high percentage rate within the various expressions he wore.

"She's probably going to get her coat," Margie said, receding inside her pink jacket. "It's wintry out here."

"Not enough brandy," Domo said, and he leaned in front of my grandparents to root around in my grandma's bag; my grandfather poked his arm, saying, *"Apád nem volt üveges!"* Then he and my grandmother chuckled while Domo squinted at them.

My mother, half laughing, said, "He's saying you're in the way, Domo. It means 'Your father wasn't a glassmaker.'"

Domo looked vaguely insulted, but the Pálinka seemed to have slowed his brain.

I sighed. "It means you're not made of glass, and they can't see through you, so go sit down." Domo went, grumbling, although he'd managed to snag some food while he was obstructing their view.

My grandmother shushed us, and we went quiet with the habit of childhood obedience. I looked past Grandma to my parents, who also seemed delighted about the imminent spectacle. They were holding hands, the incurable lovebirds. I grinned at them, then looked back at the grassy stage.

Gradually, as the darkness grew, we noticed little blinking lights in the woods, like fireflies, but more spectacular, with changing colors of blue, pink, yellow, orange, and green. We all said, "Ahh!" and clapped.

A man walked to the center of the clearing and waited. I peered at my program to see that tableau 1 was called "*The Shepherd and Szépasszony,*" I shivered. That particular fairy could be pretty scary, depending on the version.

A spotlight appeared on the shepherd. "Where is the light board?" I whispered to Erik.

He shrugged. "Over on the right, I think."

The shepherd was pantomiming work in the fields. He wielded an imaginary hoe, then paused to wipe his brow. A moon appeared: not the actual moon, which wasn't yet visible, but a sparkly, show-business moon that seemed to float just above the trees. The shepherd mimed praying to the moon, just as the farmer did in the fairy tale.

He went back to his hoe, but then one of the tiny lights in the forest seemed to grow, larger and larger, until it was a ball of gold-white light that began to move. Szépasszony was coming. Henrik was a genius, I thought, a born showman. I was actually both nervous and almost joyful at the thought of seeing her.

The actress emerged from the woods, her body glowing gold and surrounded by an aura of light. She had long silver hair which also sparkled in the moonlight. We said AHHHHH again, much louder, and we clapped. She was mesmerizing. She moved gracefully to the farmer, who dropped his imaginary hoe in surprise and fear. She spoke to him, pantomiming some sort of explanation.

"Is she going to eat him?" whispered Erik, who had learned that Hungarian fairies, historically, were not always gentle.

"No, but she'll probably kill him," I murmured softly, with a shrug, sipping my drink. "You finish this, or I'll get drunk."

Erik took the tiny cup and downed the liquid, then shoved both his cup and mine into his pocket. He was environmentally conscious—one of a million things I loved about him. "This is cool," he whispered.

"It really is." Grandma shushed me again. An eerie but entrancing music had begun to play, audible to all of us, and the fairy and the farmer began to dance. Clearly, he was bewitched by her. His face turned upward (she was taller than he) and his simpering smile spoke of endless devotion.

The fairy was smiling, laughing, as they spun around, and we clapped, appreciating the graceful waltz. The farmer, foolish and young, began to pull on the fairy's hands, as though he intended to take her home.

"Uh-oh," Erik said.

"She doesn't want to live at your boring farm," I chided the imaginary farmer. But Szépasszony could defend herself. She froze as he tried to take ownership of her, then rose to her full height. She looked literally a foot taller—how had they done that?

We all gasped as she grew tall and terrible, her glittery gown starting to look more like the scales of a dragon. She lifted her hands, and the spotlight revealed suddenly long nails, which glittered, as well, and which she brandished like knives.

The terrified farmer backed away and began to run, but

she gave graceful chase, pursuing him into the trees, from which we heard a dreadful and theatrical death howl.

Domo, who had finally finished eating, said, "Now *that* was cool."

Margie nodded, huddling into her little fur jacket. "So sad, though."

I was dumbfounded. "The production values of this thing are crazy good!"

My mother leaned toward me. "Henrik told me that their director and lighting man both have Broadway experience."

"Well, heck. It's impressive. I want to take some pictures." I pulled my phone from my pocket and turned off the flash so I could try to capture the lighting effects.

The shepherd and the fairy, now walking normally, came back out to take their bows. Our applause was thunderous. I looked around the bleachers, which were almost entirely full. Maybe two hundred people? Henrik was obviously also good at P.R.

"What's the next one called?" I asked Erik.

He used his phone light to read the program. His blond head bent forward, and I reached out to stroke his hair. Erik Wolf had his own special light, a green-gold aura that I had spotted back around Halloween, when we had attended an ill-fated dance together. It was the light of love, and of his rightness for me. It made him, inevitably, my man, my grandmother had assured me.

"The next one is called The Fairy Queen."

"Oh, I love this story. It's about a beautiful fairy, queen of all the forest fairies, who falls in love with a human man who gradually saps her magic. She has to keep replenishing it from the other fairies, and the witches that fly in the forest at night. But eventually her energy fades, and she collapses at the feet of her lover."

Erik looked at me with his stunning green eyes, luminous even in the dark. "Do any of these tales end happily?"

"Um—sometimes."

"Which means no. I remember all those fairy tales I read when I first met you, when we were trying to figure out what happened to Ava. Witches eating children, and horrors like that."

"All fairy tales are horrifying. You've read Grimm's, right?"

Grandma pulled her scarf down by the necessary inch. "The Hungarian ones are best." She said it proudly, but also a little drunkenly. I wondered how much Pálinka she had downed in the name of warmth.

Then, even though she had been the last to speak, she said, "Shhh!" and sat back with a rapt expression.

Erik grinned at me and we focused on the stage, where a gently-sparkling creature was walking about the stage, peering here and there, hunting for something. Then, with a sudden inspiration, she stood up straight, looked at the sky, and opened a giant pair of wings, which lit up with sudden brilliance that brought tears to my eyes. Wings of gold and blue and purple and pink, shimmering brightly in the light of the sparkling moon, and earning loud applause and shouts of surprise. A stunning spectacle she made, and it was all achieved with light.

We clapped for quite a while, and the fairy queen preened for us, flexing her wings and glittering as she walked.

Finally, a man appeared, tall and graceful. He did not glitter, but he was lighted in a subtle way that suggested strength and nobility. He and the fairy embraced, but as they did so, little bursts of sparkling light seemed to shoot out of her.

"Ahhh!!" we cried. The fairy became weak and sat down on a large rock. The young man bent to her, and she said something in his ear. Then he ran into the forest while she sat and flitted her wings prettily. A minute later her lover was back, accompanied by other fairies, littler ones with only one color on their wings, but still sparkling. They flitted toward their queen and laid hands on her head, her arms, her hands. Gradually the fairy queen's light grew brighter, and once again she stood, this time on the rock, and flexed her wings in triumph. She sparkled more brightly than before, and bursts of blue and gold sparked into the air.

We clapped and called "Yay!" and "Hurrah!" and I doubted anyone was being sarcastic. She was breathtaking.

The fairy bent toward her lover. She seemed to be telling him they could not be together, for obvious reasons, and the little fairies tried to pull him away. He wept, and reached for her, and she bowed her head, but shook it, refusing his embrace.

Eventually, the young man was taken away by the little fairies, and the queen leapt from her rock with new strength, flexing her wings and glittering sensationally while she looked sadly at the sky.

Then she seemed to have an idea. She held up a graceful finger, smiled, and ran to the path that disappeared into the forest. She disappeared, as well, but glimmers of her light could be seen for another thirty seconds or so.

We all clapped, waiting for her return, her reunion, and her inevitable death. Domo had turned to Margie and begun mauling her, apropos of nothing, and I poked him with the toe of my boot. "Stop assaulting Margie, or I will have Erik arrest you."

Domo laughed. Even in the darkness I could see that Margie was blushing, but she didn't seem embarrassed.

I checked on my grandma, who had receded slightly inside her hood. "You okay, Juliana?"

She raised her eyebrows at me. I didn't usually call her by her name. Her eyes crinkled in what I guessed was a grin. But then she sat up straight, pulled off her hood, and yanked down the scarf. Her face was alert, her eyes wide. She seemed to be almost sniffing the air. "Something is wrong," she said in a low voice.

On the verge of questioning her, I realized that I felt it, too—a sort of pulsing tension in the darkness, and an eerie quiet when before there had been the gentle murmuring of the audience. It was as though we were all holding our breath. Strange . . . .

The young man appeared at the edge of the trees with some of the fairies and another man who wore no costume at all, but seemed to be a stage tech. They had their heads together, speaking in what seemed to be an urgent way. Minutes had gone by since the fairy disappeared, and I realized that she had missed her cue. Presumably someone had gone to find her in the trees and remind her of what should happen next.

But I was afraid, suddenly, and so was my grandmother, and my mother on the other side of her. The three of us were holding hands, though I didn't remember reaching out.

Erik looked over. He'd known us all long enough to trust our instincts. "What is it?" he asked.

Then a scream echoed out of the woods, a terrible sound that was clearly not part of the show; the actors we had been watching suddenly sprinted down the path and disappeared. Erik stood, said "Wait here," and hustled down the bleachers in a few large strides. Then he, too, was running down the path and into the forest.

Perhaps it was inevitable that he seemed to be disappearing into a fairy tale.

I looked at my grandmother. There was ice in my core,

and it had nothing to do with the spring wind. "Someone is dead," I whispered, and she nodded. My mother's blue eyes were haunted as she said, "What could have happened?"

My father peered at me past my mother's shoulder. "So, all three of you—sense something?"

We nodded. Domo told me later that we looked like the three Fates, acknowledging the inevitability of the end of life. He and Margie stared at us, and then at the grassy stage, where now large stage lights had been turned on, dispelling all the magic and illuminating the forest path.

The crowd had begun to murmur, and a couple of brave souls ventured out of the bleachers to move toward the woods, but they were blocked by men in black, stage techs who now had a grimmer duty, most likely imposed upon them by Erik.

Clusters of people murmured, but we Horvath/Kellers sat in silence, waiting. After a long time (or mere minutes, who knew?) a man moved to the center of the stage, holding a microphone. It was our friend Henrik, and his posture suggested sadness and defeat. "Ladies and gentlemen. Thank you so much for coming out this evening to our special show. I am sad to say that there has been a tragic accident, and the performances cannot go on."

The crowd began to murmur in surprise and distress, and Henrik held up a hand. "We will contact you all via e-mail about a rain date for our production. For this evening, though, we ask that you quietly disperse, and if you would at the same time spare a prayer for a young person who needs them."

He turned and walked away, and more stage techs lined up along the stage, blocking access into the woods. Moments later we heard sirens, and soon enough the police were there, unwinding their yellow crime scene tape and ushering people toward the parking lot. We lingered, uncertain whether or not to wait for Erik. Before one of the men in black could accost us, Erik appeared and climbed back up to us where we sat, shocked.

"I'm sorry to say your instincts were correct. There has been a death."

"The Fairy Queen?" my grandmother asked.

Erik hesitated, then said, "Yes."

"Was it an accident?" asked my mother with an innocent expression.

Erik's face was grim. "No."

I met his eyes and saw the truth: there had been a crime, a murder. And Erik would have to solve it. Even as I thought this, Erik's partner, Greg Benton, appeared at the foot of the bleachers. He waved at us, surprised, and Erik held up his pointer finger to indicate that Benton should wait.

He took my hand. "I don't know how long I'll be." He turned to Domo. "You'll make sure she gets home safely?"

"Absolutely," Domo said, in a rare somber moment.

"Go," I told Erik. "They need you."

He nodded, waved to my family, and left with Benton, the two of them walking swiftly and talking rapidly.

My grandmother put her hood back up. Before she wound her scarf around her head once again, she said, "A bad omen."

"What is?" I asked softly.

"When the tale becomes real. Very bad, Hana."

Chapter Two

The Beautiful Maiden and Her Sisters

By tacit agreement we gathered at our grandparents' house. My grandfather padded around in his slippers, making coffee and occasionally pausing to rub his wife's shoulders. Grandma had recovered from the shock, but she seemed to appreciate his attentions.

Domo was studying the program from the ill-fated event. "The Fairy Queen was played by Rose Toth. That name sounds familiar," Domo said, looking at Margie. "And she looks familiar. Do we know a Rose Toth?"

Margie seemed to be doing some inward searching. "Didn't we have a Rose in our cooking class last year?"

"Cooking class?" my mother asked, perking up. "Domo, are you learning to cook?"

Domo blushed slightly. "It was a couples' class. They teach you some basic dishes you can make together. We joined for fun."

"That sounds delightful," my mother said with her bright smile. My father sat beside her, playing with her hair and looking thoughtful.

"Did Erik say how she was killed?" he asked.

I studied his face, but saw no clues about what he was thinking. "No. He's not allowed to talk about stuff like that."

"I'm sure we'll find out soon enough," Margie said. "When we left the field, a news van was driving in."

"Yuck," I said. Then something occurred to me. "You said she was in a couples' class. Who was with her?"

Domo looked at Margie, who seemed uncertain. "I think it was Arnie or Arthur or something. It was quite a while ago."

My grandmother murmured something in Hungarian, and my grandfather replied. The two of them launched into their own private conversation, which grew animated. I heard the name "Toth" several times. They pronounced it the Hungarian way—"Tote"—and seemed invested in Rose's lineage. My mother bent toward them (though my dad kept his grip on one lock of her hair) and then all three of them were speaking in their native tongue. The rest of us were out of luck, since we had never learned Hungarian.

Finally, my dad said, "What's up?"

My mother smiled apologetically. "Sorry. Mom was wondering if she could be related to the Toth family from their parish. My dad remembered that they had three daughters."

In response to her words, my grandfather was up again, scuffing his slippered way to a shelf in the kitchen hallway, from which he retrieved a slim volume that I recognized as a parish directory. Grandma got up to peer over his shoulder as he turned pages, and the two of them murmured in the language of their childhood.

Then Grandpa turned the book to show us, his finger pointing at a family picture on the bottom right of one page. "Three daughters," he said. "Teresa, Lida, and Rose."

We surged forward to study the book in his hand. "Is this a recent photo?" I asked.

Grandpa shrugged and looked at Grandma. "Taken maybe three years back, yah, Juli?"

My grandmother nodded. Her eyes seemed to have become darker, and I knew that she was feeling strong associations, either to the picture, or the events of the evening, or both.

I bent closer to study the picture. Mr. and Mrs. Toth stood proudly in the back row, their hands on the shoulders of their daughters, who sat smiling in the front row. They seemed to be in their late teens or early twenties, and posed in age order. Lida, the girl on the left, was clearly the youngest—perhaps eighteen when the picture was taken. Teresa, the middle child, not as pretty as the other two, but boasting a mane of red hair that looked both thick and soft. Lida, thin and lovely, had long blonde hair that seemed almost silver in the studio light. She smiled tentatively, as though unsure what expression to wear. Teresa's expression was confident, almost smug. And then there was Rose. Dark hair, dark eyes, and naturally red lips made her look like a character from a fairy tale, and I could see why she got a major role in Henrik's production. She was beautiful.

"Wow," Domo said. Then he added, "She's pretty. I feel bad for her parents, but even more for her sisters. I don't think I'd ever get over it if Hana died."

I swiveled my head to look at him, surprised and touched, and he lunged forward to give me a hug. I stayed there for a while, in Domo's arms. He was warm, and he smelled like one of the pleasant colognes that Margie had bought him. I rubbed my tears on his shirtfront, and he laughed.

My mother said, "Of course you would be devastated. Tragic loss devastates everyone, especially when the lost one is young and lovely." Her face was sad. My mother had told me once that after she became a mother to Domo and me, a part

14

of her felt like a mother to every child she saw. This phenomenon still affected her, and her maternal love extended to strangers not just of her children's ages, but to all ages younger.

Grandpa set the directory on the table, and my father bent to study it.

I sighed and said, "Well, I think we all need to process this in our own ways. Domo, can you take me home?"

Before we left, I made sure to hug everyone tightly. Events like this one tended to bring home the reality that not one of us is guaranteed tenancy on the earth. When I hugged my father, he said, "I love you, little Haniska."

*

I was in bed when Erik arrived. I'd been tucked in with Antony and Cleopatra, my ever -affectionate cats, and we were all reading a book—I with half-hearted concentration, and they via osmosis. Antony was sputtering out an uneven purr while digging his claws rhythmically into my blanket. Cleopatra was already asleep, lying on her back, her tiny mouth slightly open.

The only light in the room came from the fairy lights on my lovely hand-built bookcase, a gift from my grandparents and my father—and I could see the occasional jewel-toned glimmer of one of my object d'art, lined neatly and lovingly along the shelves. My feeling of sadness had morphed into one of deep reflection, and I'd been pondering the ideas of life, art, beauty, permanence. It was notable that Rose had died, not only while young and vibrant, but while performing in a pageant in which she literally glowed, the object of all eyes. I recalled the line from Shakespeare, "Our revels now are ended . . ." Which play had that been from? I took my phone from my bedside table and searched the phrase. The play, it seemed, was *The Tempest.* Prospero the magician had put on a pageant with his fairies and spirits, but then they all disappeared, and he got depressed about the impermanence of life, saying,

> *Our revels now are ended. These our actors,*
> *As I foretold you, were all spirits and*
> *Are melted into air, into thin air:*
> *And, like the baseless fabric of this vision . . .*
> *shall dissolve*
> *And, like this insubstantial pageant faded,*
> *Leave not a rack behind. We are such stuff*
> *As dreams are made on, and our little life*
> *Is rounded with a sleep."*

It struck me then that the right words, chosen artfully, could transport a reader to a place or a feeling. It felt, suddenly, as though this passage had been written about poor Rose, a soul who had faded from our sight, her "little life" spirited away, leaving us with a mystery to be solved.

A mystery that Erik would solve.

My thoughts flitted now to Erik. How strange it must feel to be exposed routinely to human cruelty or greed or recklessness. To be the stern authority who must say, "There are rules in this society, and you have broken them, and now you must face the consequences."

With a sigh, I put my book aside and lay back on my pillow, looking at the ceiling. I heard a key in my apartment door, and then the sound of Erik doing his usual routine: hanging up his jacket, taking off his shoes, padding down the hall to check on me.

"I'm awake," I said. "Come sit with me."

He moved toward me, a shadow in the dark delineated by a slight green-gold glow that was always around him, visible

Julia Buckley

only to me. He sat on the edge of the bed, waking Cleopatra, who let out a confused meow and made him laugh. He stroked her soft belly and she began a purr to rival Antony's.

'Are you all right?" I asked.

He nodded. "A shame, what happened, but not traumatizing. For her family and friends, yes."

"Yes." My mind raced around, thinking of ways that Rose could have died on that path. "Do you know who did it?"

He shook his head. "Not yet. We have some leads to follow. And the cast is being cooperative. They're in pieces, as you can imagine, and your friend Henrik has aged about a decade."

"Oh, poor Henrik. The show was wonderful, and I know he had a lot to do with how well-staged it was. All those cast members, all that work. And someone had to ruin it just to— what? Get revenge? Express anger or jealousy?"

Erik played with Cleopatra's whiskers, which she kept twitching. "Whatever caused it, the act was premeditated, and meant for Rose."

I spoke solemnly. "Do you think we should move out of Riverwood? I mean, there have been several murders since we met. Is crime increasing here?"

He shook his head again. "No. Crime rates go up and down, but crime is a constant, and has been since Cain and Abel."

I sighed. "Did you ever read that line in Shakespeare?" I recited the line from *The Tempest* for him, and he regarded me with affection.

"Hana, my philosopher and lover."

I smiled. "Perhaps you need doses of philosophy and of love to inoculate you against evil."

"Works for me," he said, grinning. He lunged at me, and the cats leapt off the bed with sounds of feline complaint, and

I kissed the policeman who loomed above me in the dark, stroking his blond hair and basking in the warmth of his golden light.

The next day I went to Fair Price Foods to pick up some Hungarian staples. I had a short list, but when my grandmother heard I was going, she made it much longer. I hunted around until I had every item checked off, and then I loitered at the counter even after my friend Maria had rung me up. She only worked part-time now because she was going to school for an advanced math degree. I asked after her grandmother, who was in prison, but making the best of it by forming friendships and teaching people to cook. She had a job in the prison kitchen, and she wrote entertaining letters to her children and grandchildren.

"She's hurting, of course. We know that. But it's not as bad as she feared it would be, or as we feared it would be. And I think when she comes up for parole, they'll see she's truly sorry. She meets with her priest every day."

"That's good to hear. I know she's remorseful."

"Yeah. Life is just crazy. Who would ever expect their grandma to end up in jail?"

I thought of my own grandma, my Juliana, reading tea leaves for a long line of inmates . . . "No one. Is your grandfather still being supportive?"

She smiled and shook her head in a disbelieving way. "You know, they were separated for several years, and we expected they'd be estranged until they died. But this whole thing—it just rocked their worlds, both of them, and he—he's almost more devastated than she is. He visits her as often as they'll let him. Reads to her, sings to her."

"Really?"

"No joke. You know what, Hana? We don't know people,

because they don't know themselves until they're tested. And even then, they have to make a decision: who do I want to be?"

I stared at her attractive face. "Yesterday my boyfriend called me a philosopher, but I think you win the philosophy prize."

She grinned. "Maybe it's a Hungarian thing. We both have the roots." She spied something over my shoulder and said, "Oh, shoot." Her face went pale. "Hana, stay here. I don't know what to say to these people, and I need moral support."

I turned to see three figures moving toward Maria's check-out line. She lifted a tentative hand and said, "Hi, you guys." When the trio reached her station, she said, "I'm so, so sorry. I just heard this morning."

Two of the three had looked vaguely familiar to me; now I realized why. These were the sisters of Rose Toth. What had their names been? Lida—that was the blonde one. And what had been the older one's name?

The one I couldn't remember was first in line, her face pale against her shining red hair. She acknowledged Maria's condolences with a solemn dip of her head. "Thanks, Maria." Her eyes flicked to me.

Maria said, "This is Hana. Hana, this is Teresa Toth." *Teresa*! That was her name. Maria turned back to Teresa, explaining me in the context of Riverwood and the Hungarian scene. "She's Juliana Horvath's granddaughter."

Now the woman looked interested. "From the tea house?"

I nodded. "I'm sorry, as well. I was at the pageant last night when—"

Teresa looked urgent. "You were at the event? We were there, too. This is my sister, Lida." She grabbed the arm of the younger woman and pulled her closer. Lida was indeed lovely.

Her blonde hair had been trimmed to shoulder length, and her blue eyes were slightly swollen with recent tears, but the beauty remained evident.

Lida reached out to shake my hand. Then she gestured to the young man beside her, who had been watching the proceedings with a dull expression, as though only his body were present. "And this is Albert. He is Rose's boyfriend."

All three of them stood there, wearing bereft expressions and viewing us with an air of helplessness, as though waiting for us to make a decision on their behalf, or to explain a terrible reality they could not yet understand.

"I'm sorry for your loss," I said again, this time to Lida and Albert. "It's so sudden, and pointless. I know you must all have been close."

Lida's eyes filled with tears, and she lunged forward with grateful hands extended. If we hadn't been behind Maria's conveyor belt, I think she would have hugged me. As it was, I took her hands and squeezed them, feeling inadequate. Teresa's gaze was aimed at the floor, as though she had decided to say a brief prayer. I found it interesting that Lida's instinctive response to my condolences had been to reach out, while Teresa's had been to separate herself, if only from eye contact.

Albert didn't become tearful, but his general air of defeat was a clear sign of grief. Life, or perhaps Death, had beaten him, his posture said, and he did not know how to go on.

"Have the police caught the—perpetrator?" I asked gently.

Teresa's eyes were back on mine, cold and angry. "No. They can tell us what happened, which is horrifying, but not who did it. They said they have dozens of people to interview, blah blah." I saw now how Teresa's grief had emerged: in raw fury. "That's fine, though. Lida and I will find out what happened, one way or another. And I won't wait for the police to get my justice."

Lida nodded, but in a lackluster way that said she didn't share this vigilante spirit. "I'm sure they'll know something soon," she said softly, touching Teresa's shoulder.

Teresa's lustrous red hair had crept over her shoulders, and she shoved it back in an angry gesture, revealing the soft heaviness of her auburn tresses. "It's so hard, especially on my little sister." With a fierce gesture, she pulled Lida to her side and locked her in place. Lida didn't struggle, but rested her head on Teresa's shoulder. "And poor Albie here only heard the news an hour ago. He was working last night, and we—were overwhelmed after it happened. We didn't think to call him until this morning."

That seemed strange to me, but what did I know about this kind of grief?

Maria's face was soft with compassion. "Can we do anything for your family? I can make food, or help with the funeral arrangements, or—"

Teresa smiled sadly. "We're good for now. The three of us came here to get some ingredients for breakfast." She pointed to a basket in Albert's hands. "We want to feed our parents, who are inconsolable right now."

I said, "My grandmother says that grief is a journey, and everyone takes a different route."

Albert perked up. "That's true," he said. "And even though people will be around you, offering support, you have to take the journey alone." His sadness had the appearance of guilt, somehow.

We pondered Albie's words in silence. Another philosopher, I thought.

Maria said, "Didn't the police have evidence? Can't they just go arrest someone?"

Lida wiped at her eyes. "At every rehearsal, Rose ran down the path to a certain point—this big square rock, where she sat and waited for her cue. Last night, the police found a rope—" her voice gave out, and she buried her face in her hands.

"A trip wire," Teresa hissed, looking around to be sure no one lingered nearby. "Someone had set it up so that she would not see it, and she went flying, falling head first on the rock." Her voice crackled with anger.

I tried to picture this. "So—they just wanted to hurt her, maybe? Because there would be no guarantee that it would be a fatal blow. Maybe it was a prank that got out of hand."

Teresa and Albert exchanged a grim glance. "They knew it wouldn't be fatal. Because they were waiting there in the darkness, holding a smaller rock. They even left it behind for the police to find, covered in Rose's blood."

"And they did it all in seconds," Albert said tonelessly. "Because that's all they had. So everything was set out for him, and he hovered in the dark like a monster, waiting for our beautiful Rose to come tripping along, trying to balance her heavy wings—" Now Albert, too, broke down, although he kept the tears at bay with several gulps that made his Adam's Apple slide vigorously up and down.

I felt desperately sorry for them all, and on an impulse, I said, "If you'd like to have your funeral reception at the tea house, I'm sure we can offer you a discounted rate."

Teresa considered this idea, her head pressed against the top of Lida's blonde hair. "That is a nice offer. I'll mention it to my parents."

I dug in my purse for a card, and handed it to her. She thanked me as Maria rang up their groceries and Albert stepped forward to pay the bill. The three of them walked away with their canvas bag, a trio both wilted and dignified.

"It's unbelievable," Maria said. "I had no idea it was so

brutal! Who would want to do something like that to Rose? She was so nice, and so pretty. Who wants to destroy goodness and beauty?"

I didn't answer, but I thought of a lovely woman named Ava, who had also been good and kind, and was the reason Maria's grandmother sat in jail, filled with regret. After a bit more conversation, I said my farewells to my friend and went to my car. I had to drop off my grandmother's groceries, the first of several errands on my list that morning.

I made it to her house in ten minutes. My grandfather was outside, examining his daffodils and tulips. He snapped some pictures; he loved to photograph his garden, and I knew he posted the pictures on his Facebook gardening page. He was quite popular in the group, my grandmother had told me with pride.

"Hello, Grandpa."

He straightened, examining his photo. "Hallo, Baby Haniska." He showed me the picture, which could have been taken by a professional. "*Ki mint vet, úgy arat,*" he said proudly in his native tongue. This was one of his favorite sayings, so I knew it meant, roughly, "He who sows, reaps."

"You're good at that flower photography. You should start a gardening blog."

He waved a careless hand. "I have enough to do." He was flattered, though, and I knew that if he had one area of vanity, it was related to his green thumb.

"I've got Grandma's groceries here."

"You can put them in the kitchen. She is visiting Mrs. Kalas. They want to talk about the poor girl who died."

"I believe it. People are in shock. I was just speaking of her to Maria, at Fair Price."

He nodded, then looked at my bag. "You got the good paprika?"

"Yes. Your meals shall not suffer." I stood on tiptoe to kiss his cheek. My grandfather was still six feet tall, though I knew at some point he would probably shrink a bit. Right now, despite his age, I could still see glimpses of the young man he had been.

I went into the house and set out her groceries. My grandfather handed me some cash. He'd scoffed at me when I had suggested Venmo. "We pay with real money," he said.

Now I tucked away the cash and said, "I've got to run. I like to make the most of my days off."

He nodded, his face serious now. "Your Wolf will catch this killer?"

"I think he will. He's got a list of suspects, and now it's time to interview them. He has an effective interviewing technique. Mom and Grandma and I got to see it, back when he was interrogating people in the tea house."

"Ah. So, he narrows it down, based on their answers."

"Yes, exactly."

He murmured something again in Hungarian—another favorite slogan that meant "It is easier to catch a liar than a limping dog." And it was true: the lies gave people away in the end. My grandmother assured me that the guilty could not remember innocence, and therefore they could not dissemble because it would reveal them. Erik agreed with her.

I gave my grandpa one more kiss and trotted back to my car. I had planned to look in on Runa, Erik's sister, who was now more than eight months pregnant. She was mostly resting, letting her sister Thyra run the company that the two of them had started together. Ulveflokk (Norwegian for "wolf pack") continued to thrive, and Thyra had found an efficient and invaluable temp to fill in while Runa nurtured her little baby.

Erik's sisters had burst into my life the previous October with the energy and enthusiasm that was innate to them. At first, I had resented their nosy questions and their imperious commands, but once I got used to the Wolf twins, I realized that I liked and trusted them. Now we were friends. Life had taken me on a variety of unexpected paths since I had met Erik Wolf, and all of them had been delightful. I smiled out at the spring scenery as I drove toward Runa's lovely apartment in Chicago.

When I stopped at a red light, a little wren flew toward my car and rested on the hood, staring in at me with beady intensity, as if we had arranged a meeting. "Hello," I said, smiling, and he peeped urgently. "What can I do for you?" I asked.

With one last glance that seemed to hold some reproach, he flew away.

Chapter Three

The Realm of Unknown Things

It was my grandmother who had told Runa she was pregnant, during what had been intended as a light-hearted reading of tea leaves. Instead, Grandma had sent us all away and told Runa not only that she had a tiny daughter within her, but that the little girl would be facing a fight to live. A pregnancy test had told Runa that Grandma was right, and an in-utero heart operation a month or so later validated the health information, as well. That was when we all realized, for the first time, that Juliana Horvath, my grandmother, shared the psychic gift that her own mother, Natalia, had possessed.

Now Runa was plump and contented, and she spent much of her down time talking and singing to the little baby that she had never intended to create. She and her boyfriend Andy had decided against having children, but not long afterward my grandmother had brought this news. Runa had felt immediately protective of the daughter that my grandmother called "a warrior." I couldn't wait to meet the little girl, whom they had decided to name Anya.

I found a spot half a block down from Runa's building

and ran to the door as someone else entered. The doorman knew me, so he waved me to the elevator, and I made it to Runa's floor without having to ask her to buzz me in.

Andy had given an apartment key to almost everyone in the family (I was family by association with Erik) because he wanted people to have access if Runa were ever in distress. Andy had proved to be a slightly anxious but very excited father-to-be. "What if Runa collapsed, and you couldn't get in there?" he had said to a group of us when he issued the keys. "Quick action could make the difference."

Never mind the fact that Anya was big and strong now, and routinely pummeled Runa from the inside, demanding to be let out. It made Runa laugh every time.

I reached her door and opened it with my key. I found Runa sitting in her sunny living room, a space that was cozy and colorful and filled with tasteful art. Runa was reading something, her hand on her giant mound of a stomach, her dogs, Lucy and Desi, lying at (and on, in Desi's case) Runa's feet.

"Hey, Runa. Hey, dogs. Hey, Anya," I said, moving toward them. I held up a plastic container. "Kiflis made by Grandma."

Her blue eyes widened. "Give that to me," she said.

I did, and I watched her devour the first one in seconds.

"Mmm, raspberry," she said, with a slight moan. When I had met Runa, she'd been thin as a reed and hadn't eaten regular meals, living off of coffee and snacks. Her pregnancy, especially the later months, had made her ravenous and newly appreciative of good food. "Your grandmother is my Fairy Godmother," Runa almost purred.

"Yeah, she's special. How's the baby today?"

"Not moving as much. And she's lower down. The doctor said that would happen in the next week or two. Getting into place. I have an appointment tomorrow, so I'm sure they'll give me all the info." She ate another kifli, this one stuffed with blueberry *lekvar,* a special jam for cookies and tarts.

I touched her arm. "You're not in pain or anything, are you?"

She sighed. "No, no pain. But I'm a whale, and I'm tired of it. I just sit everywhere, although it's kind of uncomfortable to sit now, or to lie, or to stand for too long. I'm the size of a yacht and I just want to be thin again. Anya's not the only one who wants her out of there." She was smiling, though, because she had said her daughter's name.

"What can I help you with today?" I said, looking around. "It looks as though a maid has already been here."

"Yeah, Andy has them coming twice a week because he doesn't want me to lift a finger." She fluttered her finger on the dome of her stomach, and something caught my attention.

In an instant I was next to her, examining her left hand while she grinned at me. She and Andy had become engaged at Christmastime, but her lovely diamond ring looked bulkier now, tucked into a graceful gold band. "What—did you have your ring adjusted?"

"Oh, you spied my big secret," she said with a soft smile. Really, love and motherhood had made a marshmallow out of tough Runa. "Andy was going on and on, saying 'when my child is born it will be to a married couple!' He's so traditional sometimes, my Andy."

I blinked. "I'm sorry—so you're saying that you're married?"

"Yes, two days ago. We kept it just the two of us. We can have some big event later, if we wish, but right now we just wanted it on paper. I am Mrs. Bell." She looked surprised to hear this name out loud, and then she laughed. "I think I like Wolf better. But I also like Andy, so I will be Mrs. Bell when

I am with him." She laughed again and said softly, "Mrs. Bell," as though it were a joke she wanted to remember for later.

"That's wonderful. You and Andy are perfect,together and I can't wait to see you with your daughter."

Runa stretched suddenly, her arms above her head and her legs jutting out so far that they collided with one of her devoted greyhounds. "I'm *so uncomfortable*," Runa moaned. "I feel like I have triplets in there. I've never been this heavy in my life. Luckily, I can't see the scale." She glared at me. "I told Andy this is his fault, but he just laughs. Nothing dents his happiness." Her glare faded slowly as she thought of her new husband.

I decided to distract her. "Are you hungry? I can make some—"

"No, no. Thyra and I have breakfast together every day, sort of a business meeting in my house. It's also just a chance to be together. She misses me in the store."

"I'm sure. But the breakfast meetings are a great idea!"

"Yes. I enjoy them, but Thyra feeds me too much. I'm still full. The baby is full, too, because she's barely kicked me today." She rubbed her stomach and said, "I heard Erik has another murder on his hands."

"Yes, sadly. A horrible thing. A young woman, murdered in the middle of a theatrical event. It's hard to imagine that kind of evil. Poor Erik has to pursue it."

"Who is Killing the Artists of Riverwood?" she intoned. "Sounds like a book title."

My face must have been blank. "What do you mean, the artists?"

She began to pet Lucy the dog with her toe. "Last summer he investigated the poisoning at your place. That's when you met, right?"

"Yes." My own happy memory.

"She was a talented singer and musician, the dead woman. Right?"

"Yes."

"And then in October, the artist. Kodaly, the artist who painted True Love." Runa happened to own this painting, and now, in the aftermath of Kodaly's death, it was worth a small fortune. "And then that professor. Not exactly an artist, but you said he was sort of a curator of art."

"That's true."

"And this girl—a theatrical artist?"

"I suppose. I mean, she probably had a day job, but she was performing. We were at the event."

She sat up straight, still looking uncomfortable. "Did you—see?"

"No. The event was at an outdoor theatre in Riverwood. Her first scene had ended and she ran into the woods to await her next appearance. And she never came back."

Runa looked unhappy. "I'm tired of these terrible murder stories. Erik needs to get a new job, like a mall Santa Claus or a candymaker."

I laughed. "Erik is good at his job, and you know he's the best possible person to help protect the innocent."

She sighed and yawned. "Yes, okay. But he will be a Santa to my little girl. He or Felix or my father. They can take turns."

"Your little girl has to come to the tea house for St. *Mikulas* Day in December. Although she might be too tiny for this year."

"We'll be there," Runa said. She stood up, wobbling slightly. "I have to use the bathroom."

She began to walk toward the back of her apartment. I knelt down to pet the dogs, and I heard a strange sound, like an indoor fountain. I wondered if Runa and Andy had a Zen Garden or a meditation fountain. I turned to ask her and saw her face looking back at me, her expression frozen in a mixture of surprise and fear. "My water, Hana."

My eyes moved downward to see the puddle at her feet, and everything went still and silent. A pocket of time opened up, utterly peaceful, and in that moment, I saw my grandmother's face, smiling, saying "She is a warrior." I saw Andy's face, when I told him that my vision of his daughter revealed that she had brown eyes like his, not blue like Runa's. And I saw myself, holding Runa's newborn child in my arms. I saw my great-grandmother Natalia's face, and heard the words she had confided in a Hungarian policeman many decades ago: "The forest of life has many paths. Sometimes, if you concentrate, the right path will be illuminated." In that timeless space, sent from the realm of the unknown, I knew that there would be no time for a hospital. I heard advice in my ear, soft words in Natalia's voice. "Be calm, Haniska, and soothing. She needs your confidence and your capable hands."

The pocket of time closed, and I glided forward on legs I did not consciously move. "Well, look at that! Anya wants to meet you!" I reached her and gave her a quick hug. "Don't worry about this—I'll clean it up later. Let's get you to the bathroom, and you can sit down and let the water trickle out. My mother told me years ago that once it breaks, the water keeps coming."

"Okay," said Runa, rather meekly, and we moved toward the bathroom, her hand in mine.

"The thing is, Runa—" We went into her spacious and very clean bathroom and padded across a plush rug— "I'll call Andy and the hospital, but I don't know --"

Runa was seated now, but she looked at me with a sort of misery. "I can't go to the hospital, Hana; there won't be time."

I knew that already, but I said, "Are you sure?"

She rocked a bit, back and forth. "I want to push," she

said. "I have to push, Hana!" Her voice was urgent and frightened, and I touched her hair.

"Then you'll push. Give me one minute, if you can." I ran to her bathroom cupboard and took out every towel she had. I spread several on the floor, over the plush rug, to make a soft place for her to lie. I set another huge stack of towels on the side for soaking up whatever appeared. I took two smaller towels to her sink. First, I thoroughly washed my hands. Then I took the two smaller towels and soaked them in hot water, waiting until it was practically boiling. Then I squeezed them out and set them on yet another towel. "These won't be sterile, but they'll be close," I said.

I turned to find that Runa was already on the pile of towels. A rush of water and blood flowed out of her, and I knelt down, removed the wet towels beneath her and replaced them with new ones. I was pretending I was Natalia, or Grandma, who would know what to do in a situation like this. But in another way, I did know. Something in me was guiding me.

I reached up to stroke Runa's hair. "Are you in pain?"

"A little," she said, shivering. "It's more that I just—need—to push." She did, and more of her waters flowed out. She had flung off her soaked pants and underclothes while she was still sitting on the commode, and now I knelt between her legs and looked for any sign of a baby. "Ah!!" Runa cried. "I can't wait, Hana! She's so quick."

I kept my voice soft, almost musical. "That's good, Runa! You get to meet her sooner, and in your own home, not an impersonal hospital. You and Anya will meet each other soon."

She attempted a smile, but her teeth chattered, and she bore down again. This time I saw it: the crown of a little head, matted with a mixture of fluids. A baby head, perfectly in position. *Calm. Calm.*

"I see her, Runa. I see the baby. She's doing a lot of the work all by herself, but you need to push again when you get the energy. Preferably when that next contraction comes."

Runa panted out a laugh. "God, okay. I feel the urge coming, Hana!"

"Try to breathe. No pressure, no rush. She'll be here soon."

Runa locked eyes with me. There are so few times in life that we understand something momentous is occurring, something that will change the present and future worlds. Runa and I knew this was momentous, and we shared a look of love and support. "Hana," she said, tears in her lovely blue eyes.

"You can do this, Runa. You are not just an average woman; you are a superwoman! And you are full of mother power."

"Yes, yes," she cried, determined now. "Mother power." She pushed again, and Anya's head emerged. Lightly cradling the tiny head with one hand, I grabbed one of the small heated towels, just warm now, and set it on the floor between Runa's trembling legs. Then I held Anya ever so lightly.

"One more push should do it, Sweetie," I said. "You are amazing, Runa, and you're giving life to your daughter!"

Runa groaned and pushed, and with the slickness of a dolphin the baby rushed out with another burst of water and blood, her first baptism into the world. Careful with her cord, I set the baby on the warm towel that was still clean and gently patted her. Did I need to clear her airway? Spank her bottom? It didn't seem so. Little Anya's eyes were open, and her tummy went up and down with her breathing. I dabbed gently, gently, at her baby skin, at her lovely head of blonde hair.

Runa was anxious. "How is she? Why are you both quiet? Is something wrong?"

"Everything is wonderful, Runa! Your daughter is

beautiful, and so are her fingers and her toes and her sweet eyes that are—oh my goodness, they're looking at me! Hello, Anya!"

Runa began to cry. She was still pushing, though, and I moved the baby slightly to my left while I delivered the placenta. "Let me see her, Hana," said the still-weeping Runa.

"I've just finished." I pushed aside the used towel and wrapped little Anya in the clean, warm one. Still careful of the cord, I placed the baby on her mother's chest, and soon she was nose to nose with Runa, whose tears had been replaced by wonder. She kept repeating "My baby! You are my baby!" in rapturous tones. She paused long enough to say, "Hana— Andy."

"Yes, right. Stay there and rest. I'll get my phone."

"Come right back," Runa said.

"Of course." I jogged out to the living room, which looked different now, surreal and silent. I dialed Andy at his office with a suddenly shaking hand.

"Professor Bell," he said in his calm Andy voice.

"Andy."

"Hana?" He lurched straight into fear. "What's wrong? Why are you—what's wrong? Is Runa okay? Is the baby—"

"Andy." I used the calm voice again. "Come home and meet your daughter."

"*What?*" He wasn't mellow Andy anymore. "It's so early! She's born? The baby is born? It's too early, Hana."

"*Andy.* She's delightful and perfect, and your wife is to be commended for her courage and grace. Come now."

He blubbered out things that were not words and ended the call. I smiled at the phone, then returned to Runa. Her face said that she was a woman in love. The baby's face said that she was comfortable there in her mother's arms.

"Remember that her cord is still intact. We can wait for

Andy to cut it. Isn't that the tradition?" I found the largest towel, a big blue bath towel, and laid it over Runa like a blanket.

Runa closed her eyes and breathed in the scent of her child's skin. I sat against the wall and let her rest there. Anya seemed to have fallen asleep; it had been a stressful hour for her, too. I admired her little blonde cap of hair. Like Runa's hair. Like Erik's hair. This was Erik's niece!

I took up my phone again, about to text him, but then realized it was Runa and Andy's news, and they might want to tell everyone. I put it down and leaned against the wall. I closed my eyes, as well, and I didn't open them until I heard the lock turn, the door open, the tapping sound of Andy's running feet.

He was in the doorway then, and we all stared in silence: Runa with quiet joy and exhaustion, me with anticipation, and Andy with an attempt to take in everything at once.

Finally, he said, "It happened quickly?"

Runa smiled. "So fast, Andy. Poor Hana didn't have a moment to call you or the ambulance. Anya just appeared, like someone determined to enter a room."

Andy took off his jacket and his shoes. I pointed to the sink, and he nodded, pausing to wash his hands. Then he knelt next to his wife and his baby. "She's so small," he breathed. He bent to kiss them both. I left the room and found a sturdy pair of scissors in Runa's kitchen I ran them under very hot water, then returned to the couple.

"Andy, if you were at the hospital, they would let you do the honors. Why not do it here, alone with your wife?"

He took the scissors with an awed expression and gently lifted the cord which had connected Anya with her mother. He looked at Runa, who nodded her encouragement. "We have an emotional attachment now," she said, smiling.

Andy feared that he would damage something, I felt that,

but Runa and I encouraged him, and he made a clean cut in the cord, near to Anya's little tummy. The baby's eyes opened, and she turned to look at Andy in what looked like surprise. Andy began to cry, and Runa stroked his hair.

"We had our special moment, Hana," she said. "You can call the doctor now."

As I made my way to the door, Anya made her first sound, a kind of squawk, like a chicken. Her parents both laughed indulgently, and I left them alone with their daughter, their source of joy and pain forever.

Chapter Four

A Rose Still Blooming

I sat in my car an hour later, trembling slightly. Whatever the
origin of my strange cloak of confidence, it had eventually
dissipated as the medical crew took over, bundling up Runa
and the baby and whisking them away on a stretcher, one of
them in deep conversation with Andy, who had asked me if I
could "handle things" while he went with Runa.

I had assured him that I would, cleaning the floor where
Runa's water had broken and starting a load of laundry in an
attempt to save the soiled towels. I found a lemon scented
floor cleaner and did my best with the bathroom floor.

Finally, content that the new family would come home
to order and a sanitary home, I locked their door and made
my way down to the street. Now I sat, feeling the tension for
the first time and vibrating with it. I took some deep breaths—
the kind I had advised Runa to take—and calmed myself to
an extent. I lifted my phone and called the tea house, where I
was supposed to be going next.

"Maggie's Tea House," said my mother brightly.

"Mom, it's me."

"Hana? Is something wrong?" My mother's default was always worry. I wondered if that was the perpetual burden of the mother.

"I'm fine, but I'm a little shaken up. I wonder if I can beg off today's event?"

"What's going on?" Her voice was more demanding now.

"Can you put me on speakerphone and get Grandma over here? I want to tell you both together."

I could feel my mother's anxiety through the phone as she called to her own mother, who was likely setting out the tea service for today's small group of realtors. "Okay, I'm here, Haniska," said my grandmother's voice. "What do you have to tell us?"

I cleared my throat. "I went to Runa's, just to check on her. We've all been taking turns."

Silence greeted this announcement. They were waiting for the reason for my strange mood. "Ya?" my grandmother finally said.

"We were talking and just hanging out. We discussed the murder a little bit, and—oh, Runa and Andy got married."

Predictably, some happy and celebratory sounds came through the phone, and my mother said, "Oh, I'm so thrilled for them!" She had gotten to know Runa much better over the last four months, and now she and Thyra were considered part of the Keller family (and the Horvath clan).

"Yes, well, she was feeling really uncomfortable the whole time, and she kept shifting and stretching and stuff. Then she got up to go to the bathroom, and her water broke."

"Oh, my goodness!!" my mother cried. "So, she's at the hospital now?"

"Yes. And No. There was no time. The baby started coming right away."

My mother gasped. "So--?

"I delivered the baby on her bathroom floor."

"Oh, Hana! Is—was—is the baby all right?"

A burst of euphoria surged into my core. "Yes, she's beautiful. It was magical, and seeing her, emerging into life like that—I just—it was a perfect moment. Anya is just, well, our favorite pastry chef would call her *très beau*. And Runa was incredible. But I can't quite wrap my mind around--"

"Haniska." My grandmother's voice was brisk. "This is of course how it had to happen. I am happy that Anya was in the hands of a woman she knew, ushering her from one world to the next."

My grandmother often spoke in these mysterious phrasings, ever since she had been "allowed" by my mother to indulge her psychic instincts, back when I first met Erik.

I responded the way I usually did when her thought process went beyond my ken. "Huh?"

She tsked into the phone. Clearly, her tone said, this was obvious and why was I being so obtuse? "You saw the girl at Christmas, yes? During the operation?"

"Not exactly." We, the Wolf family and I, had been gathered in a hospital waiting room while Runa and Anya underwent pre-natal surgery to fix a heart defect in the baby—the 'health battle' my grandmother had envisioned. "I was just trying to think positive thoughts, and I pictured a little blonde girl."

"Yes. You saw her face. You told her to stay with us."

"As a thought exercise. Positive thinking."

My grandmother tsked again. "You saw her again, when you went to speak with Runa during her recovery."

"Runa wanted me to touch her stomach. I just used my same mental picture."

"No, you saw the child. And she saw you. And you were

the one she needed to be with her when she made her journey. Not some doctor she didn't know."

I sighed. Sometimes Grandma was a bit too woo-woo for me. "Anyway, it went well, and quickly, and we called Andy, and he cut the cord, and now they're at the hospital. But now I'm feeling all the nervous energy, and I can't stop shaking. What if she had been breach? What if there had been some sort of problem? That baby rocketed out and Runa couldn't do anything but push."

"Oh, Hana," my mother said again.

My grandmother was still in practical mode. "You were nervous when you delivered the child?"

"No. It was weird—I just felt calm, almost serene. I was probably in shock. Plus, I wanted to calm Runa."

"Ah." She was satisfied, as though she had won an argument.

I cleared my throat again. "Anyway, I just kind of want to go home and regroup, if that's okay."

My mother said, "Of course, sweetheart. We can manage here. And I can come to see you after work if you want. I can bring you some of François's treats."

"I'll let you know," I said. "I'm not sure what I want right now."

The two women who guided my life made soft sounds of congratulations and well wishes, and promised to check on me soon, and then we ended our call. Feeling a bit stronger, I started my car and drove back to my apartment building, looking as ever like a pretty piece of driftwood in a wheat-colored Riverwood field. Our landlord had put in lilac bushes the previous spring, and I traveled from the parking lot past the fragrant buds. The scent, strong and evocative, energized me.

I entered the front hall and found several familiar faces.

My neighbor, Paige Gonzalez, stood before a charming old-fashioned buggy (I had seen it at Timeless Treasures, my favorite antique store, and given it to the family as a shower present). Tucked inside was her two-month-old baby, Daisy, who gurgled in an interested way while Paige talked to the woman in front of her. Iris, Daisy's older sister, who had essentially taken possession of the child the moment she was born, was tucking blankets carefully around Diasy's shoulders, saying in her new maternal voice, "You shouldn't push these off, baby Daisy, or you'll catch a chill outside."

I gave a quick hug to Iris and waved at Paige before I turned to the other woman, who also had a little girl with her. The visitor was my own Aunt Luca, with her newly-adopted daughter (and my tiny cousin), Jia. "Hey, Aunt Luca. The gang's all here!" Now I bent to embrace Jia, one of the most affectionate children I had ever met. As was her habit, she jumped into my arms and wrapped her legs around me. I laughed and stood up, pretending to be suffering under her great weight.

"Hello, Hana!" said Jia in her tiny voice. "We were hoping we would see you!"

She always echoed Luca's words in a sweet and often hilarious way. I held her bony little body against me, a form that was fragile yet strong. Despite her slight physique, her face still held the pudge of babyhood. Briefly I wondered about Jia's real mother. What had become of her? Why had she given Jia up? I thought of Jia's journey from one country to another, one mother to another, and then her adoptive mother had died in a collision on a busy Chicago street, and Jia's godmother, Luca, had adopted her. I sensed that more contemplation of the subject would have me in tears, so I sniffed and set her free.

"I'm glad to see you, too! Did you want to come upstairs for a visit?"

Paige smiled. "Iris invited Jia to join us taking Daisy for a walk. These two are thick as thieves these days, you know."

I had predicted a friendship between Iris and Jia, and it came to fruition when Luca decided to relocate so that her new daughter would be surrounded by family. They lived in Riverwood now, and Jia and Iris attended the same school.

"But I'll come upstairs," Luca said. "I might need to borrow something, if you have it."

"Sure. Come on up. This day has brought many un-expected visitors."

We held the door open while Paige maneuvered the lovely buggy outside, at which point the little girls stuck one to each side like limpets, cooing over the baby and describing the scenery to her.

"That's pretty adorable," I told Luca, as we made our way to the stairs.

"Oh, Jia loves that baby, and she loves Iris. What a godsend it has been for Jia to have met Iris before her first day at the new school. It made her not at all worried to walk into the room—not after Miss Angie had allowed Iris to save a seat at her table. Thank goodness she wasn't assigned to Miss Rose, or they would never have seen each other."

"That is good. What a big school, with two first grades!" Domo and I had attended St. Juliana in Riverwood, with only one class for each of the eight grades, some of the classes with as few as ten students.

"Yes, it's a perfect set-up. And I've grown quite fond of our little house. We're so close to the river that we can go to the bridge most days and feed the ducks." We had reached my apartment; I ushered her inside and straight to my kitchen.

"It is a pretty house. Grandma loves having you back in town. So does Mom."

`Luca's face grew affectionate. "Yeah, it was time. I don't know why I stayed away so long, but my dad says it's because I'm a gypsy." Luca had been only eight when her family left Hungary, but she could still speak the language, and part of the culture was still embedded in her.

"Did Grandpa actually say *gypsy?* Grandma would be mad."

"He just means I have the traveling bug. Which I do. But I need to put down roots for that little critter out there. She loves the idea of family, and she's madly in love with her new one. She's always asking to go to Mom and Dad's house, or your parents' house, or Domo's, or yours."

I'd already hosted several tea parties with Jia, or Jia and Iris, who loved to sit at the fancy table, but eventually slid away to play with my cats. One of the cats was in Luca's lap now. Cleopatra, my lovely gray, had decided that she and Luca were best friends, and she glued herself to my aunt the moment she entered my house. Luckily, Luca loved animals, and she spent the time stroking Cleo's fur and peering into her green eyes.

I handed Luca one of Erik's Diet Cokes (they shared an addiction) and we sat at the table. "You look bushed," she noted. "What's up?"

Suddenly weary, I said, "Are you sure you want to know?"

Her eyes brightened with interest, and she nodded. I proceeded to tell her about my morning, and Grandma's response.

"Whoah," she said. "Should I go out and get you some whisky?"

I laughed.

She looked thoughtful, and a bit wistful. "I always knew my mom had something. Some sort of psychic connection.

But I never knew Magdalena did. It's fascinating. Zoltan and I have nothing, not a whisper of insight. But my great-grandmother, and my mother, and now my sister. And, according to my mother, you, as well. Not Domo?"

I shook my head. "He's a bit flummoxed by the whole thing. But I think the novelty of it is growing on him."

She studied my face. "But you're okay now? After your stressful morning?"

"I'm fine. And it wouldn't have been quite as stressful if it hadn't been for the murder, which was already on my mind and kind of weighing me down."

She sighed. "The one at the Hungarian thing? Mom was telling me about that. At length." She grinned, but then grew sober. "It's unbelievable, what people do, right?"

"Yes. And I happened to meet the family of this Rose Toth, the woman who died, and they were just devastated. Her boyfriend, too."

Luca put her coke can down with a deliberate movement. "What was the name?"

"Rose Toth. She was from Grandma and Grandpa's parish, I guess. Didn't Grandma tell you that?"

"The parish thing, yes. The name, no. I hope it's not the same woman. It can't be! They would have told us," she murmured to herself, her brows creased into a frown.

"What are you talking about?" I had a bad feeling, suddenly, something I had come to call 'the misery,' which usually preceded important revelations.

"Miss Rose, at the grade school. She teaches in the other first grade. But the girls know her. I know her. I chat with her some days in the play lot waiting area while the students are dismissed. She's a lovely kid."

"And her last name is Toth?"

She sighed. "I think so." She scrolled on her phone and

found a link to a school event which included candid pictures. She opened one and showed it to me. "That's Miss Rose."

Rose Toth smiled back at me through the screen, wearing a hat made of tinsel and sporting large Christmas-tree earrings. She was smiling widely, full of fun and energy. I bit my lip.

"That's her," I said.

Luca rubbed her face with an air of defeat. "Oh! It's horrible. Thank God it wasn't Miss Angie. Poor Jia is just getting over her own mama's death. To lose her beloved teacher would be too much. She'd never feel secure again." I thought of the way Jia clung to people, celebrated all of her new relationships, wanted to be with the whole family as often as Luca could arrange it. "That would be a terrible loss," I said. "Let's hope none of Miss Rose's students is terribly fragile, in the emotional sense." I shook my head. "Who are we kidding? I would have been devastated to lose my first grade teacher. Her name was Miss Flora, and I connected her to the excitement and joy of learning. Not to mention that she was my mother away from home."

We sat and contemplated this widening of the sea of loss. I finally said, "You wanted to borrow something. What was that?"

"Oh, the class is putting on some little show, and they sent home a call for props. One of the things they're looking for is a piece of framed art to hang on the wall of their set. I remember that you were trying to get rid of something framed you had removed when you got your Kodaly originals."

"Oh! I gave that poster to Paige. She loves it, so she probably won't part with it. And I'm not letting my Kodalys leave this apartment. Erik made me insure them, actually."

"He's a wise man. Well, I'll have to choose one of my own art gallery treasures, then." Luca smiled at me. Then she got up and took her coke can with her. She gave me a big, lung-squeezing hug, and said, "Hang in there."

"You, too. I know mothering can be exhausting."

She shrugged. "Not with Jia. She makes it easy. Until her teen years, I shall be in paradise." We grinned, but then, out of nowhere, her eyes filled with tears.

"Luca?" I asked.

She wiped at her wet cheeks. "Sorry. I just—something just dawned on me, when I thought of daughters. When I talked to Miss Rose last time, after she brought out her class for pick-up, we were chatting about children. She suddenly confided that she was expecting a child. She was excited about it."

"What?" Erik didn't know this, unless the autopsy had already been performed. "Oh my gosh."

"Yeah. The memory took me by surprise. Anyway, sorry to bum you out. You rest up, and good job being a midwife to a new person."

I walked her to the door, and by the time I ushered her out, I was on the verge of tears myself. It was sad enough to know that the dead woman had been a beloved first grade teacher, but this news of a baby doubled the tragedy.

My grandmother would be furious to hear it, and I imagined her voice already, saying that this murderer was doomed to travel to the lower world with the devil, Ördög, to be stirred in his cauldron of evil souls forever. This murderer had taken not one soul, but two.

This murderer would face double the consequences for his evil act.

Without knowing it, he had summoned the sárkány, the dragons, who came in pairs to avenge the innocent and claim a debt.

Back in fall, I had sensed a metaphorical arrival of dragons as I got closer to determining who had killed Kodaly, the artist whose paintings graced my walls. Back then, I feared the arrival of the dragons, the *Sárkány,* which surely would bring trouble and violence.

But now, thinking of Miss Rose and the little child, boy or girl, who would never have a tea party at her table, I felt a surge of anger, and a rare desire for vengeance. It would be poetic justice, I thought, if this perpetrator suffered the consequences of his actions in sight of everyone.

"Let the dragons come," I murmured, and I went to my room for a nap.

Chapter Five

The Man with the Wrong Face

I woke refreshed two hours later, and my room glowed with golden afternoon light. A spring breeze wafted in, and suddenly I longed to be outside. I jumped out of bed, put on some gym shoes, and went to the kitchen to feed the cats. Then I grabbed my key and jogged down the steps to the front door. My building faced a large field, currently protected as a wildlife refuge and a place for indigenous flora. My favorite exercise was a walk down Abbott's Lane, on the shoulder of the road, where wildflowers and fragrant grasses grew and added sweet scent to the air.

I began my walk now, refreshed and invigorated by the spring-cold breeze, marveling at sturdy stalks of flax, waving patches of star grass, and the graceful quiet of Queen Anne's Lace. In the soggy areas I caught the occasional glimpse of a bog violet or some cattails, and whispering beside me always were the wheat-colored grasses mixed with spring green shoots, bowing humbly to me with every gust of wind.

I strolled for almost an hour, pausing now and then to retrieve my phone and take pictures for my Instagram page.

Like my grandfather, I liked Nature pictures, and that was mostly what I posted, aside from glamour shots of my cats and the occasional candid shot of my handsome boyfriend—and sometimes the two of us together, so people didn't think I had snipped his face out of some catalogue.

When I finally returned to what Erik called "The Driftwood Castle," I spied my handsome blond lover walking toward the front door. Apparently, he needed a break and sought some kisses from his devoted Hana. Or maybe ha had questions? I had texted him during my walk with the information that Rose was pregnant. Perhaps he needed to know the source of my information.

I reached the parking lot and crept up behind him, surprised once again by his tallness, and wrapped my arms around his middle from behind, squeezing tightly. "Hello, gorgeous. Have you come here for a little bit of Hana's Love Cure?"

As soon as the words had left my mouth, I noticed what I had not before: that Erik felt different in my embrace, and that my head reached a spot under his shoulder blades instead of at them. Shocked, fearing the worst, I let my hands fall away and took a step back as the man spun around, grinning.

It was *not* Erik.

"No," I gasped. It was almost a scream.

"Not just now," he said, still beaming. "But what a generous offer."

My face felt so hot it may as well have been in a microwave. "Uh --"

He took pity on me. "I know I look a lot like Erik, so it's a natural mistake." He stuck out a hand. "I'm Felix. And you are Hana! I've heard so much about you—that's not just a polite line, it's the truth. For months I've been hearing of all your charms, and you look just as Erik described you."

I shook his hand, dumb with shock. *Felix!* The only member of Erik's family I had not met—his older brother who lived on the West Coast.

"I'm so embarrassed," I said. "I had no idea --"

Felix offered an affable smile. "Why would you? I didn't tell anyone I was coming. I wanted to surprise Erik at work, but they said he was on a break. Greg Benton said I should try here, because Erik usually spends his breaks at your place. So, I was just trying my luck, and --"

"Yes, don't remind me of the *and* part." I managed my own smile. "Would you like some coffee or tea? Have you had lunch?"

He laughed. "I saw my parents first. My mother practically used a crowbar to get food down my throat. I think I'm full for the entire visit."

I unlocked the door. "You can wait to see if Erik does show up here, and if not, we can text him and ask where he is."

Felix followed me in, and Paige, who had darted out of her apartment to get her mail, said, "Hi, Hana, Hi, Erik." Then she looked again and said, "What?"

Felix laughed. He had a nice laugh, contagious, and I was soon giggling along. "Paige," I said, wiping my eyes, "This is Felix Wolf, Erik's brother."

Paige looked up at Felix, who had to be six foot four. "Wow. Nice to meet you," she said. "I thought for a minute that Hana was collecting tall blond guys."

"I'll talk to you later," I said as I made my way to the stairs.

"Nice meeting you," she murmured to Felix. She still looked bemused, as though I had performed a stunning magic trick in our hallway.

Felix followed me up another flight, and then watched me unlock the door and whisper promises to the clamoring cats. He shared his brother's love for animals, because within two seconds he had both felines in his arms, scratching their tummies while they sat against his chest. "Oh, and here are Erik's adopted children. He sent me pictures," Felix said. "I was jealous. We never had pets, growing up."

"Then, by all means, enjoy those two, and make yourself at home. In fact, I usually ask Erik to feed the cats, so maybe this time you can do it. The food is right next to their bowls in that plastic container."

Felix marched over to the food, looking like the King of Cats, and I realized that he also looked a lot like his father, who had reminded me of a king when I met him. With regal solemnity, Felix measured out the food into a little scoop and gave it to his brand-new acolytes.

"You and Erik—the cat whisperers," I said. I told Felix the drink choices, and he selected his brother's favorite, Diet Coke, just as Luca had done. We sat down at my table, and I said, "Well, now that I'm over the shock of accidentally molesting you, I can say that it is wonderful to meet you. Erik has told me all sorts of stories about your brotherly adventures. He misses you."

Felix nodded. "Yeah. I keep telling myself that I need to come back to be with the rest of my family. Maybe if I ever get married and have kids. Or I get a work transfer or something."

"And what's preventing you from getting married? Given the reaction of Paige—and me—you're probably like the Pied Piper of Seattle, except with women instead of children."

He shrugged. "Never really had the inclination."

"Is that so?" I started running through the list of single women I knew. "Well, let me know when you get the inclination, and I'll bet I can pair you up with the perfect person." I said this seriously, and he looked interested.

"That's right! The psychic thing. Runa and Thyra told me all about your grandma and you. And about the whole baby annunciation thing." For the first time he looked serious. "That's why I'm here, in fact. I want to be around for Runa in these last couple weeks."

I cleared my throat. "You need to call Runa."

"What?" He looked upset. "Don't tell me she's turning away visitors or something. I got an Air BnB and everything."

"Just call her. I'll give you some privacy."

With a wide-eyed look at me, he dialed his sister, and I left the room. I went to my bedroom, but even from there I heard Felix cry, "What? Runa, are you kidding me?" Then some quiet time, and another "What?"

This was followed by several minutes of soft murmuring, and then Felix appeared at my open bedroom door. "You delivered my little niece. You delivered my sister's baby, all by yourself, and you kept her calm and did all the right things and made it what she is calling the best experience of her life."

I shrugged, feeling awkward, and he held out his arms. "Get over here."

I stood up and found myself folded into a claustrophobic yet utterly comforting hug from Felix Wolf. I don't know how long it lasted; he seemed intent on hugging me forever. Then, my eyes just peeping over his shoulder, I saw the surprised face of Erik Wolf, who stood in my doorway like his brother's spirit shadow. Several expressions crossed his face: surprise, confusion, a hint of anger, and then I said, "Erik!"

Felix spun around and Erik cried, "Weebix!!"

Then the brothers were embracing, like two Thors in my little bedroom. Thank goodness I had made the bed at the start of Felix's phone call.

Talking loudly, rapidly, and over each other, the brothers returned to the kitchen, and each of them scooped up a cat.

Erik got himself a Diet Coke, and I learned, from their conversation, that Felix was in town for two weeks, that he had his own place to stay, that he had hoped to be a help to Runa and Andy, but that he wasn't needed in that way now.

"Why not?" Erik asked.

Felix looked at me, and I said, "Call your sister."

*

Felix left an hour later. I had fed both men Chicken Paprikás (Felix had reclaimed his appetite), and now Erik and I slumped on the couch, digesting. "I have to go soon," he said. "This was meant to be a one-hour break."

"I know."

His hand was in my hair, stroking it lazily while we watched leaves rustle in the tree outside my window. "I can't believe you delivered a baby. I mean, I can, but I can't believe things happened that way." He turned to me. "What was it like?"

I thought about it. "It was stressful and messy, and I was worried about keeping things sanitary, if not sterile. But in terms of seeing Anya emerge—in terms of seeing life come from life—it was awe-inspiring. To be the first person who touched her --" My eyes grew wet. "And Runa was so brave. She and Anya were both just focused on getting her into this world. Immediately." I laughed a watery laugh, and Erik hugged me.

"Just another way that my family is indebted to you. At this point, though, they're your family, too."

I touched his nose. "Why do you call him Weebix?"

He grinned. "Just a joke. When I was two and he was five, I followed him everywhere, doing what he did. The twins were always off in their own world. I couldn't say 'Felix,' but I came close. 'F' is a hard letter for a tiny kid."

"Adorable."

"Yes, that's me."

I smiled, tucking against him. "" Not to change the happy subject, but you got my text about Rose?"

His jaw tightened. "Yes."

"This might change things, right? I mean, it could be a possible motive."

Erik glanced at me with a sardonic look, and I held up my hands. "Sorry! I'm not telling you how to do your job. You know me; I'm just curious."

"Yes, I know you." He looked pleased about that. "And feel free to be curious. Whatever you learn, it comes straight to me."

"Yes, sir."

He kissed me. "And now, I have to go."

I jumped up to pack some leftover Paprikás for him and Greg Benton, who had a severe Hungarian food addiction and was half in love with my grandmother, who kept him supplied. "Tell Greg my grandma had another dream about him."

"Oh?" His eyes lit up. My grandma's dreams were not so much prophetic as they were entertaining.

I grinned, handing him my hastily-packed bag. "She dreamed that he let her shave his mustache."

Erik was still laughing as he jogged down the stairs.

Chapter Six

Three Messages

That evening my mother called. "Hana, did you talk to the family of Rose Toth and say they could have a discounted event at the tea house?"

"Oh, shoot. I forgot to tell you. Yes, I did. I thought it would be nice to help them not worry about prices for some sort of funeral meal."

"Mama and I agree. They have set up a Memorial Tea for this Friday afternoon."

"Great. I'll be back in the saddle tomorrow. Thanks for the time off."

"Of course! Have you recovered your equilibrium?"

"Yeah, I think so. Although I had another stressful incident."

"Oh no! What happened?"

I told her the story about Felix, and the mistaken identity, and why he could press charges for sexual assault. My mother laughed. I had wanted to make it funny, but I was a bit offended by the extent of her laughter; she had to hand the phone to my father, who demanded the story again, and then *he* was laughing.

"Okay, yes, I made a big giant fool of myself. In any case, Felix forgave me, and it was nice to meet him at long last."

My father was on speakerphone so that I could hear both of them gasping with stomach-cramping laughter and saying "Ahhhh," several times as they recovered. "Should I hang up, so that you two can pull yourselves together?" I asked crisply.

My mother was repentant. "No, I'm sorry, Hana. We would love to have Erik and his brother over for dinner. And you, of course." Geez, it got better and better.

She continued, "And let us know when we can visit Runa. I have a gift for her and the baby. And several of the Hungarian ladies have knitted and crocheted things. Mama has practically a whole layette of handmade things in soft pastel yarns. It's lovely."

"Runa will genuinely love that. She's emotional these days. I'm pretty sure she'll cry."

"How is poor Thyra in all of this? Her twin is getting all the attention."

I laughed. "Thyra has no shortage of attention. She and Runa saw each other every day during the pregnancy, and Runa told me that Anya's middle name will be Thyra, and—this is a secret—Runa told me that two men are vying for Thyra's affections in dramatic and expensive ways. Thyra is loving the drama."

My mother, ever compassionate, said, "Oh, but one of them will lose, and his heart will be broken."

I snorted. "Knowing Thyra, they'll probably both lose. But hopefully she won't string them along. More than she already has, I mean."

My father suddenly donned his traditional old man persona. "She needs to settle down. Look what it did for her sister."

I tried to picture Thyra "settling down," and failed. "Everyone's different, Dad."

"Not deep down," he insisted.

My mother interjected. "Hana, I'll want to talk to you about the decor for this memorial, and ideas for music and things. But I won't bother you with that tonight. I know you've had a crazy day, what with the baby, and your— introduction to Felix."

They were both starting to laugh again. "Okay, hilarious. I'll talk to you two later." I ended the call, but not before I heard my father whisper "A does of Hana love!"

Wow. For a moment I had been the hero who ushered new life into the world; now I was the buffoon who slipped on a banana peel.

Scowling, but sort of laughing, I put the phone down, only to have it ring again, as if refusing to be ignored. I saw Thyra's name and swiped the screen to 'answer.' "Hello?"

"Hana. I wanted to call and thank you—we all thank you—Mom, Dad, Runa, Andy, Erik, Felix—did you know Felix was here?" Well, thank goodness. Felix had not yet told them the tale of my indiscretion. "Yes, I met him earlier today. How is Runa? Are you there at the hospital?"

"Yes. I'm holding my niece in my arms, and she sparkles more than a sea of diamonds."

"Doesn't she? But of course, Runa would inevitably have a lovely child. Especially with Andy as the father." Then I added, thinking of my father's previous comment about settling down, "Someday *your* babies will be perfect, Thyra."

"And will you deliver them?" Thyra was an expert deflector.

"Maybe I will. I'm thinking of becoming a midwife on the side."

She laughed softly. "I imagine it was frightening. I would have been frightened."

"It was. But it was beautiful, and I'll never forget it. Did the doctors give Anya a clean bill of health?"

"They said she looked healthy and strong, and she literally just gorged herself on mother milk. We were all laughing because the kid just went on and on. Runa took to nursing with no trouble. She's on some kind of post-natal high. If you want to ask her for a sizeable loan, do it now."

I laughed. "So, what has the baby said to you?"

"She's sleeping right now after her huge meal. But she's endlessly entertaining. She let out a happy sigh, and then a huge fart—her very first fart—and her little mouth keeps up a sort of ghostly suckling, as though she wants to keep those muscles limber."

"You're cracking me up," I said, wiping tears of laughter from my eyes.

"I joke to cover up, my mother says."

"Cover up what?"

"Oh, ask her. My real emotions, my true feelings about any given thing. Ridiculous. Everyone knows my feelings about Anya Thyra Bell. She is my angel, and I will be her favorite aunt."

"When I come there, you have to let me hold her."

"Yes, yes. If you can find a time when she's not eating. Oh, and here comes her father with his lovesick look. I think I have to hand her over. He's been singing your praises, Hana. He and Runa have been vocal about their love and appreciation, practically writing odes to you. Frankly it's getting annoying."

"Oh, Thyra. You only say that to cover up your true feelings."

She laughed. "I have to hand over my precious one, so I'd better go. It's a delicate process."

"Okay."

"Hana."

"Yes?"

"I love you. I'll never forget what you did for my sister." There was nothing sarcastic in her tone now.

"I love you, too. I'm glad you are both in my life."

"Later," Thyra murmured, and the call ended.

I stared into space for a while, picturing the scene in the hospital: Runa, in a love daze, relaxing on her bed but keeping a watchful eye on her child; Andy, crooning over his tiny daughter and breathing in the intoxicating scent of baby skin; Thyra, in love, perhaps for the first time in her life, filled with a joy that she couldn't fully express. Although she'd done an impressive job, I thought.

I got up and checked the clock—nine P.M. Definitely time for one short movie or two episodes of a show before I thought about turning in for the night. I cleaned my kitchen and fed the cats. I flipped on a small lamp in my bedroom and turned back my covers in an alluring way—ready to welcome myself, I thought with a smirk.

I had just settled down with *The Proposal* when my phone rang again. "Hello?" I said, trying not to sound weary.

"Hana, Auntie Luca here."

"Hi, Auntie," I said lightly.

"I know you've had a crazy day, but I have a favor to ask of you."

Ugh. I hoped it wasn't a *right now* sort of favor. "What's that?"

"As you know, since Ji-Ji and I moved here, I've been living off of my vast wealth."

I laughed. She'd received a modest severance package

from her previous employer. It wasn't as generous as it could have been, since she did the severing, but it had helped the new mother and daughter buy their house and settle in. "In any case," she said, "I have received an unexpected job interview for tomorrow. It's a graphic design gig, and it sounds really good. I wonder if you could pick up Jia from school?"

That was a way easier favor than I'd feared. "Of course I'll pick her up. No problem. Do the teachers know that she can be released to me?"

"Yes. I texted her teacher, and I'm also sending a note in her backpack tomorrow."

"Okay. And pick-up time is--?"

"Three. Thank you so much, Hana. Just bring her to your place, and I'll pick her up as soon as I'm able."

"That's great about the interview."

"Yes! Lots of serendipity raining down on us these days."

I thought about her comment, as we ended the call, and realized that she was right. Many good things had happened in the last few months: Luca had moved back home; Domo and Margie had gotten engaged; Jia had entered our lives; Anya had been born healthy and safe; Runa and Andy had married; Erik and I were solidly together and happy, and I'd finally seen the gold-green light I had been destined to see around him; my parents and grandparents were healthy; Paige and her husband had two little girls now, named for flowers.

It dawned on me, suddenly, that there was a theme of girls running through these stories: Anya, Jia, Iris, Daisy. Another flower, Rose, had been expecting a child—would that baby, too, have been a girl?

It also occurred to me, as I got ready for bed, that I would be picking up Jia on a Monday--the day that they would notify the parents, and perhaps the students, in some gentle way, of Miss Rose's death.

How was a child supposed to process the loss of something so precious? How was anyone—Rose's family, her friends, her boyfriend, her co-workers—supposed to keep moving around the giant space that she had once filled?

With a sigh, I decided to postpone my movie. I climbed into bed, said a heartfelt prayer for those who had been born and those who had died, but also for those who had to negotiate the interval as best they could.

Chapter Seven

The Storybook School

On Monday morning, I felt refreshed and ready to accomplish things. I did a quick cleaning of my bathroom, then showered and dressed in jeans and an apricot-colored sweater. I lifted the cats onto the windowsill so that they could observe the cottony spring blossoms blowing past, and then I called my mother to make some plans for Friday's memorial event.

"Did they tell you how many people would be there?" I asked after we greeted each other. "I know it's hard to get RSVPs for a funeral."

"She thinks about seventy. Not that big."

"Okay. If you want, I'll print out that little quote card I made for the funeral brunch last year. They seemed to like it."

"Oh, yes, Hana—please do. Make about a hundred. It's always good to have extra."

"Sure. I might have to use Dad's printer if mine runs out of ink."

The previous year we had hosted the memorial of a middle-aged woman who had been popular in her community. I thought it would be nice to comfort the mourners with words, so I wrote a little poem and affixed it to cardstock so that it could be propped at every place setting. It said,

It is not my life that was an illusion,
But the belief that I am gone.
I am always, forever, etched on your soul
As you are surely embedded in mine.

It didn't rhyme, it had no particular rhythm, but I thought it was both comforting and truthful, and several people had approached to ask for the author's name so that they could quote it later. This time, I thought, I would put my name underneath.

We finished our call a few minutes later, and I got to work on the poetry cards. I found a nice quotation template online and plugged in my text. It looked sedate and elegant, just low-key enough to be appropriate for a memorial. The border was a simple black line, with one little leaf in the upper right-hand corner. I began to print out the copies; while they chugged out of my little printer, I found my black pre-cut cardstock, which I used for all sorts of stationery needs, and brought it back to the printer desk. I felt a surge of envy for Erik's desk. He had an actual office in his home, and his desk was something his parents had found at a Chicago estate sale—an 'executive desk" with all sorts of drawers that little Hana fingers enjoyed exploring. The last time I'd played with it, I found a note in the top drawer that said, "Stop snooping, Hana."

When my printer ran out of ink, as predicted, I counted what I had—forty-seven—and called my father to say I would be stopping by.

"No problem, hon. I just put a new cartridge in there."

"I'll give you some money for it."

"It's for the tea house, so we'll charge it to your mother," he joked. "It's her name on the sign, right?"

"Okay. See you in half an hour."

I spent some time with the cats, letting them chase a string as I dragged it around the apartment. Then we enjoyed a petting session during which I had to be ambidextrous so that I could pet both of them at once (they got jealous), and I chatted to them, extolling the virtues of spring.

"Did you like Felix?" I asked Cleopatra, who had been the one that Felix held during his conversation with Erik. Cleo blinked at me. I sensed that even she had a crush on the tall and handsome Felix. "Well, I'm sure you'll both see him again before he leaves. Probably many times. He has hinted that he'd like to taste more Hungarian food. Subtle, right?" I laughed at their little blinky faces.

"Okay, I'm running errands. You have food and water, and I'll see you later." Antony had already jumped into his sleeping spot in my comfy red chair, as though he couldn't be bothered with my goodbyes before he dozed off.

I locked the apartment and jogged down to my car, ready for several stops. I had brought my library books—a wonderful pile of mysteries by Jane Casey, Elly Griffiths, and Simon Mason—and the library was my first stop. I was a sucker for a good mystery, especially those set anywhere in England, so I was eating up these series books as fast as I could. All three of these writers had perfect balance, in that they could keep me in suspense, even terrify me, but also keep me laughing, sometimes right out loud.

I drove out of my lot and listened to some classical music while I navigated through town, finally pulling up at the convenient library drop-off bin, which I could access without leaving my car. I lifted the books from my passenger seat and pushed them carefully through the return slot. I'd have to drag

Erik back here with me so that we could both choose new bedtime reading. It had become a rather fun precursor to other bedtime activities.

I smiled to myself as I drove to destination two: the hospital, Runa, and Anya. I wondered if Andy had already started his paternity leave. I was guessing yes. He would be glued to his wife and daughter until they made him return.

Finding a rare spot close to the door, I tucked in my car and jogged to the main entrance. I was excited, I realized, even eager, to meet Anya again. I practically jogged in place as I got my visitor's pass and directions to Runa's floor. Then I speed-walked to the elevator and ran down the hall to Runa's door.

I peeked in, not wanting to disturb Runa if she or the baby were sleeping. I briefly glimpsed a familial scene: Runa smiling at Andy as he held his daughter's little hand in his. Andy looked up then, saw me, and burst out of his chair to fold me into a hug. "Oh, Hana," he breathed in my ear. "We are so, so grateful! If you hadn't come by, Runa would have gone into labor all alone. I don't like to think about it." He leaned back to study my surprised face, then hugged me again, after which he took my hand and led me to the bed, where little Anya was studying the ceiling with a thoughtful expression.

"She's gorgeous," I said, and I meant it. This was not the red little baby with rather mucky hair that I had held briefly the day before. This was a tiny blonde angel with carefully brushed hair and a little red bow of a mouth.

Runa smiled at me, then looked back at her baby. "Andy and I had said we didn't want children, and now we're wondering how many more we can have," she joked. "We'll have to take her everywhere, because we can't bear to be away from her."

"I understand why. What a little treasure." I edged

forward to touch her hair. Her face seemed elastic, and she changed expressions every few seconds. One moment she looked sad, and then seconds later she seemed about to laugh. Then she would simply stretch her mouth or raise her tiny pale eyebrows.

I mentioned this to Runa, who laughed. "I know, isn't it adorable? The nurse said it's totally normal, and that she's getting used to her muscles and what they do."

"What a journey she's taken. And look how well she's adapting to her brand-new world." I studied her sturdy little body. "She looks—bigger than she did yesterday."

Now Andy laughed. "My daughter has been ravenous since I met her. She's going to grow big and strong."

"I wonder how tall she'll be," I said. "Hard to imagine, when she's tinier than a loaf of bread."

We chatted for a while, all of us staring in fascination at Anya, who rested calmly against her mother's chest.

"Did you want to hold her, Hana?"

I did, but I also didn't want to disturb her. "She's so happy there, Runa. I'll hold her next time."

"Then come to our place tomorrow," Runa said. "They're sending us home today, but Anya wants to see you."

I smirked at this. Anya seemed just fine in the company of her worshipful parents. "I will. But I just wanted to dart in and say hi. I have to stop at my parents' place and get something from my dad. But I'll see you all soon." I stood up and took one of Anya's tiny hands in mine. "It was so nice seeing you again, little Anya."

Anya was still experimenting with facial expressions, but as I held her hand, she looked up at me gravely, like a miniscule ambassador, and her parents burst out laughing. "My daughter is polite," said the besotted Andy. I'd noticed that he'd managed to work the words "my daughter" into every other sentence. I was glad Domo wasn't with me, because he would have been rolling his eyes by now, and his conversation on the way home would center on how over-the-top some parents could be. I knew, though, that when Domo became a father, he would be just as infatuated with his child, or more so, than Andy and Runa were now. And why not? What a beautiful thing it was, to fall in love with your children, and to have moments of pure happiness in an often-cruel world.

At the door I turned again. Runa waved Anya's little hand at me, but Anya turned and began butting her head into Runa's breast. Even halfway down the hall I could hear them giggling and murmuring about their outrageously hungry daughter.

When I entered my parents' house, I found my father sitting at the table with a man I did not know. They spoke to each other quietly, wearing grave expressions, and I greeted them uncertainly.

My dad stood up. "Hana, good to see you." He gave me a hug, and then he stepped back. The other man, his expression sad, stood up out of politeness. I waved him back into his seat with a smile.

"Hana, this is Steven Toth. Rose is his daughter."

Stunned, I dropped into a chair across from Mr. Toth and murmured my condolences, which he accepted with a bow of his head, and looked to my father for an explanation.

"I didn't make this connection before now," my father said. "But Steve and I were colleagues at the high school. He was the senior counselor."

"I retired last year," said Toth.

"I see. I just learned that your daughter was a teacher," I said gently. "A very popular one, from what I hear."

"All three of my girls are educators," he said with a touch of pride. "Rose taught the little ones. Lida teaches art to high school kids, and Teresa gives private music lessons. She's in demand—has a waiting list." It seemed difficult, suddenly, for him to speak, as though he had a sore throat. It struck me, in a new and visceral way, that I was talking to a man whose daughter had been *murdered*. Perhaps it was the proximity of my own father, and the knowledge of our loving relationship, but the grief of Mr. Toth elicited my sympathy even more than had the grief of his daughters. My eyes filled with tears. I touched his hand, and we were all quiet for a moment.

My father said, "Detective Wolf is Hana's boyfriend. You said you spoke to him already?"

Mr. Toth nodded, his eyes on me. "Twice. He seems focused." He assessed me for a moment. "Does he—usually solve his cases? Get the people responsible?"

With a burst of pride, I said, "Yes. He won't give up, Mr. Toth. And his partner Greg Benton is great, too."

He seemed satisfied with that. "I don't want to know them. I don't want this to be happening. I want my girl back. My Rose." His face crumpled, and I thought of Andy, saying "my daughter" again and again, getting used to the sound of it, trying to believe in his own miracle, his daughter's presence. Here, on the other hand, was a father who couldn't believe in his daughter's absence. *We are such stuff as dreams are made on . . . .*

We sat with Mr. Toth as he wept into his hands. I signaled to my father, asking with a subtle gesture if one of us should hug our sad visitor, but my father shook his head. Instead, he put his hand on his friend's arm. "It's unthinkable, Steve. A cruel reality that none of you deserve. How is Rachel holding up?"

Now Toth shook his head, rubbing his eyes. "She's

sedated. It's—better for her right now. She couldn't handle the news at all."

I wanted to punch something. Punch *someone.* I wanted to find the person who crushed this lovely rose, his Rose, and pound him with my grandmother's rolling pin.

My father's hand was still in place on Toth's arm. Toth had covered it with his own hand, clearly grateful to have it there. "It must he a small comfort that you saw her that day. You said you spent the morning together?"

He nodded. "She had breakfast with Rachel and me. She always lit up a room, and she had us laughing, like always, with stories of her little students, and --" His eyes welled up again. "She told us she was going to have a baby. Rachel was in ecstasies. A first grandchild!" He gave a rueful smile, a pained thing. "That's why Rachel couldn't handle it. To lose her first-born *and* the child. It was too cruel."

I stood up and went to Mr. Toth, hugging him from behind. Now he held my father's hand and put his free hand on one of mine. He didn't seem embarrassed, though. I felt— actually *felt*—our support and compassion seeping into him, and he revived like a wilting flower in water.

"I appreciate your kindness. Both of you," he said. "It's hard. But people like you will make the way easier." I thought again of my grandma's metaphor of grief as a journey. Yes, and perhaps a long journey. I recalled Albert saying that one had to take that journey alone.

Eventually I noticed that Mr. Toth's coffee cup was empty. I went to my father's machine and found the pot was still heating. I poured Mr. Toth another cup, and he nodded at me.

"Mr. Toth --"

"Steve, please."

"Steve," I said, "the police will want to know everything

she said to you. Anything that stood out at your breakfast together. You'll want to try to remember."

He sighed. "Your boyfriend already asked me that. I can't recall, aside from her school stories, and our talk about the baby, and –" he paused.

My father leaned in. "Did you think of something?"

He looked blank for a moment. "I—there was something she said, when she told us she was expecting—about how she would have told us sooner, but she had to talk to us about some things. We were thinking maybe she needed to get Albie to come around in his thinking."

"So, Albie hadn't wanted children?" Neither had Andy and Runa, supposedly.

"I don't know—I always thought he did. I mean, I've known him for about two years, and I remember him talking now and then about family. So now I'm not sure . . . ."

I tucked this detail away to share with Erik, assuming Steve didn't do so first. Steve didn't look capable of much right now, drooping sadly over the table with mournful eyes.

"Steve, have you eaten today?" my father asked, concerned.

He shook his head. "I can't really—"

My dad stood up and went to the refrigerator, and in minutes he had made sandwiches for all three of us, beside each of which he had tucked a pickle and a pile of chips.

Steve stared at the food as though he didn't know what it was, but gradually he lifted the sandwich and took a bite. A minute later his hungry body took over, and he began to eat with more energy. My father and I talked of nothing things, giving Steve time to rest and eat. I realized that I was hungry, too, and felt grateful to my father for his nurturing.

Eventually Steve said, "I should go." He kept sitting there, though. It couldn't have been pleasant to contemplate his sad house, his sedated wife, his weeping daughters, probably a mournful Albie, as well.

"Stay for a while. Keep me company while I do the dishes," my father said, and Steve relaxed into his chair. I knew that my father liked to get all of his grading done on these rare days off, but he would never neglect a friend.

I murmured something about the printer and went into my parents' office to make the rest of my copies, after which I carefully glued each sheet to the black cardstock. I looked at the clock when I finished and felt a punch of urgency in my gut. I packed the cards in my purse and hurried to the kitchen.

"I've got to run, Dad," I said. "I have to pick up Jia, and the school lets out at three."

My father's face brightened at the mention of Jia. She was his unexpected new niece, and the two of them had bonded immediately over sports. My dad had been re-watching the Cubs World Series win, and Jia had climbed into his lap (she loved sitting on laps). My father had answered her questions, of which there had been *many,* and she had nestled closer against him with each of his deep-voiced responses until she had fallen asleep against his chest. The whole family loved the story, but it wasn't one to reflect on now, with poor Steve sitting in front of us like an empty shell.

I gave my father a hug, and Steve stood up to hug him, as well. "Thanks again, Jack. You've been a great friend to me today."

My father returned Steve's hug, and I saw his face over Steve's shoulder. His expression was furious, at least for an instant. It was clear that my father, like me, wanted to get this perpetrator in his sights.

Steve and I walked out together, and I said that I would probably see him Friday at the tea house. He didn't seem aware of the event – "the girls are handling that"—but he was pleased that it was happening. We spoke for a moment on my parents' porch. "Your dad is a good man," he said. "I didn't know who to turn to, and then I remembered that he lived close by. It was nice of him to take me in."

I nodded. "He feels terrible for you. So do I."

He thought about this. "You know, when Rose left our house after breakfast, she said, 'Don't forget to come see our show tonight. It's that outdoor stage, right by the woods. We'll all be watching you gather from there, like the fairies that we are. It's going to be spectacular. My costume is a show-stopper!"

He sent me an ironic look. We didn't need to say it aloud. Rose had indeed stopped the show.

Steve left then, walking gingerly down the steps as though he were twenty years older than his age, and moving with dragging steps toward a nondescript car parked at the curb. He folded himself into the driver's seat, and the car soon drove away.

All of the euphoria I'd felt at seeing Anya had dissipated with the reality of Steve's grief, his wife's despair, his daughter's demise. Dispirited, I drove to Longwood Academy. I'd visited the place once or twice when I'd been invited to one of Iris's recitals. She usually spent the time staring at the other children on the risers and moving her lips up and down, fishlike, as though this would fool adults into thinking she was singing. This memory lifted my spirits slightly. Iris was always a day-brightener.

The school, a basic institutional-looking structure, was distinguished by two special things. First, one had to negotiate a little wooded driveway to find the building, itself tucked into an acre of woods. Second, as a nod to this wooded location and the fact that it was a primary school, the architect had designed the front facade to look like a charming little cottage.

The children were enchanted by it—at least the tiny ones were. The fifth and sixth graders tended to march in with embarrassed expressions, as though they hoped no one other than their equally-horrified classmates saw them enter such a structure.

The building was undeniably charming, as was the wooded lot, and when the children began to flow out, dismissed a class at a time, I had the sensation that I was watching a cartoon. Tiny little figures—the preschoolers, surely—went darting out, exuberant and leaping, before finding the safety of their parents' arms.

I edged close to the main entrance, where several teachers stood at what seemed to be appointed posts. Perhaps I was still reeling from my recent shocks, but I had the strange sensation that someone was watching me, perhaps from the woods around us. I gave in to the feeling and turned to look into the trees behind me. Had I seen motion there? Or was it merely a forest fairy, the kind that Rose had been portraying when she went too far into woods of her own?

The thought chilled me.

Chapter Eight

Watering the Mice

I caught the eyes of one of the teachers and waved. "I'm picking up Jia Horvath today. I'm her cousin. Her mom called it in?"

Th woman, short and bosomy with dark hair and kind brown eyes, said, "Yes, I spoke to Ms. Horvath myself. You are Hana?"

I stuck out my hand. "Yes, Hana Keller."

She shook it and said, "I'm Edie Pembroke, the Principal here at Longwood."

"Nice to meet you. I'm also a good friend of Iris Gonzales, who is my neighbor and the custodian of our building."

Edie Pembroke laughed at this. "I believe it entirely. Iris is a force unto herself."

A child hurtled toward us and flung herself at the woman beside me. "Bye, Mrs. Pembroke!" said a breathy little voice.

Edie Pembroke bent to give the little girl a generous hug. "Goodbye, Gretchen! I will be so excited to see you again tomorrow!"

The girl moved away, beaming, and Edie Pembroke

looked genuinely thrilled by the encounter. She spoke to me in a low voice. "She used to be so shy that she would barely greet her own friends. It took her teacher two months to get her to speak aloud in class. But we kept working on it. We were Team Gretchen. And she is transformed."

I thought I might have seen a tear in her eye, and I opened my mouth to say something when another Pembroke fan shot toward us in a blur. This child, though, had flung herself at me, and I realized as she made contact and almost knocked me down that it was Jia.

I picked her up, and she wrapped her limbs around me in the expected way, letting her backpack fall to the ground. "Hi, Hana!"

"Hi, sweetheart. Did you have a good day?"

"Yes," she said, looking shyly at Mrs. Pembroke.

The principal reached into the pocket of a capacious cardigan. "Jia, do you know what your teacher told me today?"

Jia shook her head. Mrs. Pembroke looked directly into Jia's little face. "She said that you read a page out loud to her and did not make one error!"

Jia's smile was huge. "I did," she said. I loved the way that children were willing to accept compliments and tell the truth about their pride in themselves.

Mrs. Pembroke's hand came out of her pocket with a blue button that read, "I am a Longwood Lion!"

"I think you deserve to wear this. Do you know why?"

Jia shook her head.

"Because you have come from a different school and bravely walked into a new class and made friends of students and teachers alike. Not everyone can find such courage when they come to a new place. You have a special talent for befriending people. Longwood Lions are all about friendship."

She smiled into Jia's awed face. "And because of your excellent performance in reading today."

She reached out and attached the pin to Jia's little sweater. "I'm proud of you," said Mrs. Pembroke. I was impressed with the woman; not just with the way she made each student feel special, but because she made each of her actions on their behalf seem monumental and memorable. Something the children could tuck into their hearts. Even I sort of wanted a button now.

"Wow, Jia! What a special thing to get from your principal! What would you like to say?" I asked. Jia was still clinging to me like a bony monkey.

"Thank you," she whispered.

Mrs. Pembroke patted Jia's head with great affection. "You are welcome. Oh, and here's Mr. Bevington. Do you like art class, Jia?"

Jia nodded again, her big eyes moving to the man who now stood before us, looking pale and a bit sick. He said, "Do you have a minute, Edie?"

"Of course, Bruce. This is Jia's cousin, Hana Keller. Ms. Keller, this is Bruce Bevington, Longwood's art program director."

I reached past Jia and shook his hand. "How do you do?"

He offered a rueful smile. "I've had better days." He did in fact look rather disheveled, as though the children had knocked him down and attacked him with his own art supplies. His brown hair was messy, and his apron was paint-spattered and wrinkly. "This was a rough day for the kids, but even more for the teachers, I think."

Edie Pembroke looked at me with her brows raised. "I'm not sure if you saw our announcement on the website--?"

I shook my head. "No, but I figured it was happening

today." I looked at Jia, who was waving to a friend, and then said, "I was at the event where it happened."

Both Mr. Bevington and Ms. Pembroke looked horrified, and I nodded. "I did not know her, but I've met a lot of people who loved her, and I know what a loss this is to you all."

More children had gathered around the principal, and she bent to speak to them. "Hello, my lovely lions! Did you have a fine day?"

The little ones talked at once, in a cacophony of responses. Mrs. Pembroke laughed. "Wonderful! I am impressed by your energy! Be sure to help your parents if they need it today. Because in being good family members, we are also being good--?"

"Citizens!" piped the little voices, along with Jia's, which yelled right in my ear.

I gave her a fake-stern look and said, "Okay, I'm putting you down now. No problem with your little lungs, Cousin."

Jia giggled as she slid down the front of me and ran to join the little circle around her principal. Mr. Bevington sent me a weary smile. I ventured, "Were you good friends with Rose?"

He reddened slightly, and I feared I had made him angry with my question, but he answered calmly enough. "Yes. She was a kindred soul. Loved art, and had an artistic sensibility. She and I painted the backdrops together for the school plays."

That was the sort of activity that bonded people, something that extended beyond the school day and allowed for more casual conversations. "I'm sorry," I said.

He nodded. "I haven't wrapped my head around it yet. When I go home, it will feel more real. Especially when she doesn't call to hassle me about my latest art project. Sometimes, she said, they were too nouveau." He attempted a smile. Then his expression changed into an aggravated frown. "Oh, God," he said.

I turned to see another man coming out of the building just behind a blonde woman in a light trench coat. He was saying, "I do apologize again," to the back of her head as she marched away. She was definitely displeased with him, and she glared down at her pink, manicured nails, one of which was short and jagged. Perhaps he had bumped into her and caused her to break a nail? In any case, she rapid-walked toward the parking lot, and he moved slowly into the throng of people. He was a tall, fussy-looking person with wire-rimmed glasses and a rumpled grey suit. With an air of importance, he removed a watch on a chain from his vest pocket and studied the wathface.

"Is that a pocket watch?" I whispered to Bevington in amazement. The man looked like an old-timey train conductor.

Bevington snorted. "It is. And I assure you, its primary function is not timekeeping, but performance. I think he fancies himself a sort of children's tv character." He sent me an apologetic look. "I guess he's okay, but I am *not* in the mood for his theatrics just now."

The man was saying, "All right, children, be on your way. The gates will be locked in a few minutes!"

"He always wants to get home early," Bevington said. "He and his wife are in the amateur theatrical society, and they usually have play practice. I don't know how Edie puts up with him."

"He's a teacher, or--?"

"Vice Principal," Bevington murmured as the man came toward us.

"Hello," he said. "How is everyone today?"

Bruce Bevington didn't dignify that with an answer, but he said, "This is Hana. She's picking up little Jia, our new girl."

The man thrust out a long hand. "I'm Adam Partridge, the vice principal here at Longwood."

78

"Nice to meet you, Mr. Partridge." I shook his hand; he hadn't looked like a muscular person, but his grip was surprisingly strong. I made a little mental note of this, then looked around for Jia.

Bevington sighed now, looking suddenly exhausted. He said. "Hana was at the performance where it happened."

Partridge's face went white. "You—were there? Several of us went to the dress rehearsal, but not the Saturday show. Did you actually see--?" he paused, not sure how to go on.

"No. She ran into the woods as a part of her performance. I guess—someone was waiting for her there."

That silenced all of us. Edie Pembroke had finished complimenting her little charges, and they had flown to meet their parents. She returned to see us all looking glum. She grew brisk. "Bruce, if you still want to talk, we can do so in my office." She turned to me and said, "It was nice meeting you, Hana."

"You too," I said. "Jia, let's get going." Jia skipped to my side, and I waved briefly to Mr. Partridge, who nodded at me before tucking his watch away.

In the car, I looked at Jia as she went through many painstaking steps to buckle herself in. Her little face was ridiculously cute, and I tended to stare sometimes, enjoying the sweetness. She would grow rapidly, as Iris had done, as Anya would do. "So, you had a nice day today?"

She nodded. "We had story time and art time. Usually, we just have one or the other." She thought about this, and her features became pensive. "Mrs. Pembroke came to our room for a serious chat."

Edie's words, I was guessing. "Oh? What was that about?"

"She said the teacher in the other first grade had an accident, and she passed away." Her face crumpled slightly.

"That's sad. Did you know that other teacher?"

She shook her head. "I just saw her every day when we lined up. She was really pretty, with long hair. Me and Iris said she was like a princess." Her sadness was increasing. I didn't want to deprive her of a chance to express her feelings, but I also didn't want to make her sadder than was necessary.

"Did Mrs. Pembroke give you all some ideas about how to remember her?"

She dipped her little chin in assent. "She said that if we pray, we could pray for her, and if we don't pray, we could think of her family and save special pictures of her in our minds."

"That's nice. Good advice," I said. We were driving past the river, headed toward my apartment, and a fresh, spring smell came in my window. I darted a glance at Jia and saw fat tears running down her cheeks.

"Do you want me to be quiet so that you can feel your feelings?" I asked.

She shook her head. "I want you to say something."

I thought for a moment. "When I was little, and I was sad, my great-grandmother Natalia would take me into her lap and say, '*Miért itatod az egereket*?'"

She wiped at her tears with a little hand and studied me with a wise expression. "That sounds like my mom's homeland language."

"Yes. Do you remember what it's called?"

"Hunkerian."

"Yes, Hungarian. The language of Hungary, where my great grandmother, and my grandmother and grandfather, and your mother, and my mother, and our uncle Zoltan were all born."

She was quiet for a while, then said, "What did your grandma say, but in English?"

"My *great*-grandma."

80

"Yeah."

"What she said meant, 'Why are you watering the mice?'"

Her eyes grew wide, and she laughed through sparkling tears. "She didn't say that."

"She did. Because she said that when a child cried, since they were so close to the ground, their tears became a drink for the mice. Or a little shower, maybe."

She giggled again. "Maybe the mice *need* some water."

"They probably do. That's why we all cry sometimes, but the mice like the tears of children best. It's healthy to cry when we're sad, so the mice are getting healthy food."

She sent me a wry look. "You're making that all up. It's not healthy food!" She called this out with another giggle, and I felt a burst of gratitude to Natalia, who was never far from my thoughts and always an inspiration.

Jia and I shared some lemonade at my house, along with some Nilla wafers. Jia put one wafer in each cheek and told me she was a chipmunk. My instinct was to see how many I could shove into my own mouth, but I said, "Be careful not to choke, Jia." Parenting was no fun.

Jia made me teach her the mice saying in Hungarian. She practiced until she could say a recognizable version of it. When Luca got to my place, Jia ran to her, gave her a hug, and said, "Mee-et unterikuz ezraket!" A noble effort. Luca's eyes widened, and then she made a show of looking around.

"Are we in Hungary? Is my grandmother Natalia here? It sounds like someone's been quoting my grandmother!"

"I am!" Jia shouted. "I spoke Hunkerian!"

Luca knelt and held her daughter close. "And have you been watering the mice?"

Jia nodded. "I was sad. Miss Rose passed away." Her large, kind eyes threatened to fill again. "Hana said it was healthy to feel my feelings, but then she said I was watering the mice."

Luca sent me an approving look over Jia's head. Then she told the little girl, "Of course, she's right. Her great-grandmother told her that when she was little. And her great-grandmother was my grandmother. Does that make sense? And Hana's grandmother is my mother, Juliana."

"When you were little, did you water the mice?" Jia asked, playing with Luca's dark hair.

"Oh, yes. My brother Zoltan called me a water spout."

Jia giggled, then sighed. "It's important to express your feelings."

"You are so right," said my Aunt Luca. She looked very pretty in that moment, her dark hair loose, her eyes bright, her cheeks pink with excitement. "Hey—are those Nilla wafers? I suppose that's good enough celebration food." She swooped up her daughter and ran into the kitchen. "Because I got the job!!"

Chapter Nine

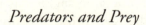

Predators and Prey

On Thursday evening I sat on my couch, popcorn bowl on my lap, tucked against Erik Wolf's solid shoulder, listening to *Dracula*. In addition to our library book nights, we had begun the habit of listening to an audiobook together, bit by bit, on certain evenings after dinner. The pastime allowed us to unwind, relax, and kiss when the urge arose. We had started with that particular spooky classic a week earlier, when we had found, in a random conversation, that neither of us had ever read it.

The book had been delightful so far, not only because it was heavy with Gothic tropes, but because there were, to my surprise, many references to Hungary. The first narrator, Harker, begins his tale in Budapest, through which he has passed while on his journey from England to the Transylvanian castle of Count Dracula. Harker speaks of the beauty of Budapest, the loveliness of the Danube, and the surprise of a new spice he has never encountered but loves at first taste: paprika.

Erik had grinned at me, and I said, after my initial surprise, "Of course. No one can resist it."

Later, inside Dracula's castle, Harker meets an extremely eccentric man with weirdly sharp teeth who never joins him at dinner. "Red flag," Erik had murmured. Dracula, at one point, gives a long speech about his people, and how Transylvania was made up of four groups, including "Magyars in the West, and Szekelys in the East and North."

"So, a bunch of Hungarians," Erik noted.

"Right? No wonder they always got Hungarians to play Dracula. Bela Lugosi was Hungarian. So was that little guy with the weird voice. Peter Lorre," I said.

"Peter Lorre wasn't in *Dracula*," Erik had observed.

"Whatever. Also, at one point the count offers Harker his plum brandy, which he calls, what? Slivovitz? But it's *obviously Pálinka*."

We had found the little Hungarian touches to be one of the highlights of the book to this point, although the suspense, and the character list, kept growing. Tonight, we were following the travails of poor Miss Lucy Westenra, Dracula's gentle prey, who kept being drained of blood and having to receive transfusions to revive her. Four different men performed this duty at different times, reanimating the feeble Lucy.

"Apparently they didn't know about blood types back then," Erik observed, digging for the caramel-flavored bits and avoiding the cheese.

"You're supposed to eat them together," I scolded. "It's a taste pairing that satisfies the palate." I took the bowl back and smashed a handful of popcorn in my face in a way that Miss Lucy would have found unladylike. Erik laughed.

"Her well-meaning boyfriends are going to kill her if they pump the wrong blood type into her," he noted.

I set the bowl aside, feeling indignant. "God, she's such a *victim!* Is this how Bram Stoker saw women?

Erik paused the audio with a flick of his remote. "Not all the women in the book are like Miss Lucy. She's just a fragile little flower." He grinned at me.

"Blech." He laughed again, reclaiming the popcorn to do his careful picking. "Here's how it should have gone down, the *first* time she woke up with barely any blood inside her. She should have said, after being revived, "Listen, something seems to have taken away all of my blood. In addition, I have these mysterious, itchy wounds on my neck. You guys are doctors—figure it out, and put some guards outside, and don't just say how worried you are!"

There was a pause, during which I realized I had kind of yelled the last few words. Erik put the bowl down between us. "Makes sense. But also, maybe you're feeling upset about victimized women in general right now."

"I'm always upset about victimized women. Lucy is *prey*. Poor Rose Toth was *prey*. I'm sick and tired of predators in a supposedly civilized society. Not to mention that it's an unhealthy and dangerous way for men to view their female equals."

"You can't assume Rose's predator was a man."

"You know what I mean, though."

"Yes," Erik said, putting the bowl on a side table. His face became sad.

I felt guilty then. "I'm sorry, my sweetheart. I'm bumming you out," I said, smoothing his hair and kissing his nose. "This is supposed to be our mellow hour."

"It's also a time for us to talk, if we want to. So, vent away."

I shook my head. "No, I've said my piece." I relaxed my rigid posture and leaned against him once more. "Tomorrow is the memorial for Rose. Family, friends, co-workers will be there, I expect."

"Your grandmother already told me," Erik said, grinning at the memory. "She's bought into the new image she's created of me as a protector. The cop in wolf's clothing."

"Well, I'm glad she told you, because I forgot until just now. Will you be there?"

"Greg and I will both be there. Your mom suggested that we just pretend to be guests, since our last undercover effort apparently didn't fool people."

"Domo said that cops look like cops, and that their badges would shine to outer space."

"Your brother talks like an experienced criminal."

I offered him a wry smile. "I think he was one in another life."

Erik slapped his thighs. "Okay, subject change. I was chatting with Paige downstairs when I got here. She said that the penthouse apartment is going to be available. Apparently, Tim the computer guy is moving to California. The siren song of Silicon Valley is luring him."

"Oh wow. Well, good for him. He'll probably make tons of money."

"Yeah. So, I thought you might want to claim the apartment."

I turned to him, surprised. "I might--? That place costs at least double what I'm paying now. Probably triple. It's way bigger. Three bedrooms, two baths, giant windows, bedroom skylight, modern stainless-steel kitchen . . . . "

Erik frowned. "Did you—date Tim at some point?"

I laughed and hugged him. "No, I didn't date him. He had a New Year's party there a couple years ago, and he invited all the tenants along with his friends. It was a brilliant strategy, because our invitations ensured that none of us would complain about strangers or loud music, and we neighbors got to know each other better. Plus, Hana could nose around, holding her champagne glass and looking casual while she scoped the real estate."

"Ah. You certainly seem to admire it."

"I do, of course. But it's not like my cats and I need three bedrooms and two baths."

"No, but you and I might like the extra space if we moved in it together. And we'd have two salaries with which to pay our rent."

I turned, meeting his beautiful green eyes. "You're saying you want to move in together?" The final word disappeared because I was suddenly breathless.

He took my right hand in his. "Do you?"

"Well—yes! I would love to move in together! And now that you mentioned Tim's apartment, I want that, too!"

His smile was extremely wide. "Seems silly to have two rentals when I'm always here."

"It does. When is Tim leaving?" A part of me was already imagining my furniture, and Erik's, in Tim's apartment. And Runa and Thyra could help us decorate—Runa especially had excellent taste. And I would finally have space to hang my Kodaly paintings! They were large, framed oils that I'd obtained in October, and I had longed for wall space to do them justice.

"Are you decorating in your mind?" Erik asked, laughing.

I stuck out my tongue. "Yes. And there's no room for your stuff."

He leaned in close and touched his lips to mine. "That's okay. I don't need much stuff. I just need my Hana."

For the next several minutes I lost myself in some enjoyable popcorn-flavored kisses, pressing my body against Erik's until we both grew excited. Erik spoke softly, in his seductive voice. "Seems like we're at a crossroads here. We can keep listening to *Dracula,* or we can turn it off and have some couples time."

"How many couples were you planning to include?" I joked weakly, plucking at the buttons on his shirt.

He smiled. I loved his smile. "Just us. The cats can wait out here when we adjourn to the boudoir."

I laughed, and Erik's phone sounded, with its thrilling ring tone: the *Mission Impossible* theme.

"Hold that thought," he said, standing up to retrieve his phone from the kitchen table, where he'd tossed it, and his keys, when he arrived.

Normally, holding that thought wouldn't be a problem, since I found sexy Erik enthralling, but in an instant, I had gone from excitement to dread, filling with *the misery* I had felt when Aunt Luca told me about Rose. This feeling had become more and more palpable to me as my psychic instincts increased. I cried, "Don't answer it!" just as Erik reached the kitchen and switched on the phone.

He appeared in the doorway and sent me a surprised look as he said, "Hello?" Then he listened for a while, his brows furrowed. He managed, "Dad, just say it!" and listened some more. His face grew pale, and he sat down suddenly, right there on the kitchen floor. I stood and edged closer to him, sensing the imminent pain.

"Where?" Erik asked tersely. Then he said, "Okay, see you there," and he ended the call. He sat for a moment, staring at the doorframe, seemingly deep in thought. I felt his turmoil, and I knew that he needed some quiet time. I supposed it was as true with Erik as it was with Jia—he needed to feel his feelings.

Finally, I walked to the doorway, knelt beside him, and wrapped my arms around him, Tense, afraid to ask, I said, "What is it? Is it the baby?"

He cleared his throat. "It's Felix," he said.

The misery flooded in, and I knew, somehow, that another predator had done its work.

Chapter Ten

In the Dark

For the third time in a few days, I entered the hospital lobby, this time clutching Erik's hand. We checked in at the desk and received our visitor's passes. We had traveled without conversation, for the most part, because I sensed that Erik needed and wanted the quiet for processing events and emotions, and that my mere presence provided enough comfort. He was gripping my hand tightly, so I struggled to attach my visitor's pass one-handed. Then we were racing to the emergency ward, where we found Erik's entire family in the lobby—his parents, Runa, and Thyra. Andy must have stayed with the baby. All of the Wolfs hugged each other in greeting, and then they all hugged me. Erik's mother hung on to me for a long time, so I tried to send calm and comfort into her. She finally pulled away and said, "Thank you, Hana." She managed a tiny smile, but I could feel her fear.

"What do we know?" Erik asked briskly.

"A doctor came out a while ago and said they were doing a cranial MRI, checking for any bleeding or bone fragments," Thyra said quietly. Her blue eyes glistened with unshed tears.

"Is your boyfriend on duty? The one who works here?" Erik asked her.

She nodded. "His name is Rolf, Erik, as you know. He said he'll keep us apprised, too."

Erik's father tried a bit of bluster. "I'd like to get a straight story. We don't know what in the world happened! How did he come to be unconscious in a parking lot?"

I looked away, hurting for them, and saw a woman sitting on one of the chairs against the wall—a woman that I knew. "Maria?" I called.

She looked up and brightened when she saw me. She walked over and said, "Hana, what are you doing here?" Her gaze moved to the tall Wolf clan, then back. Something dawned on her then. "Oh my gosh, he's one of *them*!"

Runa, despite her maternal softening, had summoned up her most imperious look. "Who is one of whom?"

Maria looked confused. "The man in the parking lot. Felix."

Erik's whole family surrounded her now, their expressions greedy. "What do you know about Felix?" Mr. Wolf asked.

Maria stepped back, startled. I put a hand on her shoulder and said, "This is my friend, Maria. Maria, I think you know Erik. These are his sisters, Runa and Thyra, and these are his parents, Magnus and Marta Wolf."

"Nice to meet you," she said uncertainly.

"Felix is their son and brother," I added. "Do you know something about what happened to him?"

She hesitated, then took a breath and began. "It was at the store. He was buying a few things, and it was almost closing time. He was chatting with me, you know, kind of flirting. He asked when I got off work, and I said in about ten minutes. He said he'd like to take me out for a drink." She looked nervously at the Wolfs.

I said gently, "Why don't you all give her a little room?"

Erik and his family all made an effort to step back and soften their facial expressions. Erik said, "Then what happened?"

"I tried to hurry up when I closed my register because I didn't want to keep him waiting. I didn't want him to get bored and leave," she confessed, her face growing pink. "I grabbed my jacket and jogged outside, and he was lying there, in the parking lot. He was bleeding from his head."

Erik was easing into cop mode. "Did you see a weapon?"

Maria lifted her chin. "No, but I know what it was."

We stared, mouths open, and she said quickly, "Tom, my boss, keeps stacks of firewood against the building all year long. The stack wasn't ten feet from where he was lying. I think someone hit him with one of those little logs."

Erik was on the phone. He walked across the room and talked in a low voice. I knew that he was talking to Greg Benton.

Marta Wolf said, "Are you the one who called the ambulance?"

Maria nodded. "I felt so bad. He's such a tall guy, and I'm guessing his head took another blow when he hit the parking lot. But I knew he was alive because he was breathing normally and there wasn't a lot of blood." She sent an apologetic look to Mrs. Wolf.

"Thank you for doing that, dear," Felix's mother said.

"The ambulance came very quickly," Maria offered. "In just a minute or two, it seemed."

Mrs. Wolf studied her. "You're Hana's friend. Are you Hungarian, as well?"

Maria looked surprised, but she said, "Yes. half Hungarian, like Hana."

To my surprise, Mrs. Wolf looked pleased, for reasons I couldn't fathom.

Erik came back. "Greg has been on the case for a while now. Maria was right; they found the log. It's been taken into evidence."

A gasp went around the group, and Magnus patted Maria's shoulder.

Then a man with longish brown hair and a trimmed beard materialized next to Thyra. I had seen him before—he had also appeared when we three women had been attacked in the back room of Ulveflokk, the clothing store run by Erik's sisters. Though Thyra was reputedly dating around, I found it interesting that this was the man who showed up in emergencies.

He was hugging Thyra now, seemingly an embrace of comfort and support, but obviously a declaration of love. Instead of looking embarrassed, Thyra looked briefly smug before she said, "What do you know?"

Rolf beckoned us to a rather empty corner (we had barely noticed the other emergency room dwellers) and sat us down. "The MRI has revealed no bleeds or bone breaks."

Erik's mother let out an inadvertent groan of relief. I was sitting beside her, so I put my arm around her, and she clutched at it.

"There is a great deal of swelling due to the concussion, so he needs to be under observation. If the swelling increases, they might have to open the skull to release the pressure."

This time it was Magnus who groaned.

"How likely?" Erik asked in a clipped voice.

Rolf studied him. "We can't know that now, but it's a great, great thing that he was brought in so soon after the injury. No matter what happens now, they'll have it under control."

Runa wiped at her eyes. "Is he conscious?"

"Not yet. If they need to operate, then they'll put him into a temporary coma." More gasps. Rolf held up a hand. "Again, that would be a good thing, for his own protection. If they determine that he doesn't need to be opened up, then he'll probably be conscious in two or three hours." He looked at Thyra's parents apologetically. "Thyra said to give it to you straight. And this is, from a medical perspective, fairly good news."

Magnus nodded. "Thank you, son."

Rolf sort of bowed to us, touched Thyra's hair, and disappeared.

Thyra said, "You can't tell, but he's actually quite relieved. That means Felix will be okay."

Runa sniffled. "He was visiting us just a few hours ago. He called Anya his little sunflower." She wiped her eyes. "Ah, I have to call Andy." She stood up and walked shakily out of the room.

I realized that Maria had not been invited to the corner where the Wolfs (and I) heard the update. "Do you think it would be good to share this with Maria? She seems very worried over there."

Magnus stood up. "I'll go get her." He walked across the room and bent toward Maria. He was clearly turning on all of the Wolf charm. I looked at his wife, who was chuckling. "Watch out for those Wolf men, Hana. Although I suppose it's too late for you."

I was still half-hugging her, and now I gave her a happy squeeze. "It is much, much too late." We laughed together, and then she said, "I'm glad. My Erik has never been happier than this, not even as a child." She beamed at me, and her lovely blue eyes shone.

"I'm so glad. And I'm so glad Felix will be all right."

She turned toward me. "Have you met him?"

"That's kind of a funny story." I figured my embarrassment might be worth it if I could make her laugh, so I told her about my assault of Felix. She began to giggle, then to laugh out loud, and suddenly she couldn't stop. Tears streamed down her face, and her husband appeared, looking concerned. Thyra took charge of Maria, moving with her to another couch and telling her what we knew.

"Marta?" her husband asked.

Erik's mother pointed at me. "Hana made me laugh. Ah!" She wiped at her streaming eyes. "I'm okay now. Stress relief." She turned to me. "Tell Magnus that story."

I pretended to frown at her, and then I told Erik's father how I had met his oldest son. His laughter was much louder than hers, and he said, "I doubt Felix minded that, at all! Having this little Hungarian Fairy fly up to him and offer her love!" He clutched at his stomach while he laughed.

I looked at Erik, whose face was both grateful and relieved. My own expression must have been wry, at the very least. *Little Hungarian Fairy*, indeed.

Thyra and Maria returned, and Thyra let out a long sigh. "So, we just have to wait here for three hours and go crazy?"

An idea occurred to me. I wasn't sure if it was a good idea, so I pulled Erik aside and ran it past him. His face brightened, and he assured me that it was an excellent thought, for several reasons.

So I left the ER and found an empty hallway, where I pulled out my phone and called my grandmother.

*

Half an hour later, at 9:45 in the evening, my grandmother was in her element, warming and serving Hungarian food to the entire Wolf clan. Runa and Thyra had met her before, but

Erik's parents had not, and they had worn fascinated expressions since they were introduced.

My grandmother's goal, it was clear, was to stuff them all into a stupor in order to dull their fear and anxiety. She had started off strong with servings of Chicken Paprikás and fluffy egg dumplings drenched in gravy, Hungarian Beer Bread, Székely gulyás, and Töltött káposzta (stuffed cabbage). Her kitchen smelled so good, and the food tasted so good, that at first her guests simply moaned.

"Juliana, this is truly delicious," said Erik's mother, who was, despite her worry, moving rapidly through the contents of her plate. I halfway believed my grandmother had cast some sort of spell on them.

Grandma marched to the table, her face flushed and determined, and began plopping second helpings of Paprikás on each plate without asking if people wanted more. I was about to protest, but Magnus made a loud, happy sound and shouted, "You read my mind, Juliana!"

My grandmother's face was smug as she thanked him and moved back to her stove. Grandpa was in the room, too, chatting in Hungarian with Maria in one corner of the room. I was glad Maria had been welcomed into the fold by everyone. It must have been traumatic for her, too, to find Felix lying there, bleeding . . .

Erik had been quiet, ploughing through his food with his usual devotion. I knew that some part of him loved me for my Hungarian food connections, but that was understandable.

Runa and Thyra had been talking, too, and now Runa called, "Juliana, you must meet my Anya. She has to say thanks to you."

Amidst the sudden wave of thanks from the entire Wolf family, Grandma came to the table and deigned to sit down.

"I look forward to meeting," she said. "Your little girl is healthy, yes? And happy?"

Runa looked ready to cry. "Yes. And her daddy is happy to have her all to himself tonight. I'll have to leave soon, though, to feed her." She glanced at her phone. Apparently, Andy had not yet sent an SOS. Thyra leaned affectionately against her sister, but her eyes were on my grandmother as she said, "It's nice to have you watching out for us."

My grandmother laughed. Marta Wolf leaned forward, her eyes bright. "Would you say that your—gift for knowing things—was hereditary?"

Grandma shrugged. "My mama knew things. Found a kidnapped baby for the police." Erik's parents gasped. "And I knew, too, from childhood. My daughter Magdalena is coming to understand her gift, and Hana --"

"Hana is catching up with Juliana," said Runa firmly. "She sees things, and she feels warnings and things like that."

Now all eyes were on me. "Not really," I said, and forked some food into my mouth. Erik paused his eating long enough to reach out and touch my hand.

Marta leaned toward my grandmother, hungry for something other than food. "Would you be willing—I don't know—to tell me if Felix will be all right?"

My grandmother, ever compassionate, took Marta's hand in both of her own and said, "Tell me about him." Marta began to talk, and through her words we could feel her bond with her first baby, her blond boy, who had been a charmer since toddlerhood, and was generous, like his siblings, but, unlike her youngest, Erik, he was outgoing and spontaneous. "And he loves to flirt with women." Marta's eyes darted to Maria, who sat listening at her end of the long table. She blushed slightly, relegated as she was to be just one of the "women" flirted with by Felix.

After a few minutes, my grandmother smiled, and the room went silent, awaiting an annunciation. "She is smiling," she said.

More silence. I thought, panicking, did she mean an angel? Had Felix died? Were angels smiling at him? A glance around the table told me that many of the women present had developed similar anxieties about her words.

"Who is smiling?" Erik asked softly.

My grandmother's eyes creased with laughter. "She is laughing, smiling at his joke."

"Who? A nurse? Is he awake?" Marta squeaked, her face pale.

"Yes, yes. Awake and demanding. Asking for this and that. Weak, but not dying." My grandmother seemed to come back to herself and was just in time to receive Marta's hug, which was hearty and long-lasting.

As with the popping of a balloon that releases air, so did this news relieve the tension in the room, and we looked around at each other, well fed and ready for good news.

A little cat strolled into the kitchen then, a marmalade-colored feline with a pretty face and an imperious expression. She took no notice of the people at the table, but made a beeline for my grandfather and jumped into his lap. This would not have been an unusual sight, except for the fact that my grandparents did not have a cat.

"Ah, hello Bálinka!" Grandpa said, petting the little cat's pretty head. "You come to visit, and taste some food?"

Grandma muttered something in Hungarian, half frowning.

"What's with the cat?" I asked.

She shrugged and pointed at her husband. "She flirts with him for weeks, and he finally lets her in, like the fool shepherd who is lured by Vadleány."

Grandpa laughed. "You are jealous of a cat." But his look was fond, as always.

Grandma, the center of a rapt circle, said, "*A macska terhes*"

"What does that mean, Grandma? I only made out 'cat.'"

Grandma sighed and actually rolled her eyes, which I don't think I'd ever seen her do. I looked at Grandpa and Maria; the latter was laughing. "She said the cat is pregnant," Maria said, and everyone laughed.

My grandmother murmured mutinously and narrowed her eyes at my grandfather and his little ginger cat. "You wait,' she said. "Soon he will have a box with a velvet cushion, and then little toys with bells inside, and then cans of food. The house will be filled with cats."

Grandpa sent her a big, loving smile, and she melted, right in front of me. After all this time, he could win her heart with a smile. Erik had seen this, too, and he reached for my hand.

Runa had to return home. "Tell Felix I'll see him tomorrow. Tell him I love him," she called, and then she dashed off to find her own husband and her hungry baby.

Erik and I were the last to leave. We thanked Grandma repeatedly; Erik assured her that she had done a great deal of healing with her delicious food and kind hospitality. We offered to stay and help with the dishes, but she pushed us gently away, pointing at my grandfather. "That one will help me—he and his cat."

I grinned at her. "This was a nice thing to do, Juliana."

She shrugged, her face rosy with pleasure. "Ya. Go on and take care of the other Wolf. Imagine, I had a house full of them!"

We laughed and went out into the spring chill. Erik said, "My brain has been working overtime."

"I can tell."

"Why Felix? If it was a random attack, why didn't they take his wallet? The hospital showed me the contents of his pockets, and everything worth stealing was there. Why hit a man over the head with a piece of wood? It's brutal."

"Like Rose Toth's death. A brutal blow to the head."

"I was thinking that, too. But what possible link could there be?"

We pondered this as we climbed into his car. "At least tomorrow you can get some more information. Did you and Greg get your cover stories together?"

He nodded. "I'm a former student of Steve Toth. We have his permission to say that. Greg is Mrs. Toth's second cousin. We're still Erik and Greg, but he's a Toth, and I'm a Fox."

"You sure are," I said. "You don't need to work after we visit Felix, do you?"

"No."

"Good. We'll go home and talk about our dream apartment."

"That sounds nice." He reached out and ran a hand through my hair. "You know what?"

"What?"

"I think I see a light around you, too. It's a shimmering bronze, like your hair."

"Wow, fancy." I sent him a lazy smile. He put his hand back on the wheel and we pulled into the hospital parking lot. He had been supportive of his family, kind to my grandparents, attentive to me. But I could almost read his mind, and there was only one thought that dominated, a loud drum beat that could not be suppressed.

Why Felix? It said, again and again.

Erik parked the car and jumped out as I was still collecting my purse from the footwell. I glanced up to see him under the parking lot security lights: tall, blond, athletic. The Wolf men: so attractive, I thought, and remembered how I made Erik's parents laugh with my story about Felix.

The story about my foolish mistake, how I crept up from behind . . . Without warning, *the misery* returned like a giant wave, and I bent in half, afraid I would be sick.

Erik had my door open in an instant. "Hana? What's wrong? Babe, are you okay?"

I sat back up and leaned against the seat, feeling shaky. "I know something," I croaked, my throat dry.

He squatted beside me. "What is it? Is this about Felix?"

I nodded, my eyes closed. When I opened them, he gave me his hand, and I clutched it tightly in both of mine. "Ow," he said, with a little smile. "Out with it. What did you see?"

"They didn't hit Felix," I said.

"They didn't--?" He studied my face. "Don't worry, we'll catch him. But we have to face facts: yes, they did."

"No, what I'm saying is, they don't think they hit *Felix.*" I turned to him, and I could feel that my eyes were wide and intense. Erik's eyes grew wide, too, as he anticipated my words.

"They thought they were striking *you.*"

Chapter Eleven

The Jealous Room

"Look at Benton," my grandmother whispered, laughing. "He is a boy at church. See the hair? And the little curl?" Greg Benton did indeed look clean and polished. He wore black jeans with a white shirt and blue suit vest. There was a mismatched quality to his clothing that was his attempt to confuse anyone contemplating his ensemble.

"Eirk's not much better," I said with a sigh. "He looks like a knife salesman." Erik was wearing one of the wrinkly suits he used to wear when we first met. Underneath it he wore a turtleneck and a Bolo tie.

My mother stood next to us, also laughing. "Stop, my stomach hurts." Then, wiping her eyes, she added, "In fairness, we should thank them for trying to not look like policemen. This is a much better disguise than last time."

"A little better," Grandma corrected, still grinning.

I poked her in the side. "I think Benton trimmed his mustache for you, Grandma."

She grabbed her stomach and stuck out her tongue, as though she was suddenly sick. "And his wife kisses him, even with that."

I laughed again, then straightened. "I see Mr. and Mrs. Toth. Mom, do you want to greet them while I start bringing out sandwich trays?"

My mother narrowed her eyes. "We don't start the trays until everyone is seated. You just don't want to face their sadness."

"Well, duh," I said, feeling mutinous.

"I will go," Grandma said. "I can give them some peace." She swept out of the room before we could say a word. My grandmother did have a special gift, and when she wished to do so, she could calm an anxious heart. Her own mother had possessed that gift, as well, and had somehow passed it on to her daughter Juliana. I remembered a story that Henrik Sipos told me—a story I would never forget. As a baby, decades ago in Hungary, he had been abducted and his parents were in agony, wondering what had happened, where he was, if they would ever see him again. He was found and returned to them because of my great-grandmother Natalia's period, After little Henrik came home, Natalia had met his poor mother, who still felt guilty about her child's abduction. Natalia embraced the traumatized woman and the latter was filled with comfort and peace. That peace was the second gift Natalia had given her.

Grandma was speaking to the Toths, holding their hands, leading them to a table. Mr. Toth was nodding, and Grandma tucked Mrs. Toth into a chair and spoke in her ear. The woman turned to her suddenly, and Grandma put her hands on either side of Mrs. Toth's face. Tears streamed down the woman's cheeks, but she was smiling—smiling!--at whatever my grandmother was telling her. Her husband looked dumbfounded. My mother and I, too, stood with our mouths open, watching the magical effect of my grandmother's empathy.

"I shouldn't be surprised," my mother murmured. "But I always am."

"Yeah, me too. It's like having a Wonder of the World in your family. Like the Colossus of Rhodes is your brother."

My mother smirked at me. "Did you get enough sleep last night?"

"No. The whole Felix thing."

She sobered. "God, yes. First Rose, now Felix. I'm glad Greg and Erik will figure this out soon."

Yes, that was to be hoped. I moved backward to see our pastry chef, François, adding tiny dollops of cream cheese to the tops of artistic sandwiches. "They look amazing, as always," I told him, and he nodded his acknowledgement (and his agreement).

"I have news today," François said to his sandwiches. His focus was legendary.

"Oh?"

"Claire and I have found an apartment together. Near the river—very nice. We moved in yesterday."

"How exciting! Congratulations!" I couldn't hug him while he worked, but I gave him a pat on the shoulder. "Erik and I are talking about doing that very same thing!"

He finished his task and looked up with a triumphant expression. "It feels good, having a place together, planting our roots—is that the expression?"

"Close enough." I smiled at him.

"Our living room is large, with a wide window that has a view of the river. Do you know the first thing I put in this room? My Kodaly painting. The one you got for me. I love it every day."

François had fallen in love with a painting by the artist Kodaly; as fate would have it, Runa and I had Kodaly paintings, too, as did my friend, Katie. François's masterpiece was a picture of a man at the top of a mountain, celebrating life and sunrise. Kodaly had been a genius with creating light on a canvas, and the painting was indeed invigorating and inspiring. I was glad to think of it in François's new home. "I'd love to come and see it," I hinted.

He waved a vague hand in the air. "Yes, we will have everyone over when we have finished moving in."

"That's great. I'd better get moving," I said, with a glance at my watch. I jogged to the back wall, where our large teapots sat on warmers, and transferred several pots to a rolling cart and moved into the tearoom. The atmosphere wasn't as sad as I had feared. Several people were greeting each other with smiles and embraces. Mr. and Mrs. Toth were still sitting at their table. She was reading the card I had set on her plate, and when she finished, she leaned toward her husband to show it to him. He pulled her against him and kissed her hair, and a sudden lump rose in my throat. Determinedly, I pushed the cart to the center of the room, and my mother and grandmother joined me, each of us lifting a pot from the cart and traveling to assigned tables where we began to pour tea.

The Toth's daughters had joined them, along with Albie, Rose's erstwhile boyfriend. A few other family members sat at their table. I began to pour tea, and when I leaned between Lida and Teresa, the latter said, "Thanks for this, Hana. Our family appreciates your kindness."

I met her eyes, which were sad, but also still a bit angry. What was Teresa angry about? asked my brain, while my mouth said, "Of course. We hope that you find it restful. Grieving people forget to tend to their own needs," I said, repeating something I had heard my mother say many times.

"And we can use the microphone, right?" Lida asked. "We have some people who want to speak about Rose."

"Yes, absolutely. My grandmother is our sound technician, and she checked everything just before you all arrived."

"Thank you." Lida sipped her tea and closed her eyes. Then she turned to her sister. "Rose would have liked this place."

Teresa nodded her agreement, her angry eyes flashing, then pointed at Albie. "He's got a poem to read."

Albie managed a smile and a shrug, and I left them to their tea. "If you need refills, just raise a hand," I said. "The sandwiches will come out in a couple of minutes."

They seemed happy with these arrangements, so I moved to the next table, which seemed to consist entirely of Longwood Academy staff. I recognized the principal, Edie Pembroke, and the art teacher, Bevington. Vice Principal pocket watch was there, too—what had his name been? Partridge, I recalled just as I reached the table. I saw recognition in several pairs of eyes, and I said, "I'm Jia's cousin. I picked her up yesterday."

Edie Pembroke nodded vigorously. "Oh, of course— Hana Keller."

"You remembered. I'm impressed. You have so many names to recall."

She shrugged and pointed to her temple. "I have a little file cabinet in there. Anyway, Hana, I think you know Bruce Bevington and Adam Partridge? That's Adam's wife Rita beside him; they are both gifted performers in Riverwood's amateur theatrical society." A thin woman with gray hair waved to me, acknowledging Edie's compliment. "And this is Ursula, our indispensable front office representative—" she pointed to a woman with blonde, curly hair and a dimpled smile. Then she pointed at a familiar-looking woman who sat to the right of Mr. Partridge. "And this is Angela Morris, our other first grade teacher. You've probably heard her called Miss Angie." *Miss Angie.* I had seen her from afar when she dismissed Jia's class. I waved to Jia's teacher, about to speak, but Edie Pembroke went on to introduce a few teachers from the upper grades who had also befriended Rose while she was at Longwood School.

I realized, at second glance, that I recognized the blonde woman—Ursula—as the one who had preceded Mr. Partridge out of the school on pick-up day. She had looked annoyed about her broken nail, and he was stuttering out an apology; I had the idea at the time that he had done something oafish. Miss Angie struck me as familiar, not just as someone that I had seen peripherally. Perhaps her picture had been in one of their parent publications, which Aunt Luca sometimes forwarded to me for one reason or another.

I was pouring their tea as I spoke, expressing my condolences at the loss of a colleague. "I have heard so many good things about her, and I feel grateful that I saw her performance at the Hungarian Tableau Theater."

Miss Angie pulled nervously at her dark ponytail, wearing a haunted look. "You were there?"

I nodded. "She was lovely. It's unfortunate that the evening will always be a sad association, because she moved and danced with such artistry, such grace. She shone brightly."

Miss Angie nodded at this and wiped at her eyes. I wondered, suddenly, why none of these people had been at the performance. Had Rose not mentioned it to them? Not wanted to invite colleagues because the Hungarian group was a separate part of her life? But then again, Bevington had said something about a dress rehearsal, and some of the Longwood people viewing that event.

"You're one of Jia's guardians?" Miss Angie asked, touching my arm as I poured her tea.

"Yes. I'm officially her cousin, but more like an aunt."

Angie's face brightened. "She is a delight. I love having her in my class."

I smiled. "Good to know. I'm glad she has Iris—"

Angie laughed. "Oh, Iris! What a character that one is. The two of them are like a comedy duo."

I smiled, catching the eye of Ursula the receptionist, who smiled, too. My eyes moved to Bruce Bevington, who wore an intense expression as he stared into his teacup. I wondered if he fit the "tormented artist" stereotype. He was dressed well enough, and certainly less disheveled than he had been the previous day, but there was something under the surface of him—of many people at this table—that went beyond sadness. I wondered . . .

By the time I finished pouring at my assigned tables, people had begun to wander up to the stage. Mr. Toth, my father's friend, went first to thank everyone for coming and to say that the family was most grateful. He maintained his composure, but the pain in his eyes, when he spoke of Rose, made me look away.

When he stepped aside, his daughters moved to the microphone. Lida talked of her sister's beauty and kindness. "She was always protective of me, as older sisters tend to be. I think having two little sisters was what got her interested in primary education. She loved little children. And she was looking forward to having children of her own."

A wave hit me then—a giant roller of emotion that emanated from the audience. I staggered under the unexpected onslaught, looking around to see if my mother or grandmother had felt it. Grandma wasn't in the room, but my mother stood three tables away; she had pressed herself against the back wall, and her skin was paler than usual. Oh yes, she had felt it, too. We exchanged a shocked glance.

I was having trouble determining the primary emotion in the mix that had followed the mention of Rose's dream of children. There was melancholy, of course, but also guilt, and anger. Resentment, too, I thought, and even—envy?

My grandmother had wheeled out the platters of sandwiches, so my mother and I went to claim our trays to deliver to tables. Erik and Greg were seated with different groups. No one seemed to have questioned their legitimacy as relatives of the Toths, and I had seen, from the time we started pouring tea, that they were listening avidly to the conversations at their tables.

Teresa was speaking now, her voice toneless. "Rose and I were close all of our lives. We confided in each other, and we trusted each other. I will always remember what a good sister she was." She glared out at the listeners with a furious expression, and I realized that she was trying not to cry. "A week or so before Rose was killed, she and I had a fight." I saw, out of the corner of my eye, that Erik had sat up straight in his seat. "I won't go into the details, but it was significant enough that we weren't speaking to each other, and then I heard the terrible news that she was dead." Teresa's expression now would have broken the heart of a misanthrope. "I hate the person who killed my sister, not only because they deprived her of her life and her hopes and her future—" she wiped angrily at her eyes—"but they deprived me of the chance to resolve my differences with Rose, and to tell her that I loved her one more time. Rose, I hope you can hear me now. I love you, and I will always be your sister, and I will see you again one day to offer my apologies and my love."

She walked quickly off the stage, followed by Lida, who cried openly, and I heard several sniffles from the crowd.

Albie walked up then, a diminished and dispirited figure. He put his mouth close to the microphone, like a rock star, and began reciting what turned out to be a truly awful poem. Suddenly I wanted to laugh, probably just to break up the relentless sadness in the room. On silent feet, I headed for the break room, fearing that nervous giggles would bubble to the surface and win me the disdain of everyone assembled.

I made it to the back, where I found François looking scornful. "I feel insulted, as a lover and a Frenchman," he said.

I pulled in my lips, trying to lock out amusement. "He's speaking from the heart."

"He is speaking rubbish. The rhymes are forced. An embarrassment. He rhymed "sweet" with "neat." François looked sick to his stomach. I knew that he had written many a poem for Claire, often in French. But he let me read one or two, and they were beautiful.

"Poetry is a good outlet, François. Cut him some slack."

François glared at me. "He abuses the art." He turned and stalked to his table, where lovely little cakes awaited frosting.

I went back to the doorway in time to receive another gust of emotion. What was going on? Grandma and my mother moved swiftly toward me. We met each other in the doorway and my mother closed the door. We moved to the table near the cubbyholes in the back wall and sat down. "You felt it?" my grandma asked.

We all said it together: "Jealousy." The joint response, immediate and sure, surprised me, yet at the same time it did not. After all, we had been able to narrow the feeling to this precise emotion. I could not recall a time that all three of us had shared a reaction, much less one this strong.

"Who is jealous?" my mother asked. "And why?"

Grandma said, "A man at one table was talking about Hungarian food. About the Kolbász he had for dinner yesterday. Benton was next to him, and he was jealous. The man would pay a thousand dollars for a pot of Paprikás." Grandma smirked. She enjoyed mocking Greg Benton, but I knew she secretly loved him.

My mother was solemn. "Poor Teresa is jealous of everyone who was on good terms with Rose. She's in a lonely place."

Grandma and I nodded our agreement. I said, "I suppose Mr. and Mrs. Toth are jealous of every parent in the room whose children are safe and alive."

Now that her joke about Benton had been delivered, Grandma had become grave. She was allowing herself to fully feel the vibrations around her. Suddenly she sat up. "It is about the child," she said. "The jealousy has something to do with Rose's poor unborn baby."

We stared at her for a moment. "Who would be jealous of that? A woman who could not conceive?"

That idea floated around us for a while. Then my mother added, "Maybe one of her sisters envied her happiness? Teresa said they had been at odds."

"But why would her jealousy cause an actual fight between them? Isn't jealousy more of a hidden emotion?" I asked.

Grandma folded her hands. "We need to know what their fight was about, of course."

This was true, I supposed, but none of us had the right to approach Teresa and ask her to confide something private. I sighed.

Grandma said, "Is it certain that her baby was fathered by the boy out there? The one who read the dreadful poem?"

"Merci," murmured François, who routinely eavesdropped on our conversations.

My mother picked up on this idea. "If Rose were pregnant by another man, then Albert—is that his name? — would certainly feel jealousy, assuming he knew he had been betrayed."

I considered this. "Based on everyone's stories, Rose

doesn't seem to have a reputation as a cheater. So, who would even be in the running as a potential secret lover?"

"The sisters know," Grandma said. "Sisters would know everything."

I glanced at my watch. "We have to go out there soon. I'm going to run to the bathroom while I have a chance."

My companions waved me on. As often happened when I left the conversation, they switched to Hungarian, and I left the room to the comforting music of another language—one I had always found particularly alluring.

Out in the hallway, I listened, attuned to calls for a waitress, but all I heard was the slight droning of a voice saying that Rose had been a nice colleague and beloved by children. Other than the voice, I heard only the clattering of teacups on saucers.

On the wall to my right hung a tapestry that all the tea house staff treasured: the World Tree. My mother had purchased it from my friend Falken, an antiques dealer, and he thought that it was authentically Hungarian. The tapestry, a brilliant weaving of glittering threads and yarns in a multitude of colors, depicted a tree with three levels of existence. The high branches represented the spirit world, and was filled with gods and goddesses with peaceful faces. The trunk of the tree held all of humanity, along with some earthly magical creatures like fairies and witches, but mostly just people of all kinds—adults, children, women, men. Their faces reflected every emotion: happiness, sadness, joy, anger, surprise, regret. My favorite figures were the ones experiencing love, like the young lovers holding hands, or the mother looking into the eyes of her baby. That one reminded me of Henrik and his mother, back when he had been a baby. A child who was lost, and then was found. The idea of his mother's joy in their reunion had never left me.

My eyes drifted down to the earth beneath the tree: the lower world. There in the center sat Ördög, the shape-shifter, the creature of dark and evil who took joy in bringing souls to himself. He stood grinning before a cauldron filled with desperate people who would be stirred into his sad assemblage of lost souls. Those who had made regrettable choices, those who had done wrong.

I heard the bathroom door open behind me, and suddenly I was awash in feeling-- a jealous rage that swept through me like a storm. Before me, Ördög grinned and grinned, his face weirdly illuminated in the dark lower world until it was all I could see. Everything else seemed to shrink into darkness except for the evil soul-catcher, who wallowed in sin. His head began to expand then, as all else receded, and the air left the hallway, left my lungs, until I could feel nothing but Ördög's hooves on either side of my head, his blade-like tail wrapping around me, drawing me down, down, to the place of wretchedness.

And then all light was gone.

Chapter Twelve

Respite and Renewal

I returned to consciousness and the lovely blue eyes of my mother, who bent over me, concerned. I realized that I was back in François's room, lying on an upholstered bench near the window.

"Are you all right, darling? Did you skip breakfast this morning?" my mother asked, wearing her anxious mother look. Grandma's face appeared as well, her expression assessing.

"You saw something," she said. "Or you felt something."

I nodded. "I saw Ördög. He was grinning at me and growing larger and larger, trying to trap me in his arms and pull me down. There was someone --" I swallowed, realizing my throat was dry -- "Someone behind me. They came out of the bathroom."

"Men's or women's?" This was Erik's voice. He had held back, apparently, giving the women their chance at me, but now he knelt beside me.

"I don't know. But there was so much emotion. Rage, jealousy. I was drowning in it, and I couldn't breathe."

Benton must have been nearby, because I heard Erik say,

"Make sure no one has left, or leaves now. I want every name, and a photo, before people depart."

"Yes!" I called to Benton. "Because he is here, the killer, and still angry."

I thought of Teresa then; perhaps everyone did. Grandma said, "Can you sit up?"

Several arms helped me into a sitting position. I still felt faint, and rather sick. François approached and lifted a cup of tea to my lips. It was a sweet gesture, and I smiled at him. "Merci," I said.

Erik's eyes held mine now. "Are you all right? Do we need to take you to the hospital?"

I shook my head. "No. It's just---it was terrifying, being pulled into hell. Into the darkness, and knowing I would never escape."

I looked into my teacup, but I knew that glances were being exchanged above my head. "I'm not insane," I said. "I just have some of *him* or *her* in me. And I want to get them out."

Grandma understood this explanation. "I have felt that. And my mama used to feel it, as well. Sometimes she would go straight to bed after she had one of her visions. They overwhelm."

"I get that," I agreed. "I felt that my senses were overwhelmed. All I could see was his face, that devil's face, grinning at me. The way you would in a nightmare."

My mother pulled me into a giant hug, forcibly holding me against her. This contact was instinctual, perhaps, but it was the right instinct. I felt some of my terror and sickness fading away with the physical presence of her love. I clung to her for a while. "That helps," I said into her hair.

François, always a man of action, said, "Who is this person? I will go and find him."

"I don't know," I admitted again. "Can we ask the crowd who was recently in the bathroom?"

Erik sat thinking, chewing on the inside of his mouth. "We'll make some inquiries. Did any of you see someone in that hallway?"

No one had. "I talked with a man from the school," François said. "But that was ten minutes before Hana went out there. I made a pit stop."

"Who was it?"

François shrugged. "A young man, good looking, but not as much as me," he said with simple egotism. "We talked about art."

"That's probably Bruce Bevington," I said. "He's the art teacher at Longwood."

"We both admire Kodaly. I told him I had a painting. How I had been able to purchase it for a pauper's price. He was jealous."

The word *jealous* had our trio of women stiffening slightly.

"I would guess he was," my mother said mildly. "The whole world has discovered Kodaly now, and his art is in demand." Her blue eyes, sad and beautiful, reminded me of Kodaly's painting, *Magdalena's Eyes*, for which my mother had posed.

"I told him you had two Kodalys," he added. "He said he would love to see them all. That he had tried painting in Kodaly's style, and it was difficult."

"Huh. Well, if he was there ten minutes earlier, then he's not Hana's person," Erik said. "I'm going to run out and help Greg." He squeezed my hand, then kissed it, and then he was gone.

Grandma looked at François. "Desserts ready?"

"Oui," he said automatically, looking thoughtfully at me. Then he snapped to awareness and said, "I will load them."

My mother told me to stay put. "Mama and I will pass out the desserts. You need some recuperation time."

I didn't disagree, but nodded, thankful, and closed my eyes. I spent some time meditating on beautiful things: Anya's birth, Anya's sweet face, Jia and Iris, Runa and Andy, Erik's green eyes, Felix— that last one reminded me of the attack, so I started over. Erik's and my new apartment, Domo and Margie, paintings by Kodaly, my family, living and dead, my friends Henrik and Falken, Katie and Eduardo, Paige and Paul. Thyra and whoever finally won her heart. My uncle Zoltan and aunt Luca. My new friend Livia and her fiancé, Hans. The beautiful tea set Zoltan had given me for my birthday. All the beautiful art in the world . . .

"Hana," said François, who had returned to my bedside. We were alone in the room.

"Yes?" I rubbed my eyes; the light seemed too bright.

"I will now ask you something, and you must answer right away."

I smiled. François and his games.

"Two quick questions in a row."

"Okay."

"This person behind you. What you felt was some of what they felt? Yes or no."

"Yes."

"And this person in the hall: was it a man or a woman? Go."

"A woman," I said automatically, and we stared at each other in surprise.

*

My mother and grandmother wanted to send me home, but they didn't want me to drive. Erik said that he would take me and have my car returned to me later. I moved through the tea room half an hour later to wait at the front door while Erik pulled his car under the awning. Before I reached the door, Bruce Bevington approached me. "Hello. Hana, right?"

"Yes. How are you, Mr. Bevington?"

He bowed in greeting. "Bruce is fine. This is a nice memorial event. Respectful. Thank you for making the hall available." His words were polite, but his veneer was thin as ice, I felt it, and in the depths beneath that surface there was a vast grief.

I nodded my acknowledgement, and he said, "I spoke with your chef. We got to talking about art, and about Kodaly. He's a particular favorite of mine, and the French guy --"

"François," I offered.

"Yeah, François said that you own a couple of Kodaly paintings."

I smiled, still giddy about this reality. "Thanks to that man's generosity, several people I know possess a painting by him."

"Amazing. If there was ever a time that I could take a look at them, I'd really appreciate it."

"Well—sure, I guess that would be fine. Just call me here at the tea house in a week or two, and we can arrange something."

He thanked me, then said, "François showed me a picture on his phone of his own Kodaly."

"His proudest possession," I said.

"It should be." His face was fervent: the expression of an acolyte.

A wave of sorrow swept through me. If only Will Kodaly could have seen the power of his art, the joy and awe that it brought to the people who viewed it.

Erik's car pulled up outside, and I said, "Here's my ride. I'll talk to you later, Bruce."

"Thanks, Hana!" He nodded once and turned back to his table, where everyone seemed to have been observing our conversation and would now be plying him with questions. As he approached, Ursula the receptionist pulled out a chair and looked at him with an expectant smile.

People were so curious about other people, I mused. I wondered if Rose Toth had been subject to the same kind of scrutiny at Longwood. Of course she had. She was young and pretty. She was also expecting a baby. Did her pregnancy make her the subject of gossip? Had everyone at the school known that she was pregnant?

I started moving toward the door, giving Erik a little wave. For some reason I turned back to scam the room. The first face I saw belonged to Edie Pembroke, who was staring directly at me, her countenance a picture of worry.

I smiled at her and left the building, tucking into Erik's passenger seat. He reached across and squeezed my hand. "Doing okay?"

I nodded. "But I'm glad to be going home. For some reason, I'm really tired, like I walked a hundred miles."

He squeezed a little harder. "You can climb into bed, and I'll tuck you in with the cats and a cup of tea. I'll read you one of those Hungarian fairy tales as a bedtime story."

I laughed. "I've been reading mysteries lately. But we both have enough mystery in our lives at the moment."

His hand slid away from mine so that he could grab the wheel to make a turn. "That's for sure." He treated me to a quick green gaze, then looked back at the road. "So—this experience you had—I don't want to make you re-live it, but was there anything significant or memorable, like the scent of someone's cologne, or the sound of a voice?"

I shook my head. "No sensory detail. That was part of

what made it scary. I saw nothing, I heard nothing, but I *felt* something."

Erik thought about this as he drove, and I pondered my own thoughts. We traveled in a contented silence. When we arrived at The Driftwood Castle, my green-eyed boyfriend ran to my side of the car and helped me out as though I were an invalid. He marched me up the stairs and said he would feed my cats while I changed out of my uniform.

I emerged minutes later in a pink sweatsuit. It was a favorite of mine because the material was particularly soft. Erik smiled at me, his face tender. "You look like a little flower."

I kissed him. It was around lunchtime, so I assembled some quick turkey sandwiches and we ate a companionable lunch. Then, as promised, he escorted me to my bedroom, tucked me into bed, and lifted my curious cats onto my blanket.

"Thank you, dear," I joked.

"You rest now, okay? I think your moments of insight are psychologically draining. Just relax and don't try to solve any of those mysteries we spoke of."

I shrugged. "I'll probably sleep. You should know something, though."

Erik grew alert. "What's that?"

I told him about François's little experiment, and how I had answered that the murderer was a woman.

Erik trusted my instincts too much to dismiss this entirely. "I'll share that with Greg. Maybe we'll shift our focus."

"Okay." I yawned, and Erik stood up. He bent to kiss my forehead and smooth my hair. "Get some sleep, beautiful Hana. I'll see you tonight. Maybe we can visit Felix together."

"I would like that."

I was already drifting into sleep when I heard the soft click of the apartment door as it closed—and locked—behind him.

*

I woke to hear my door opening. Hadn't Erik locked it? Then I heard the voice of Katie, my best friend. "Hana? Where are you?"

"In bed," I called.

Katie's pretty face appeared in my doorway. She was dressed for work in a power pantsuit of pearl grey, and she was clutching one of those huge pads that business people put on easels, covered with statistics. "Hey, pal!" she said brightly, putting down her chart and sitting on the bed beside me. "How are you doing?"

I smiled. "I'm fine. How did you even know--?"

"Imagine my surprise when I got a call at *work* from your *grandma*."

"Oh my God."

"Yeah. I was half afraid she saw something terrible in my tea leaves," she joked. "But she told me about your whole Gothic fainting spell. Pretty cool, actually."

"That's me. Cool Gothic Hana." I studied Katie, confused. "Why did Grandma call you?"

Katie shrugged and reached out to smooth my bed head. Her hands were soothing. "She thought you could use a friend."

As usual, I realized, my grandmother was right. I had been thrilled to see Katie's face in my doorway. "Well, I could. I just want to hang out and relax and not think about people getting killed or attacked or anything."

Her brows rose. "We will do that. But I think I need some updating."

I told her about Rose Toth, and the tea house hosting the memorial event. I shared the news regarding Felix, and how I feared it was Erik that someone had wanted to silence. I explained how they looked similar, and that even I had been fooled when I approached Felix from behind.

Naturally, Katie focused on this last detail, and when she had finished laughing—bent over and clutching her stomach—she wiped her eyes and said, "Sorry. That's just such a funny picture. You going up to some big tall stranger and offering him --"

"Yes, yes, hilarious." I scowled at her.

Katie, ever the pragmatic person, clapped her hands. "Okay, here's what we'll do now. We should probably make chocolate chip cookies—?"

"That goes without saying."

"And then we can go one of two ways. We can hang out and eat dough and make each other laugh."

"A hard option to beat," I said, relaxing against my pillow.

"Or we can use that big pad over there to jot down everything we know about each woman connected with Rose, and see if you can come up with anything for Erik. And his poor brother."

I narrowed my eyes. "Did Grandma tell you to bring that pad?"

Her brown eyes widened to express her innocence. "No. I came up with that my own. Remember when you had that girls' tea party at Christmastime? That was so fun! We need to do it again."

She was right, I realized. A part of my brain began planning. This time I would invite Livia, my new friend from the days before Christmas. And maybe Sparkle, from Stones by Sparkle? Maybe not. We didn't exactly know each other, and yet there was a sort of connection . . . .

"Anyway, we ended up talking about the murder on the campus, remember? And we all kind of Nancy Drewed our way to some key information."

"That was pretty amazing."

Katie, bright as a bunny, sat up straight and sent a significant glance to the pad.

I laughed. "Cookies first!"

"Of course!" she said happily, and I followed her to my kitchen, where we unearthed a rather elderly bag of chocolate chips. The cats circled our legs, pleased to see some activity.

"Will you be in trouble at work?" I asked.

She tossed her head. "They can't do without me. Besides, Eduardo will cover for me."

Eduardo was her devoted lover. She broke up with him at one point, but he had won her heart, and her renewed devotion, through persistent and romantic gestures. I loved him for it. "Good old Ed," I said. "Are you two still--?"

She sent me a brilliant smile over her shoulder as she rifled for my flour and sugar canisters. "Oh, yes. We are, indeed."

I felt the wave of contentment and happiness coming from her, and then I was happy, too.

She pointed at Antony, my black cat, who was trying to pull my sock off. He'd gotten a good hold of the floppy toe, and he yanked persistently, his paws planted. "You feed your voracious cats, and I'll start on the dough."

"A wonderful plan. Jot eggs on my shopping list there, would you? We'll be using up the last of them. But for a very good cause."

Katie had uncapped the vanilla extract; she inhaled the scent and crossed her eyes in a comical show of pleasure. "Pure vanilla. I wonder why people don't huff this stuff?"

"Have you seen the price of vanilla extract? For a tiny bottle like that?"

Katie recapped the bottle and set it down. "It's been too long, my friend, since we made cookie dough and caught up and pondered the cost benefit ratio of huffing vanilla."

"It has!" I finished pouring crunchies into the cat bowls and put the food back in a low cupboard. Then I stood up and hugged my best friend. "It really has."

Chapter Thirteen

The Path of Possibilities

Katie stood beside her giant pad, now perched on my step-stool. It was clear that Katie had been born to give presentations. She wore her authority and efficiency like impressive badges, and I was on board immediately. "So," Katie said in a brisk voice while she popped the lid from her Sharpie. "You told François that you thought it was a woman who overwhelmed your, uh, spirit. So, let's list women, and how they might be connected to Rose."

"Well, there are her sisters. Teresa and Lida."

Katie wrote in neat letters: *Teresa Toth*. Then on the line beneath, *Lida Toth*.

"And are they viable suspects?"

I adjusted my position on the kitchen chair, uncomfortable. "Normally, I would say no. But Teresa is angry. I saw it when I ran across her at the grocery store, and she admitted it at the memorial today. She said she had been in a dispute with Rose when she died."

Katie's brows pulled down, like an angry emoji. She wrote, "Motive" next to Teresa's name.

"And Lida?"

I shrugged. "I don't know a lot about her. She's the youngest. Seems to admire both of her older sisters. She almost seems kind of—like a follower. Not in a bad way."

Katie frowned again, but wrote nothing next to Lida's name. "Who else?"

I sighed. "Okay, let's see. There are her colleagues at the school. Angela Morris—they call her Miss Angie---is the other first grade teacher. Apparently, they were good friends. In fact, a lot of people were there from the school today, and they all seemed devastated. Several of them were women."

"Names?"

"The principal is called Edie Pembroke. Very motherly, great with the kids, seems like she's married to the job. Although the kids do call her *Mrs.* Pembroke. Maybe she's actually married? I guess I got a single lady vibe from her, but I didn't get an evil vibe. Just the opposite, in fact. But when I left today—"

"Yes?" Katie leaned toward me, her dark hair slipping like silk over one shoulder.

"She looked worried. Not sad, but worried. And I wondered why."

"So, we have Edie and Angie. Who else?"

I thought back to the people at the table. "There was a secretary. Sorry! Front office representative. Named . . . Ursula! I didn't catch her last name. Cute and dimply. Not obviously evil. Oh, and there was Mr. Partridge's wife, Anita. No—Rita. And some other teachers that I didn't meet. Women and men. I think we had a sign-in book, so I can check it later."

Katie had written down Lida, Teresa, Angie, Edie, Ursula, Rita. The list did not inspire me or bring about any revelations. "Maybe we should list the men, too. My answer to François was not scientific, or anything."

Katie made a new list and pointed at me. "Shoot."

"Okay. There's Albie, Rose's boyfriend. No one knows the state of other people's relationships. If they were fighting, or one of them cheated —"

"True." She added Albie to the list.

"Then at the school, there's Mr. Partridge. He seems to have a good marriage, but his wife is maybe sixty, and at the school he's surrounded by young, cute women."

"But those women would have to like him back. Is he attractive?"

"*No.*"

Katie laughed. "You just made the funniest face!"

"It's not just his physical self, which is underwhelming, but he's kind of—affected. Like he's posturing all the time for an audience."

And what's his first name?

"I'm not sure."

She picked up her phone. "Let me check their website. Longwood?"

"Yes."

"Okay, got it. Click on Administration, Faculty, and Staff . . . Oh, Mrs. Pembroke is darling! Like a Teddy Bear, somehow. Okay, here he is: Adam Partridge."

"Yes, Adam."

She studied his picture. "He's not attractive, but he's not unattractive. He looks like the standard boring administrator."

She set down her phone and wrote Adam's name on her pad. "Next?"

"I didn't meet any male teachers except for Bruce Bevington. He's good looking, passionate about art. Seems to be devoted to the kids." I pondered my conversations with him. "He and Rose were very good friends. She used to call him after school and just shoot the breeze."

"Flirting?"

Antony jumped in my lap and turned on his high-decibel purr. That meant he was hungry. I picked him up and carried him to his bowl, then set him down. "He said no. Implied that it was just an affectionate friendship. But --" I opened a cabinet and retrieved two cans of Fancy Feast. Antony started circling my legs in a manic way. Cleopatra, obviously just awakened by the sound of a can snapping open, strolled in and sat by the bowls, looking groggy and expectant.

"But what?"

"He's attractive. For a lot of reasons. Her boyfriend Albie, by comparison, seems kind of --"

"Lame?"

I laughed. "Not that bad, but just sort of passive and uninteresting. He wrote a love poem as a eulogy, which should be sad and romantic."

"But it wasn't?"

I snapped open the second can. Antony was doing fast motion laps around my feet. "François called it 'rubbish.' Said that he was ashamed as a Frenchman and a lover, or something."

"Wow." She studied her marker, her brown eyes thoughtful.

"I talked with him after the memorial today. I got waves and waves of grief."

Katie's right eyebrow rose. "*Did* you?"

"And now I'm thinking about it, if Rose did have an affair with Bruce, then the baby's paternity is in question."

Katie pointed her Sharpie at me. "And it gives Albie a motive."

I lifted the bowls and filled them with wet food, then

returned them to their place on the floor; the cats moved like an incoming tide, making little snarfing noises. "Gross," I said, laughing. Then I turned to Katie and pointed back at her. "But it might also give Bevington a motive—or Partridge, or whoever her hypothetical lover might have been—if in fact that lover did not want to be a father or be exposed as a cheater."

"Is Bevington in a relationship?"

"I don't know. I don't think so . . . . ."

"One other person would have a motive," Katie said, turning back to her pad.

"Yeah?"

"The woman, of course! The wife or girlfriend of the hypothetical boyfriend."

I made a hmph sound. "This is all pretty much nonsense. We're basing this on nothing."

Katie set the marker down and whirled to face me, hands on hips. "I disagree. These hypotheticals are all questions the police would invariably ask as they try to find a killer. Was there an affair? Was there bad blood between her and a family member, or her and a friend, a colleague, an acquaintance? They'll look at all of it. And you have the ability to come closer to an answer because you *feel* things."

"Okay, good point," I said. "I also taste things." I grabbed another cookie and took a huge bite. "So good," I said with my mouth full.

Katie laughed and took her own cookie. "They are good. We should be bakers. Hana Kate's Bakery." I gave her a thumbs-up. Then she regarded me with a curious expression. "So, I'm going to use François's technique. We have –" she turned to count – "nine people on this list. Do we need to add more?"

I closed my eyes, letting my mind relax. Then I opened them. "No. I think that list is good."

Katie's eyes grew huge. "That's amazing! You have to tell Erik that! Only nine suspects—they can work through those in a couple of days!"

"You would think," I agreed. "But there's something about this—the brutality of it, and of the attack on Felix—that makes me think we haven't hit some hidden well of emotion. The one that was bursting with jealousy today. But *who* is jealous, and *of whom*, and *why?*

Katie waved a hand. "You've done your part. The rest is for the cops to determine." She took out her phone and snapped a picture of our suspect board. "I'm texting this to Erik," she said. "I'm going to tell him he can narrow it to these nine."

"Nine," I said. The number chimed inside me.

"What?"

"That number is important. Nine." I closed my eyes. When I opened them, Katie's face was in front of mine, wearing a jubilant expression.

"You mean, like the nine months of pregnancy?"

The chime within me rang again. "Yes."

Katie took a cookie and handed it to me like a prize. "Then it's about the baby," she said. "This murder was about the baby."

What had my grandmother said, while we huddled in the back room this morning? *It's about the child. The jealousy is about Rose's unborn child.* And now Katie was echoing that very same theory.

The chimes rang out inside me, triumphant as church bells. If my grandmother had been there, she would have insisted that my *inner eye* was opening.

"Yes," I said, feeling almost weary. "It's about the baby."

Chapter Fourteen

The Fairy of Darkness and Light

Erik and I did visit Felix that evening. We entered the hospital, holding hands, and found our way to the fourth floor, where Erik's brother sat up in his bed, head bandaged. A nurse fussed around him, clearly looking for reasons to stay in the room. Felix barely saw her. His face lit up when we entered, and he said, "Thank God! I was getting bored out of my mind."

Erik moved forward to touch his brother's shoulder. "How are you?"

"Fit as a fiddle, to borrow Mom's expression, as long as I don't move my head. If I do, it's a different story. But they say the pain will recede in a day or two."

I joined Erik at the bed. "I'm so sorry this happened to you."

He clasped my hand in his. "I will say Riverwood seems less welcoming than it once did."

Erik waited until the nurse left the room. Then he said, "Any idea what happened? Did you see anyone before --"

"I'll save you some trouble there. I don't even remember leaving the store. The last I recall I was talking to a pretty girl—

dark hair, dark eyes—and trying to lure her out for a drink. I wish she would come to visit me. I forgot her name . . . . "

"It's Maria," I said. "She's a friend of mine."

Felix's lovely blue eyes moved to my face. *"Is* she? Well, that's great. Next time you visit, bring Maria, will you?"

Erik's face remained serious. "Maria happened to be the one who found you. She called the ambulance and tried to tend to your wound. She's been traumatized by the experience."

Felix's face fell. "Oh, no. Poor kid. Maybe I should get her a thank you present. Hana, what do girls like after they encounter a bleeding man in a parking lot?"

I couldn't help but laugh. "I don't think there's a greeting card for that one. I do think a verbal thank you would suffice."

He leaned carefully back on the pillow behind his head. "So why do you think they did it? It wasn't for money, and it wasn't a carjacking. The nurse told me my wallet and keys are still with my clothes."

Erik looked slightly guilty. "Hana has a theory that you were not the target of the assailant. That maybe they mistook you for me."

Felix's brows rose, and he turned his head toward Erik without thinking. He hissed with pain and closed his eyes as he rode out the wave of pain. Momentarily, he said, cheerfully enough, "Impossible. I'm much taller and better looking."

Erik said, "From behind, we are similar. After all, Hana mistakenly--"

"Yes, we all know what Hana did," I said quickly. "No need to rehash that particular event."

Felix grinned. "Oh, but I do like to recall it. Such a pleasant memory . . . . "

"Weebix, this is serious. You saw no one in the store that looked suspicious?"

Felix squinted. "I don't know that anyone else was in the store. I was distracted by the lovely Maria. I think—there might have been a guy by the beer cooler. And someone in the aisle with all the shampoo and stuff. A woman, maybe. It's kind of fuzzy."

"Okay, no problem." Erik patted his brother's blanketed leg. "I am going to insist that when you get out of here you move out of your rental and move in with me. I'm in a secure building, and that way I can give you some protection."

Felix frowned. "That would cramp my style, bro. I have places to go, women to pursue, new babies to visit."

"You can do all of that. Preferably with a companion." When Felix began to protest, Erik said, "Someone tried to kill you, Felix. I'm not letting them get anywhere near you again."

Now Felix looked chastened. "Okay, I get it. But do me a favor and find this psycho soon, so I can be a lone wolf again."

I pointed at him, smiling. "You'll never be a lone wolf. You're part of Ulveflokk."

He managed a careful eye roll. "Yeah, I know. My sisters have been laying it on thick." He smiled, though. "I know they love me. Not to mention Mom and Dad, who are threatening to seal me inside a bubble while they seek military intervention."

Erik smiled for the first time. "They all love you, and so do I, and we're glad to have you back in the Midwest. This is not the reunion we hoped for."

Felix was quiet for a moment. Then he said, "Okay. Staying at your place would be fine. It beats going to our parents' house and having Mom force-feed me through a tube."

Erik laughed. "Good."

"Hana, could you grab my water from the table there?" Felix asked.

I practically dove for the water, and I held the straw to Felix's lips. He drank gratefully, then pushed the cup gently away. "Thanks." He closed his eyes for another minute or so, then opened them. "So, this Maria. What's her story?"

*

Erik and I returned to my apartment; the cats greeted us as they would the long-lost. Erik and I were hungry, so I threw together a quick snack of grilled cheese and potato chips.Neither of us had eaten dinner. We sat in my kitchen, listening to the happy crunching of Antony and Cleopatra, who were dining with us via their mat on the floor. Erik's phone rang, and after glancing at the screen, he swiped it on and said, "Hello! Thanks for returning my call." He stood up and walked into the living room, where he paced around while he talked. I heard him say, "Yes, very interested. What's the asking price?" A pause. Erik's voice again: "Really? Well—yes, I think so. If you can send me that paperwork, I'll look it over and have it back to you tomorrow."

When he came back in, he looked jubilant. The gold-green light around him seemed to be sparking slightly, and his green eyes glowed. My Erik was the o*nly* Wolf with green eyes. I studied his handsome face, his strong body, and experienced a burst of desire. "What is it? The apartment?"

"Yeah. He said we can do a viewing tomorrow. But get this: he's planning to convert the rentals to condos. He's going to offer current residents the chance to buy at a discounted rate. So—he's putting the penthouse up for sale. It would be ours, Hana!"

My thoughts whirled. A place with Erik. A place that we owned together. An airy space full of light, with high, arched ceilings and polished wood floors . . . I forced myself back into sensible mode. "Can we afford it?"

"I can provide a nice down payment. You picked a boyfriend who saves prudently."

"That was my first criterion," I joked.

"And after that, well, we pay a monthly price, just like we do as renters. Except this time, we'll be paying down something we'll own at the end. With neighbors we already know and a great location."

"Yes!" I cried. "Yes, yes, yes! And we'll throw a huge housewarming party for the sole purpose of showing off our elegant home."

"Oh, my. The fairy of vanity has landed on Hana's shoulder."

I giggled. "This is exciting."

"Yes, it is." He stood and brought his empty plate to the sink. I lifted my own plate and joined him.

"I'll miss this apartment, though. It's my first place, my Hana palace. And it's got that beautiful homemade shelf that my dad and grandparents made! Do you think we can move that?"

"We can do anything. And by that I mean that your dad and grandpa can do anything."

I laughed. "And I'll miss this spot, where I first kissed you. We might have to befriend whomever moves in here and ask to stand here now and then."

"Of course," he said, with mock solemnity.

I slid my arms around his waist. "I love you."

He kissed my hair. "And I am enthralled by you, my Vadleány."

The cats joined us on the little kitchen rug, settling into comfortable positions. They seemed to know that Erik and I would remain on that spot for some time, clasped in each other's arms. When we finally stepped apart, ready to adjourn to the living room, the cats were fast asleep.

After Erik fell asleep that night, I pulled a book from my shelf.

It was a volume of Hungarian fairy tales, quite old, and had been an important clue for Erik when we first met and he was trying to solve the crime of murder in our tea house. I thought I had recalled a story in the book about human beings and their motives for cruelty. I turned the old pages carefully, scanning the text, and I finally found what I was looking for in a story called "The Fairy of Darkness and Light." The story was about a woodland fairy that people rarely glimpsed in the daytime, but often found in the nighttime because she glowed. This reminded me, with a sharp pang, of Rose and her glittering fairy costume, illuminated in the trees and creating a sense of magic. I began to read.

The Fairy of Darkness and Light

A woodsman had befriended a wolf, and the two of them would walk together each day to whatever job awaited the woodsman. The man and the animal would talk to one another in a way that other humans and animals could not, and their friendship deepened through their dialogues. One day another man came with his saw to chop down a tree near the place where the woodsman toiled. Seeing the wolf, who sat calmly in a clearing, waiting for his human friend, the interloper pulled an arrow from a quiver on his back and shot the wolf.

Alerted by the wolf's howl of pain, the woodsman arrived and found his friend prostrate and bleeding. He shouted at the other man: "How dare you! It is evil to kill a creature that means no harm to you! You fear what you do not understand, but your ignorance gives you no right to take a life." The other man ignored him, finished sawing down his tree, and departed.

The woodsman knelt beside his dying friend and wept. The obscene arrow still jutted from the wolf's chest; the woodsman did not think he should remove it, so he stroked the wolf's fur and told him that he was not alone, that he, the woodsman, would stay and share his suffering and pain. In the twilight, as the wolf's breathing became ragged, a fairy emerged from the woods and knelt on the other side of the wolf. "You feel great love for him," she said, studying the woodsman.

"I do. He is my friend," the woodsman answered, weeping openly. "Why, magical fairy, are people so cruel?"

The fairy smiled a sad smile. "We cannot stop people from choosing the darkness." She watched the woodsman's sad face and added, "But we can seek out those who dwell in the light." Just then she began to glow brightly, and she rested her hand on the wolf's wounded chest. Slowly, the arrow began to emerge of its own accord, and life grew in the wolf's eyes.

As the woodsman stared, astonished, the fairy took the arrow, which had emerged fully and bore no sign of blood, and broke it in half, then threw it toward the woods. "Let the beaver use it for his dam," she said. "But let it never harm a living thing again." To the wolf, she said, "You have been granted another chance at life because you live in the light of a friend's love. Its brightness drew me here, and its glow will continue to illuminate your path."

The man, crying now with joy, thanked the fairy again and again, bowing at her feet. She touched his head and said, "All living beings should have a friend as devoted as you. Always keep to the light, my friends, and you shall be happy."

She rose and glided toward the woods, and in her absence the world was far less bright. But the man and the wolf now had the light inside of them, and they walked together toward the man's woodland hut, where he sheltered the wolf from the elements in his wide front porch. The man, exhausted by fear and relief, told the wolf, "I am sorry for what you suffered. I am ashamed to be of the human race."

The wolf studied the man. "But you are a credit to the human race. You befriended me when you could have called me an enemy. Because of that we have both learned the path of peace. We must do as the fairy said, and keep to the light. It is all anyone can do on a darkening path."

The man patted the wolf's head. "The first light I can provide tonight is a warm fire in the hearth. And we can share a meal of stew and bread."

The man and the wolf remained friends until they were both old, and when the wolf finally lay dying after a long life, he told the man, "You have always kept me in the light, and for that I thank you. When we feel dark, others can give us the gift of light. And when others walk the dark path, we must bring our light to them." The old wolf died then, and his companion sat, his hand on the animal's large head, loving him even as he said farewell.

The man buried his friend near the cabin. The next day, he went out in search of the wolf's mate, for whom he and the man had built an elaborate den, warm and safe from the elements. The mate, smaller and sleeker than the male, sat in front of her den, snarling at a man who held a huge knife and clearly wanted to kill her pups.

The woodsman lunged forward, and with all the light he possessed, he faced the man. He glowed his warning, and the man, stunned, dropped his knife and ran. The man turned to the wolf and said, "He is gone. Come and bring his pups to an even safer den."

The wolf's mate now understood the man, as the wolf had once done, and she led her three pups to the man's cabin, where he showed them the warm porch and protective wooden walls. The female, tired now after her fright, lay down in relief, her pups tucked around her. The man nodded and went inside his house.

That night, when the man blew out his lamp, a light remained. Surprised, he turned and saw the Fairy of Darkness and Light looking through his window. She smiled at him and nodded her head, and the man felt the light of her approval. "You kept to the light," she said, and he could hear even through the closed window. "And peace is your reward."

Indeed, from that day on, the man lived in harmony with his animal friends, the female wolf and the three offspring of his best friend, and he knew that his life had been a gift. When he died as a very old man, his fellow woodsmen buried him and carved him a beautiful tombstone, and his wolf friends stayed near it always, because no matter if it was day or night, the stone glowed like a beacon in the dark and lonely forest.

I shut the book, thinking. What stayed with me, after reading the story, were the woodsman's words, "You fear what you do not understand, but your ignorance gives you no right to take a life." Was violence the result of fear? Had someone killed Rose Toth in such a brutal manner because they *feared* her? Or did they fear something she represented? Or did they simply "dwell in darkness" and choose violence as a conscious act of sin?

After my dialogue with Katie, I was fairly certain that Rose Toth's baby was part of the motive for her death. Did someone fear that the baby would create problems? Was someone afraid that his paternity (if Albie was not the father) would be found out? Then I remembered that strong feeling of jealousy at the tea house event. Had a woman been jealous of Rose's impending motherhood? But surely, that was no reason to *kill?*

With a quiet sigh, I set the book on my bedside table and turned off my tiny booklight. I nestled up against Erik's back, letting his heat and peace seep into me. There had been so much joy, with the coming of Anya, the visit of Felix, the chance of our new home. But there had been so much unhappiness to counter each of those joys.

Nestling my head into the crook of Erik's neck, I tried to channel the words of the fairy. *Stay in the light. Stay in the light.*

Ultimately, it was all that we could do.

Chapter Fifteen

The Return of Magdalena

I was doing the breakfast dishes and studying the poetic light of the late March sky when I saw a car pull into my parking lot. I knew at once that the occupants were there for me; I dried my hands and went to peer out of the larger window in my living room. To my vast surprise, François emerged from the driver's seat. François had never been to my apartment before; I had no time to process this fact before I saw that his passenger was Bruce Bevington, the art teacher from Longwood. I thought of the expression that Domo's Margie used when she was surprised: *What in the big wide world?*

I was in front of the buzzer by the time it rang, and I immediately unlocked the door for my unexpected visitors. I was intrigued now, and a bit nervous. François spotted me as the men emerged from the stairwell, and he waved. "Hana, I am sorry I didn't call you first."

I waited until they reached my door, then said, "Hello, François." I turned to Bevington and added, "Bruce."

They both looked a bit sheepish now, but they moved eagerly forward when I invited them in. The cats made their usual demands for fealty, and the men gave them the equivalent of a pledge in the form of petting and ear-scratching. I laughed, and said, "Well, now that you're here, you can see one of my Kodaly paintings immediately." I pointed at the wall above my couch, where Kodaly's painting of Keszthely, Hungary dominated the room with its energy and color. François gasped, and Bevington moved forward, like a man under hypnosis, until he stood right in front of the Kodaly original. "Sublime," he breathed. "There's just no one like him."

François spoke quietly in my ear, as though we were in church. "This is why we came; he and I had said that on Saturday we would look at one another's paintings. Like visiting two tiny art museums. He has a small Kodaly in his foyer, and he is looking to buy more. Do you remember, when I first saw the painting that you helped me to buy? I was so emotional, yes? And today, Bruce also cried. Something about that canvas, the triumph and the joy—it moves me every day, Hana."

"Yes," I agreed. "I would never part with mine, if that's what you two were thinking."

François looked scandalized. "No! Of course not. We are just appreciating, seeing as much of his work in person as we can."

Bruce Bevington said, "May I take a picture, Hana?"

"Sure." I watched as he poked at the screen of his phone, choosing his camera and light settings. He lifted it and snapped several pictures of the artwork. "It's spectacular," he said. "The way he creates motion and light, the way he translates his affection for the place through color and the slant of the buildings . . . ." He sighed. Artists are nourished by art, and Bevington was like a plant leaning toward the sun. "I can't wait to show this to my students."

"I have another in my bedroom. I don't know if François

told you, but I bought both of these at a garage sale. I handed the money to Will Kodaly himself."

Bruce turned, open-mouthed. "What? You met him?"

"Yes. I'll never forget it." I felt happy at the memory of our meeting, but then I'm sure my face fell. "As it happened, it was the day he died."

Bevington had just closed his mouth, but now his jaw dropped again. "That is unbelievable! I have to hear all about it!"

I shrugged. "We didn't speak for long, but it was a special encounter. I was devastated by his death. Anyway," I said, trying to change the tone, "I'll show you the second one. Come this way." I had hung my second Kodaly, a lovely study of a woman standing in front of a fence and a field of flowers, on the wall opposite my bed. Both men rushed forward to examine the painting. It should have been awkward, even embarrassing, to have two men in my private sleeping chamber, but our love for the artist bonded us in a way that made the rest of the room irrelevant. "There is something about the way he paints women," François said. "I have seen several of his portraits now, and I can't quite *pinpoint*-- is that the word? The effect is so powerful."

Bevington nodded. "There is always soft light upon them. He loves them with his light." He looked briefly away from the canvas. "He reveres women, respects them. He makes them glow with power."

"Yes!" cried François, and I nodded my agreement.

"I hadn't thought of that," I said. "But I've seen several of his portraits of women, and they all have a special beauty. I would say that he paints poetically."

We all stood, awed by the painting that used the likeness of Cassandra, our local librarian, who had dated Kodaly at one time.

"There are three paintings of his, all studies of women, that bring me to tears," I said. The men turned to look at me. "One captures the reunion of a mother with the baby boy she feared she would never see again. The joy on her face, as she runs toward him—there is nothing else in the world for her at that moment. Just her child." I wiped at my wet eyes. "See, it gets me even as a memory. I'm not sure where that one hangs now. In the home of some devout collector, I'm sure."

I had their undivided attention, a rarity in these days of distraction and buzzing phones. "The other is owned by Erik's sister, Runa. It's called True Love, and it captures the moment that Kodaly realized he was in love. And the woman—a beautiful woman with her dark hair blowing around her face—is indirectly the reason he died."

"No," Bevington breathed. And then, "I would give anything to see it. And to hear the story."

François knew some of the story, but his face suggested that he, too, would like to see the painting. I nodded. "We can arrange something. Runa just had a baby, so she's busy right now."

I led the men out of my bedroom and back to the first Kodaly, which they studied again. "What about the third?" François said, his eyes on the painting.

"What?" I stared at him.

"You said three paintings of women. You have told us about two."

"Oh, yes. Well, the third one is the most personal of all. He painted my mother."

Both men whirled. "Did I know this?" François demanded. "I do not think I knew this!"

I shrugged. "We don't own the painting. My mother posed for him because the painting was meant to raise money for charity. When it was finished, my mother said that my father desperately wanted to buy it, but he couldn't afford it at the time. It sold at auction for six thousand dollars."

"It would earn so much more now," François assured me.

Bevington was looking at me, his eyes narrowed. "What was the name of the painting?"

"Magdalena's Eyes. That's my mom—Magdalena Horvath Keller. She does have beautiful blue eyes, but he made them into something magical. I'd love to see it in person; I've only seen a photograph."

Bevington was back on his phone, poking the screen and then scrolling. "There's an art auction site that I check all the time. Their mission is to put great art in everyone's grasp, not just the rich. I always search it for the name Kodaly and a few other artists that I love. I just saw a couple of Kodaly pieces yesterday . . . got it! Look what we have here."

He turned his phone toward me, and there was a picture of Magdalena's Eyes, listed at an auction house called "Art Alliance." The company's philosophy, according to a banner at the top of the site, was "to bring great art to all people, regardless of income." The price being asked for the painting was $5000.

For a moment I saw only white; then I saw my father's face, and a giant realization dawned: his birthday was in fewer than two weeks. "What's the web address?" I asked. "I'm bidding on it."

"Five thousand?" François asked. "Does the tea house pay this well?"

I shook my head. "No. But my brother is wealthy, and he'll pitch in, and so will Margie and Erik. And I can give it to my father for his birthday. We can, I mean."

"That's a big smile," Bruce said. "Here, I'll send you the link. Get it fast, because not much stays on the site for longer than a day or two."

I knew that he was right, and I felt a sudden terror that I wouldn't log my information quickly enough to secure the sale. My hands were shaking as I began to fill out the purchase form. The men watched, expectant.

"I never thought I'd have to use that maximum amount on my credit card," I said. "But I can't miss this chance! I wonder why it's even on sale?"

Bruce said, "I read about it earlier. The owner passed away, and his children are selling a great many of his paintings."

"Ugh. Okay, I'm pressing *submit*." I did so, with a shaky finger.

Nothing happened. I looked at Bruce, who said, "Sometimes the server is slow. Give it a minute."

I waited, tapping my foot. We sat down on my couch, and I set the phone on my coffee table. As often happened in the fever created by the love of art, a feeling of indispensability engulfed me. I *had* to have the painting. I n*eeded* to see my father's face when he opened it. I *had* to provide this gift to both of my parents because it was a personal symbol of their love. My heart thumped in my chest; then I covered my face in despair.

"Oh no! It's not going through. Someone else got in before me."

"Hana," said François, his voice fat with satisfaction.

I uncovered my eyes. The phone still lay there, but now there were words on a bright yellow background: *Your purchase has been completed.* Underneath this was some shipping information and an estimated date of arrival.

I shot up, my arms in the air. "Yes!! Oh my gosh, I never expected this to happen today! Or any day! Bruce, you are the best!!"

They stood up, too, and I hugged them each in turn. We laughed the shared laugh of people who value art above all else.

When my euphoria faded enough for me to think rationally, I said, "I'm a terrible hostess. I have tea and coffee, and I have chocolate chip cookies. Any takers?"

There were. We sat at my kitchen table and talked about art, and the art of food, and teaching art. François, the expert baker, said that my cookies were "very tasty" and that he was not ashamed of them. From François, this was like a blue ribbon, and I basked in all the good news of the day.

After eating several cookies, Bruce said, "Well, I'm glad I could point you in the right direction for that painting." His eyes met mine. "I wonder if I can ask —?"

"You want to see Runa's painting."

He shrugged. "It's an obsession. Not as bad as drugs or alcohol, though, right?"

I took a sip of tea and wiped my hands on my napkin. Then I hunted out my phone and dialed Runa. When she answered, I switched to speaker. "Hi, Runa. I'm here with my friends Bruce and François. You remember François, right? He --"

Runa laughed. "Oh yes, the delectable little French boy who makes delectable treats," Runa said.

"You're on speakerphone," I warned.

"I assumed," Runa said, not at all embarrassed. François had turned red, but pretended that Runa's predatory regard did not frighten him. Runa and Thyra had enjoyed teasing him ever since they met him at the tea house, on a day when they were, of all things, hired bodyguards for me.

"Uh—okay. Well, both of these gentlemen are big fans of Will Kodaly."

"Then they have good taste," she said. "Hang on, I have to switch breasts."

Now both men looked uncomfortable. Bruce was suddenly concerned about something he saw out the window, and François was studying a blank page on his phone. "She's just breastfeeding, "I whispered.

This information did not lessen their discomfort by one iota.

Runa was back, laughing. "Anya is voracious. I'm proud of her. She gets fatter before our eyes."

I knew how much joy this would bring Runa and her husband, Andy; after all, little Anya had almost died before she was even born. Now their baby was thriving, and it gave them a sense of satisfaction and security. "That's great. I can't wait to see her again."

"Come any time," she said, her voice serene.

"When I come by, can I bring these two so that they can say hello to Anya and also look at your Kodaly?"

"It's not for sale," Runa warned.

"No. I mean, yes, they understand that. They just like to see the works in person. They've viewed several now, just in Riverwood."

"Yes, that's fine. Pick a time and text it to me. I'll let you know if it works."

"Thanks, Runa."

I ended the call, and we spent the next ten minutes comparing calendars. We found we could all make it the next day, Sunday, at 1 pm. Runa approved the time via text, and the men were both pleased.

"Thank you so much, Hana," Bruce said. He looked so relieved that it made him appear tired.

I studied him while I refreshed my tea with some hot water. "Tell me something, Bruce. This quest of yours isn't' about Kodaly or Runa now. It's about Rose Toth, right?"

His face closed a bit, but he said, "Why do you say that?"

"I know you said the two of you were great friends. But you were more than that, weren't you?"

Perhaps it was the intimate setting—all of us at my kitchen table—or perhaps it was the fact that we had just shared two victories. But something in his face relaxed, and he said, "Of course we were. You never met her, Hana. If you had, you would have understood how, just, *alluring* she was. The first time I met her I wanted to touch her. It wasn't only a sexual response; she was the kind of person you just wanted to connect with. She had charisma. You—I, at least—felt this strong desire to be a part of her life. Just in the first minute after introduction." He sighed, using his finger to sweep up some cookie crumbs.

"You loved her."

"After a couple months, yeah. We loved each other."

I kept my voice gentle. "And the baby?"

His eyes filled with tears. "It was mine. She and her boyfriend had been over for months. They hadn't told many people yet. She was kind. She wanted to be considerate of him, to let the news filter out gradually, when he was ready. I think she also wanted to avoid telling her parents about breaking up with Albert, for whatever reason. I said I could wait for the public stuff. We were together, that was all that mattered."

"So, the world thought Albie was her boyfriend." I had a sudden realization. "And Albie presented himself as her boyfriend at the funeral. Didn't you want to say something?"

He shrugged. "I've barely been able to function since this happened. François dragged me out today, and it has helped a lot, having a focus, getting into the fresh air. At the time, I didn't care. I mean, what did it matter who was dating her or whose child she was carrying? They were both dead." He wiped his eyes, and tears gathered in mine, too. "We were excited about the baby. We were looking at houses on weekends."

François put a brotherly arm around Bruce Bevington. I wondered if Bruce were the first male friend he had made in

America. He squeezed Bruce's shoulder and said, "He is sick with sadness. But today we have fed the patient with beautiful art, with friendship and tea and cookies. Weeks of this will get him to a solid ground, where he can remember with a smile."

Bruce looked surprised, and pointed to François as he met my gaze. "This guy is something special, isn't he?"

"Yes, he is. We would be lost without him, for many reasons." I turned to our pastry chef. "François, have you ever told Bruce the story of Runa and our landscaper?"

The moment I alluded to had occurred on that same day, the bodyguard day, when Runa and Thyra, both with police training and Black Belts in karate, had roamed the tea house like tigresses impatient for the kill. Runa went out for a perimeter check, and our poor gardener, Janos, had trudged past with his trowel and Thyra had labeled him as an intruder. Before any of us could react, Runa had flown through the air like a vengeful fairy, taking down Janos and pinning his arms behind him. Janos, in turn, had treated us all to some primo Hungarian swears.

François related this, through his laughter, to Bruce, who was soon laughing, too. "More stories like that, please," he joked. The laughter had brought him some relief, but now that I knew the truth, I realized that his grief had been evident all along—something in his eyes that spoke of an inability to quiet his restless thoughts.

I put a hand on his arm. "Thank you for telling me. I will be discreet, but I do intend to share the information with Erik Wolf."

François said, "He's the policeman investigating—the tall blond man—you have most likely seen him."

Bruce nodded, then raked both hands through his hair. "I don't know why I didn't tell them. I haven't been able to concentrate, or sleep, or decide what to do."

"I understand," I said, going for a soothing tone. Whether or not Erik would understand was another question.

"We must go," François said, looking at his watch. "We will see you tomorrow, Hana." It was strange, having a weekend free, and seeing François out of the confines of the tea house. We were colleagues, for the most part, but over the past few months it had become apparent that we were also friends.

They moved to the door, then turned in a final farewell. I waved, smiling, and they left. I sank onto my couch and the cats jumped up beside me for a debriefing. My thoughts whirled. Rose had been pregnant with Bruce's child. Rose and Albie had no longer been a couple. Bruce had sounded sure of that, but I wondered if Albie had been as certain. He seemed to have been under the impression that Rose was the current love in his life. Had the Toth sisters also been under that impression? I sat up straighter. Or had Teresa known that Rose had broken things off? Was that why she had been angry? After all, Teresa seemed fond of Albie.

Still . . . if Rose had been carrying Bruce Bevington's child, then Bevington had no motive to kill her. But Albie did, and correspondingly, if any woman had set her sights on Bevington, perhaps she, too, would have a motive? I shook my head. Jealous love wasn't something you killed for. Was it?

Kodaly returned to my thoughts. He *had* been killed by a jealous man. The thought of it made me sick. The waste of wonderful life, a prodigious talent, all because of a resentful heart.

And then a feeling came back to me: the waves of jealousy in the tea house, so strong that we had all felt it, we Horvath/Keller women, and one person's negative emotion had overwhelmed me. My unexpected swoon was the reason Katie had come to see me, why we had worked on her big white chart, why we had determined that the root of the thing was the *baby*. The poor little baby.

I called Erik. He said, "Hello, Hana," in such a sexy voice that I almost swooned again.

"When do you think you'll be home?" I asked.

"We have the viewing tonight at eight, right? And I'm hoping to eat before then because I'm starving. I'll aim for six-thirty."

"Good. I have a lot to tell you."

"About your growing love for me?" he joked.

"Yes. But also, about your current case."

I could practically hear his gears switching, clicking into cop mode. "Like what?"

"It's a long story, but I got some information today from Bruce Bevington. You'll want to hear it."

"Did he happen to leave crucial things out of his statement?" Erik said crisply.

"The baby was his," I said. "He's grieving. So, find some gentleness."

There was a silence. "All right. We'll talk over dinner. I don't want you to think I take you for granted or think of you as some kind of servant, but—"

"I'll have a hot meal ready."

"Oh, thank God," he said, and I laughed as we ended the call. I needed to have a talk with him about not skipping meals.

The thought of eating more meals made me think of Domo, and the chat I needed to have with him. I poked the third number on my speed dial, and Domo answered. "Hey, Han. What's up?"

"Are you at work?"

"Nope. Home early, drinking a beer, and admiring the beauty of my fiancée."

"Great. Do you have a minute to talk about Dad's birthday?"

A sudden rustling suggested he was sitting up in a panic. "Did I miss it? No, wait—it's not for a couple weeks."

"No, you didn't miss it. I had been wondering what to get him, and I just happened across the perfect gift—so I bought it. But it was expensive, and I'm going to need people to pitch in."

"Sure, I'll pitch in. What did it cost?"

"Five thousand dollars."

I think he spit out his beer. There was a wet sound, and then some swearing; he seemed to be rubbing something. "Five *thousand* dollars? What did you buy him, a second wife?"

"No. Dad only has eyes for his current wife, and that's why this present is so perfect."

"I'm on the edge of my seat."

"Do you remember that painting that Will Kodaly did of mom? I never knew about it back then. I think I was off at college. He called it Magdalena's Eyes."

"Of course. Dad was so hilarious when that guy came over. He was always hovering, and asking Mom if she needed anything."

I laughed. "Grandma said Dad made excuses to do all kinds of yard work because Kodaly was painting her out in the garden."

"Yeah, so what—you framed a print of it for him? But that wouldn't cost thousands of dollars. Did you get ripped off, Hana?"

"I got the painting itself. You know that Kodaly's work is out of our price range these days."

"Yeah."

"But there's this auction site, and sellers are encouraged

to set affordable rates. The original buyer died, and his kids are selling a bunch of his paintings. I couldn't resist, Domo."

To my surprise, Domo said, "No, you did the right thing."

"Really?"

"Of course. I know how much Dad wanted to buy that painting. But he was paying college tuition for two kids back then. God, he's going to love this. I am happy to go in on this gift with you." A soft sound in the background. "Yeah, and Margie is obviously in on it, too."

"Can you cover half?"

"We'll cover whatever you need. I'll Venmo you some money."

"Thanks, Domo."

"No, thank you, Hana. You have always been a thoughtful little person. Margie says that gift-giving is your love language, whatever that means. But I appreciate it. You're a good daughter and little sister."

Relief flowed through my veins; I felt it spreading like warm water. "Thanks, big brother."

"No problem. I'm going to kiss Marguerite now."

"You do that. I have to figure out what I'm making Erik for dinner. Love you!"

My brother Domo said that he loved me, too, and I was smiling when we ended the call.

I looked at the cats, who purred beside me. I think they were actually pleased to have heard Domo's big loud voice. "What do you think? Chicken Paprikás? Or maybe Székely gulyás?"

They blinked at me, looking sleepy. Laughing, I told them to enjoy their nap (which they would undoubtedly take piled on top of each other), and made my way to the kitchen in quest of dinner ingredients.

*

My mind was full of holidays as I gazed around the penthouse of my building, clutching Erik's arm with excitement. We could host Christmas parties here; I would climb a ladder to hang pine boughs under the lovely arched ceiling, and two slim, elegant little trees, glowing with white lights, could flank the brick fireplace, while candles and pine boughs and delicate Christmas deer would adorn the wide mantel. The big tree would stand before the generous floor to ceiling window in the living area. The place was so big that we had room for a piano, around which we could sing Christmas carols with our friends. And oh! Halloween parties would happen here, with everyone in costume and Erik and I sneaking kisses before we opened the door to Iris and Jia, dressed as something unpredictable and waiting for candy with imperious little faces. In summer we could make tiny sandwiches and lemonade and Sangria and sit with friends at the giant dining table we would have to buy to fit the space (Falken could help me find the perfect one), and I would sit tucked under Erik's arm, proud of our grand home and laughing at the antics of Antony and Cleopatra, who would definitely enjoy running down the long hallway that led to the bedrooms . . . and I would enjoy the bedroom, with its skylight view of the stars, and I'd enjoy the bed I shared with my handsome lover . . ..

"Hana?"

"Yes? Sorry, I was daydreaming." Two men were grinning at me: Erik, and Jon Kantner, the owner of our building.

"I'm guessing you like the place?" Jon asked. "It helps that Tim has moved out a lot of his furniture already. You can really see the bones of the place now."

"Amazing bones," I murmured.

Jon nodded his approval. He was a big, hearty man with a large middle and ruddy cheeks. His avuncular charm had probably helped him in his Real Estate career (ours was not the only building he owned), and it was certainly effective as a way to win me over. "Come on back, let's look at the bedrooms."

There were three; Erik had suggested that we each have an office, initially, before we turned one of them, perhaps, into a nursery. The master bedroom had its own adjoining bath, and another bathroom sat between the two additional bedrooms. All of the rooms had real wood-plank flooring, polished to a shine, and generous closets with shelving and hanging rods. The master closet was a walk-in, something I'd never seen in real life. My hand tightened in Erik's. The golden-green aura around him seemed to be glowing more brightly this evening.

The moment felt magical. I was standing in a space that held my future.

Erik smiled down at me. "So, we'll take it?"

"We will!" I cried, hugging him. He still smelled like gravy. He'd had to inhale his chicken and dumplings when he got home late, and then we'd raced upstairs to meet Jon outside the apartment.

"Great!" Jon said, smiling. "I'm glad to sell to such good tenants. I know you'll take care of the place. We'll be forming a condo association after the other units are sold, and I think you two would make great co-presidents."

Erik laughed. "My schedule is pretty sporadic, as is Hana's. But I'm sure we'll be involved somehow." The men gravitated toward the kitchen, where Jon had set some paperwork on the counter. Erik had brought a check to secure our offer. I should have been right beside him, as a co-buyer, paying attention to all the financial details and contractual obligations. And I would do so, at the closing. But right now, I needed to drift around the place that would be ours, imagining it with our furniture, our rugs, our possessions.

I walked down the hallway with its glowing wood, its pristine, cream-colored walls, and peered at the men in the open-plan kitchen, staring down at documents with frowns of concentration. Erik was slightly disheveled after a busy day, but he looked handsome to me, and a swirl of affection and desire made me grin, probably in a way that Domo would call "love-stupid."

I did love him. It seemed suddenly that I had always loved him, since the day he was born.

A stray thought floated over my happy daydream. Had Albie loved Rose this much? But they had already parted. He must have accepted the separation. Mustn't he?

Another drifting thought: had some woman loved Bruce Bevington? Had she seen him as a future conquest? A present one? Had Rose seemed like an interloper, a thief, a destroyer? What if I found out, at this point, that Erik was in love with someone else? That she was going to have his baby?

I studied my boyfriend: his beautiful golden-blond hair, his intelligent face, his tall form. My plans for the future had twined themselves around him, keeping him rooted with me in the same ground, growing with me in the sunlight of our love. Another woman, wrenching him out of our Eden, leaving a gaping hole in my life? How would I feel?

The misery rose up in me. I did not think I was a woman who could ever kill. But like any human being, I could probably hate. And I would hate her, the thief-woman who stole my love, my life. And if I had been a different sort of person—one without the supportive family, the happy upbringing, the healthy relationships, the loving friends—then perhaps that hatred could lead me to kill. Or could it?

I looked down at my hands; my fists had clenched slightly as I imagined the terrible scenario of loss. Could I kill? No.

But could I understand why someone else would kill, in the circumstances I had imagined?

With a sigh, I acknowledged the truth to myself: yes, I understood. Yes, I could envision the jealousy that would twist into hate and madness. Something good could turn ugly, destructive, obsessive. I thought of the Fairy of Darkness and Light; how quickly, really, one could morph into the other, if life brought unexpected change. Yes, that deprived lover *would* kill.

And I was fairly sure that they had.

Chapter Sixteen

A Small, Silver Voice

I called my friend Falken on Sunday morning. Falken and I had bonded over our love of antiques and beautiful objects, and I wanted to know if he was aware of the auction site Bruce had shown me.

"Art Alliance?" he asked me. I could hear his pen scratching as he wrote it down. "I don't know that I have heard of it."

"You won't believe what I found there yesterday. Well, a guy named Bruce found it, but he showed me and I bought it."

"Oh, my. Was it porcelain?" His voice was gentle, pleased for me, because Falken was a good friend.

"It was a painting. It was *Magdalena's Eyes*."

"Oh, wonderful! And you bought it? I'd love to see it up close."

"Yes. It was more than I could afford, but my brother is going to bail me out. We're giving it to my father for his birthday."

"Dare I ask what they wanted?"

"Five thousand."

He whistled. "And yet, nowadays, that's a steal."

"I know!" I hugged myself. "It was serendipity. I can't wait to see my father's face! I'm going to have Margie take a picture and Erik take a video."

He laughed. "By the way, I'm glad you called. I have a lovely little Hungarian something for you."

"I can't even look at it. I've gone beyond the bounds of responsible spending, so I won't spend again until I pay off that painting. Or Domo does," I added, and Falken laughed again.

"I'll save it for you," he said. "It will keep."

"Thanks, pal. Okay, I have to go. I'm headed to Runa's place. Did I tell you she had her baby?"

"No, how wonderful! The little girl is fine?"

"Yes. She's beautiful." A sudden memory of Anya, newly born into my hands and blinking at me, sent happy shivers through my limbs.

"All is well in Riverwood," Falken said in his soothing voice.

We said goodbye, and I pondered his final words. If only they had been true.

*

Runa's apartment was as lovely as always, though a bit more cluttered. A baby carrier with a sleeping Anya in it sat beneath a beautiful tapestry. Boxes of diapers sat stacked against one wall, and a breastfeeding pillow sat on the arm of the bright blue couch. Runa saw my gaze drifting back to Anya and grinned. "When she falls asleep, we don't have the courage to move her to the crib. We value the free time too much."

I felt a pang of guilt. "Oh! We won't take up too much of that precious free time."

She shook her head. "We do like seeing adults. Partly to show off our beautiful girl, and partly to speak words to human beings. All we do right now is coo at her." She couldn't suppress her smile.

"And—you feel all right?"

"I feel great."

And she looked great, too--almost back to her original slimness and smelling like some expensive perfume. Andy sailed in then, holding a plate. "Runa, here's your sandwich. Hi, Hana! Nice to see you! Did you notice my daughter there against the wall?"

"I did. But I won't go too close. I don't want to wake her."

He smiled. "She'll wake soon enough. She seems to think that at some point we'll start charging her for the milk, and she has to get as much of the free stuff as she can. That little girl of ours can pack it away."

Clearly, Andy was still in his "my amazing daughter" mode; it was actually quite adorable.

"So, you're on paternity leave?" I asked.

"Yup. Until the end of April."

"That's awesome. You get to learn Anya's personality together, and she'll be used to both of you giving hugs and kisses."

"Runa gives something I can't, but I think Anya finds me an acceptable second choice." Andy grinned at me; his hair was messy and his eyes were tired, but ironically, he looked quite attractive. Runa seemed to think this, too, because she went to stand next to him and kissed his cheek before taking her plate.

"Would you like something to eat, Hana?" Andy asked.

"No, no thank you. The guys should be here any moment, and then we'll be out of your hair." I felt nervous now, like an intruder and a time thief.

Runa sat down with her plate, and Andy tucked in beside

her. Runa's two greyhounds, Lucy and Desi, were both wedged into one of the blue chairs situated across from Runa's matching couch. Runa followed my gaze and said, "They're pouting. We haven't walked them yet, and they seem to understand that the baby is going to get more attention. But my dear husband has promised to take them for a nice run."

Andy nodded, still smiling. I thought he may have been smiling since the moment of Anya's birth. "Yes, I will, as soon as I make sure my wife receives the proper sustenance."

"Isn't he sweet?" Runa asked, looking not at me, but at Andy's adoring eyes. They kissed, this time on the lips, and I exchanged a glance with the greyhounds, who seemed to be saying, "Do you believe these two?"

Moments later the bell rang, and Andy leaped up to answer it. Runa finished her sandwich and set the plate on her coffee table. When Andy ushered in François and Bruce Bevington, she stood and smoothed her silky blue pantsuit. "Runa, you know François. And this is Bruce Bevington. He teaches art at Longwood, and he is a huge fan of Will Kodaly."

Runa shook Bruce's hand and smirked at François, who blushed. "You are intelligent, then. Intelligent people like Kodaly, because his paintings speak not only to the heart, but to the mind."

Bevington nodded, bright and excited as a groupie.

Andy murmured his agreement, then said, "I'll take the dogs now, love." Runa shot him a dazzling smile, and Andy seemed stunned by it for a moment before he remembered to put his body in motion and find leashes for the sulking dogs. Once they saw what he was holding, they leapt gracefully from the chair and loped over to Andy, smiling at him with their doggy teeth and wagging their tails like mad. "Pushovers," Andy said quietly to them. He had obviously grown fond of her dogs; in fact, everything that had once been Runa's seemed very much both of theirs now. I wondered if that was how it would feel for Erik and me when we moved into the big apartment . . .

Runa walked over to the baby carrier, where Anya still slept, looking like the tiniest of angels. Runa smiled down at her, then turned. "So, you want to see my beautiful painting? My husband bought it for me more than a year ago. One of the best presents he ever gave me. Come this way."

The men followed her, on a quest for beauty. "I'm glad I knew you were coming, so I had time to make my bed," Runa said over her shoulder. Her long blonde hair looked clean and shiny, as though she had washed it that morning. We followed her into the large bedroom, where the painting in question hung across from her bed. Bruce and François crowded in front of it like rude patrons at a museum.

"Exquisite," François said. A moment later, eyes fixed on the canvas, he dashed away a tear.

Bruce Bevington was equally fascinated. "Whoever would have thought that you could *show* what falling in love looks like? That you could capture the *moment,* that blend of excitement and confusion and sheer joy?

He turned to Runa, his face solemn. "Whatever your husband paid for it, he got a bargain. Even if it cost a million dollars."

Runa nodded, understanding. "I am spoiled. I see it every day, every morning and night, and it transports me to a higher place. The whole point of art, is it not? And it reminds me how much I love my Andrew Bell." She held out her left hand to admire the ring on her finger. It was a sizeable diamond—I wondered how much money Andy had spent in order to lavish Runa with gifts—and it glinted in the light of her bedroom chandelier.

Bruce stared at her, his expression stiff and frozen—a

cross between a smile and a grimace—and Runa looked up at him. "I'm guessing you have been in love," she said. "You have felt that lightning bolt moment yourself."

Bruce nodded, not smiling.

"I have, as well," said François. "My lover, Claire --"

But Runa was still looking at Bruce. "It's painful, isn't it? The woman in the picture is still alive, but the man is dead. He died for love of her, did Hana tell you? A jealous man had him hunted down and killed, because he loved the woman. Really, it's like something out of a myth, or a fairy tale."

"In my case, it's the woman who is dead," Bruce said. "And the man who is left broken-hearted." There was something in his voice then, a ragged, broken quality that I had not heard before. Pity washed through me, and I stepped closer to put a hand on his forearm.

"I'm sorry, Bruce."

He patted my hand, then turned to Runa. "The painting is called True Love, is that right? Do you mind if I take a picture of it? The morning light in here will be perfect."

Runa started to reply, but we all froze as an unfamiliar sound reached our ears—a sweet, tiny, silvery sound that I realized was Anya vocalizing, calling for her mother. My hands flew to my cheeks. "She's not crying," I said, amazed. "She's—talking!"

Runa's grin was triumphant. "Yes. She's had several dialogues with Andy and me. When we're not dumbfounded, we are laughing our heads off. Hang on, I have to feed her." She slipped out of the room. For a moment, I heard them conversing, mother and daughter, as she lifted Anya from her carrier. The pure and beautiful moment transformed the space, making it inspiring as a church.

Bruce took several pictures: first, the painting as a whole; second, close-ups on the two lovers' faces, and finally, a close up of Kodaly's signature. François took a picture, as well, and then asked me to take a photo of him beside the painting.

A minute later we shuffled silently out of the room. Runa sat, smiling at nothing. Then she looked up at us. "Hana, come and hold her. She wasn't even that hungry. I think she just wanted someone to cuddle. She's sleepy again, very peaceful. Don't be afraid."

I moved across the floor and leaned down to take the small bundle into my arms. She was light and warm, and she smelled of powder and baby skin. I tucked her against my chest and put my nose in her wispy blonde hair. "I should probably hold her every day," I said, half joking.

"You probably should," Runa agreed.

I walked toward the men, who stood uncertainly near the exit. "Meet Anya Bell," I said.

They bent over the baby; both François and Bruce were obviously charmed by Anya, but I realized, too late, that the sight of her might cause Bruce pain. His eyes filled with tears, and I said, "I'm sorry."

He shook his head. "Not your fault. Not anyone's fault, except one."

I walked around a bit with Anya, murmuring soft nothings into her tiny ear while her eyelids fluttered and then gave up, staying shut in a new slumber. Her mouth was curved into a smile, but then it reversed itself, and she seemed ready to cry. A moment later, she was smiling again.

I laughed softly and stroked her velvet cheek, her tiny arm. I examined her miniscule fingernails and grinned at the dimples in her little elbow. What a beautiful, perfect child. My grandmother needed to see her. I walked back to Runa. "Hey, we're having a birthday party for my dad on April 12th. Can you and Andy and Anya come? My grandmother will be there, and I know she's dying to see the baby."

"Of course!" Runa sprang up from the couch. "I'll jot it on my calendar. What time?"

"Around two, I think."

Runa left the room just as Andy came in the front door, looking flushed from running the dogs. The slender canines did, in fact, look happier, and they moved on swift long legs into the kitchen, where I could hear them slurping water from their bowls.

Runa returned and slid into Andy's arms. He kissed her hair and smiled at nothing in particular. Mirroring him, I kissed the thistledown hair on Anya's sweet head and handed her back to Andy, who was already holding out his arms. "I promised we wouldn't stay long, so we'll be on our way. Thank you for sharing the painting, and for sharing Anya. Both experiences were uplifting," I said.

My two companions, who had edged even closer to the door, reiterated their thanks, and the three of us left the apartment. I had not even noticed while basking in the light of love in the apartment, but I now saw, through a small hallway window, that it was raining.

"Rain," Bruce said, his voice dismal.

François, ever buoyant, said, "I will run ahead and get the car. You wait at the entrance. Hana, I will drive you to wherever you parked." He bolted down the stairs, a man with a mission.

I stole a glance at Bruce as we descended the stairs. "Did you enjoy the Kodaly?"

"It was marvelous. Perhaps my favorite so far. The woman's face is so beautiful, but her expression makes it – ethereal. I fell in love with her a bit myself. I wish Kodaly were alive, and that I could talk to him."

Yes, how nice that would be. "Talk to him anyway. Did I tell you he was psychic?"

He stopped on a landing. "What?"

"We have it in my family, whatever you want to call it—second sight, extrasensory perception—and Kodaly was interested in us for that reason. He felt that he too had the gift, and wanted to talk to us about it. He died before he could."

Bruce thought about this information, his face bright with emotion. "But why does that mean I can talk to him?"

"Oh, well. It might not. But once, when I was in trouble, I called out to Natalia. She was my great-grandmother, and she had the strongest abilities of all of us. She once helped the police to find a missing child."

"Wow," Bruce said, stunned.

"Anyway, she died years ago. But I called to her when a man was chasing me. Long story. I was running, panicking, not thinking clearly. I asked her for help, and it was like a light went on. I could hear her voice, and I knew where to go."

"Wow," he said again.

"Obviously you could argue that it was just my mind, using her image to find a solution. Perhaps it was."

"But you don't think so."

"No."

By some quiet consent, we began our descent again. Bruce said, "Do you have this power?"

"Yes. But I only recently discovered that I do."

"So—can you tell me what happened to Rose?"

"Not exactly. I just get sensations. On the day of the memorial, the one at the tea house?"

He nodded.

"I felt someone's strong emotion. Grief, yes, but a stronger one than that."

He looked at me, and I said, "Jealousy. We all felt it---I, my mother, and my grandmother. We are sure it was the motive."

We were at the door now, but there was no sign of François's little grey Audi. Bruce Bevington was thinking hard. "Jealousy of whom? Rose?"

"Perhaps. And I wanted to ask you: did you date women before Rose? Perhaps one of her sisters, or someone at the school?"

He shrugged. "I mean, yeah, I dated. Not once I met Rose. But she had only been at the school for a year. I went out with some people before that."

"Who? Anyone who still feels upset by the breakup?"

He looked surprised. "Listen, I'm not perfect, but my breakups tend to be amicable. I'm never out to hurt anyone."

"Right. Would you be willing to tell me who you dated? At Longwood, let's say?"

Now his face flushed slightly. "This is kind of embarrassing. I dated several women. It's not like I intended to just make my way through the staff. The connections just happened naturally and ended naturally."

"How long did they last?"

He shrugged again. "One, a couple of months. Another, maybe six months. A third, a year or so. And there are a couple women I socialize with, just as friends. No physical stuff involved."

"Okay. Names?"

He sighed. "Angela."

"Miss Angie? The other first grade teacher?"

"Yeah. And Cheryl Pratt. She wasn't at the memorial; she's on maternity leave."

"Okay. And?"

"Ursula and I had a short fling. She's already dating a new guy. Henry, or Harvey or something. And sometimes I'd grab a drink with Rita if she came to pick up Partridge and he wasn't finished, uh, administrating." He grinned. "I doubt

Rita has any interest in me, but she's a fun conversationalist. We liked to chat about theatre arts versus visual arts. How they inform one another." He sighed. "And then --"

"Yes?"

"I go out with Edie sometimes. Totally platonic. We just go to a bar once in a while for some wine, venting about curriculum, or scheduling. About Mr. Partridge, sometimes."

I couldn't picture Edie Pembroke dating anyone. She seemed to me like one of those fertility symbols, buxom and motherly, made to comfort children. "And she knows it's platonic?"

"Of course she does!" he snapped. "I'm not some lady-killer." He paled, regretting his choice of words. "I'm just a regular guy, trying to find a woman I can spend my life with. And I found her."

He looked away from me, and I put a hand on his shoulder. "I know. I'm sorry. And thank you for telling me this. I'll share it with Erik"

He sniffed, then said, "I can tell you that none of those women committed murder. They work in a grade school, for God's sake."

"Right. Regarding Rose's sisters. Did you know them? Date either of them?"

He shook his head. "No. But I did realize at that memorial that I went to school with one of them. The older one. I'm pretty sure she was in my homeroom in high school, maybe a couple of classes. Everyone called her T-Rex because she had a temper. But she was popular, as I recall."

T-Rex. Teresa, a creature of destruction? Teresa, who had a temper, even as a teenager? Teresa, who was angry with her sister at the time that Rose died?

My thoughts whirled around as we looked out the

entrance and saw François pull up in front of us, beckoning, his face urgent, because he was in a no-parking zone.

We darted through the rain and dove into his car.

As we drove away from Runa's building, the dominant image that stayed with me was that sound, pure as a chime, of Anya calling to her mother. How quickly people learned to love, I thought.

And how great the pain of a love denied.

Chapter Seventeen

Trapped in the Witch's House

Aunt Luca called me the next morning. "Hello, my sweet! Jia told me how much fun she had when you picked her up from school. She was very proud to show off her principal and her schoolyard, and for her friends to see you."

"How nice. Children are so full of good will."

"They are. They put us all to shame, corrupted adults that we are. Anyway, I have orientation today at the new job, so could you pick her up again? I know I could ask Magda or Mama, but you were so popular --"

"Yes. I'd love to pick her up. It felt so cool, being a school mom."

She laughed. "It's new for me, too. And it is special, I think because we know how fleeting these days will be. It's funny—Jia was always my friend's daughter. But then all of a sudden, she was mine, and I felt this-- fierce possessiveness. And then I realized that feeling was love, and a desire to protect her. It's amazing how quickly I loved her as my own."

I thought of what Runa had said long ago, when she first realized she was pregnant: that she had found out how long it takes to love a child—from the first moment you know of her existence. And then, inevitably, I thought of Rose. When I picked up Jia, perhaps I could check on Bruce to make sure he was emotionally healthy.

"Thanks, dear niece. I owe you dinner at our house."

"I would like that! Can I bring Erik?"

"Of course! I need to get to know him better."

We ended the call with promises to compare calendars.

I went to the mirror to adjust my Maggie's Tea House uniform: black skirt, white blouse, and apron embroidered with Hungarian patterns. I tightened the apron tie and tucked some stray hair into my work bun. Erik had left hours earlier, and the cats, already sated, were asleep in a pile on my bed.

Today's event had been booked by a Riverwood law firm which was honoring its partners and associates after a very good quarter. They had paid for the "deluxe" package which required more expensive tea, more intricate pastries, and real flowers at each table. My job was to pick up our sheaves of roses at Blossoms, our preferred florist. They gave us good deals on truly exquisite blooms. We had decided on a color theme based on the firm's logo. They were called Peterson and Bright, and the names of the two founders were set apart with complementary colors: Peterson was blue, and Bright was a pale orange. We were going to use a plain white tea service with a gold border at the cup rims, but we'd alternated blue and peach cloth napkins on the plates. The company logo, a sun over the word "Bright" and the god Apollo, gold and blue, above Peterson, served as a striking inspiration for our palette. I had found Renaissance-looking statues of Apollo at a craft store. They were merely papier mâché forms, unpainted, so my mother had whisked them into her backyard and sprayed them gold. Now, a thoughtful Apollo sat on each table, and soon, roses tinted blue would be tucked into vases alongside the most beautiful shade of peachy-yellow. The whole thing was going to look magnificent, and of course we would provide our usual excellent service. They had asked for background music, so my grandmother had created a playlist of classical pieces that seemed appropriate to the occasion. The dais was ready, along with the microphone, so that they could make congratulatory speeches and give out their awards and bonuses.

When I reached Blossoms, I hopped out of the car, noting that the March air still held a chill, and then I remembered: it wasn't March anymore. It was April 1st. Shaking my head at the bizarre rapidity of time, I walked into the glorious scented atmosphere of the florist and greeted Rania, the owner. Rania's family was from Kuwait, but she had been born in the U.S. and spoke with all the obligatory American slang. She looked like a princess, with long dark hair, dark eyes, and dark, long lashes. She had zillions of admirers, including Peter, the mail carrier, and the man who owned the restaurant next door to her business. Those were just two of the recent ones—it was an endless flow. Rania greeted me and said that she would be right back with my flowers.

She darted into the back and returned with two buckets full of those lovely apricot-colored roses, as well as the blue-tinted roses that evoked thoughts of the sky. "Just take the buckets," she said. "You can bring them back on your way home. I'll tuck some baby's breath and purple statice to help you fill out your bouquets if you need them." She saw that I was still studying the roses, and added, "Yes, aren't they superb? And smell them. Cheap roses don't have much of a scent, but these --"

I put my face near the flowers and inhaled. I was rewarded by that distinct, floral-raspberry scent of garden roses. "Yum," I said.

"Yes." Rania's dark eyes flashed with pride, and she skipped behind the counter to ring up the sale.

I was examining the flowers. "As always, these are perfectly pruned."

She nodded. "That's my wonderful Omar and Jessica in the back. You hear that, Jessomar?"

Someone yelled "Thank you!"

"Jessomar," I said, grinning. "Like a celebrity couple."

Rania laughed, revealing pretty white teeth. "It's just easier." She handed me a credit card slip to sign. "So, you have a luxury package today?"

"Yes. A law firm. Mom is excited; she's been negotiating with them for us to be their regular place for business events. She's good at that."

"Great! And we'll be your regular florist." She grinned, too.

I studied Rania for a moment. "Your arrangements are always so inspired. Do you like art?"

She clapped. "Love it. All sorts, but especially sculpture. And certain painters. I tend to like those floaty watercolors, Japanese or otherwise. Why do you ask?"

"No real reason. You just seem to be a font of creativity." But I did have a slight ulterior motive. Someday, when Bruce was on the mend, I might send him to Blossoms and see if anything . . . bloomed.

Rania handed me my receipt and ran a professional eye over the flowers in my containers. She nodded, pleased. "Okay, you're all set. As always, I ask that you take pictures. I'll put them on my site and reference your tea house."

"And we'll list you on *our* site as the provider of our enchanting blooms."

We shook hands in a jokey, theatrical way, and I bundled out with my heavy buckets.

In the ten minutes it took me to drive to Maggie's Tea House, I played 80s radio and heard a bouncy song by Katrina and the Waves, and a bluesy number by George Michael. I liked them both a lot. My dad had commented once that 80s music was special because everyone was so distinctive—that there were fewer sound-alike acts back then. Naturally, my father was biased about the music of his youth, but I'd been listening to this station for about a week, and I was starting to agree with him.

When I entered the tea house hall, my family rushed toward me, and I was subjected to a careful inspection of my person. They had not seen me since the day I fainted, and they were doing a wellness check.

"I'm fine," I said. "And thanks for sending Katie to me, Grandma."

"Yes. It helped?"

"Very much." I set the buckets down and gave hr a hug, then embraced my mother. "You two are the best," I said. "And it looks like you got a lot done this morning." The room was already half-decorated, tablecloths and dishware in place, the Golden Apollos glinting in the chandelier light. "Yes," my mother agreed modestly.

"Look at my roses," I said. My mother knelt and breathed the scent. "Oh, paradise," she enthused.

She looked up at me, and my whole body filled with butterflies. She would be as surprised as my father by the painting of her. I couldn't wait.

A glance at my grandmother told me that she had picked up on something. "You have a secret," she said. Not even a question.

"Not really. I can tell you now. Erik and I are going to move in together."

They both congratulated me and clapped their hands, but

something was off. "You're not surprised," I said. "Did Erik already tell you?"

Two pairs of wide, innocent eyes looked back at me. "No, no," my mother insisted. "We are surprised."

Liar. Fine—they could keep their secrets, and I would keep mine.

I got to work putting the lovely flowers into vases at each table, using the baby's breath and statice very minimally so that the roses dominated the visual. With the Apollo statues and the glowing candle on alternating white and navy tablecloths, the overall effect was stunning: elegant, lush, almost mysterious. "I love it!" I cried.

Grandma was back on the stage, tinkering with her sound machine. "Yes," she said. "Magda, you will get pictures?"

"Yes!" my mother agreed. "Let me do that before any people arrive."

She darted around the room, capturing the elegant scene on her iPad from various angles. "Now I have to work on the tea," she said. "And François has outdone himself."`

He had. When I put my spring jacket in the back room, he was slicing a beautiful Dobos Torte. He had already created trays of sandwiches on flaky croissants and mini quiches Lorraine that filled the room with the fragrance of bacon and buttery crust.

When he finished slicing, he said, "I still have the painting in my mind. That woman's face! The beauty of it, and the sadness. How is the whole world not in love with art?"

I shrugged. "They don't know how to open their eyes."

"Or their souls have shriveled," he said darkly, picking up a pastry bag. His expression changed to one of concentration as he deposited custard into newly-baked cream puffs.

I was unable to quell my childish instinct. I said, "Can I

lick the cream bowl? Or the chocolate bowl, once you drizzle it on?"

He looked up at me, his face unreadable. "You Americans. Such creatures of instant gratification."

I refused to be cowed. "You French. Putting pastry above all."

He grinned. "The bowl is by the sink."

I skipped over and found both the bowl and a little spoon. I began scraping. François continued to grin as he finished with his custard and put the little pastry "hats" on each puff. Then out came the chocolate icing, which he drizzled with a generous hand over each little dessert.

"You really are talented, François," I said, wiping custard from my bottom lip.

"Oui," he agreed, still drizzling.

"Do you think you and Claire will get married?" I asked, trying to ambush a genuine response from him.

He never even paused. "Oui," he said again.

I sighed. For some reason, I thought of Albie. "Remember the guy who read that poem the other day? At the memorial?"

Now he was all drama, acting the part of "irate man." "Why would you remind me of this?"

"Because I have a question."

"Ah? What?"

"Putting his level of talent aside --"

"If only I could."

"Putting it aside, did you get the impression that it was – heartfelt? Or did it seem kind of --"

"A sham? A show of a man grieving? Oui. Yes."

The idea that Albie was less than devastated by Rose's death had never occurred to me before. Now, simply by talking to François in the room where he had ridiculed Albie's poem, the moment had come back to me. And in retrospect, the performance had seemed wrong, somehow.

I nodded slowly, setting the bowl and spoon in the sink. "Why do you think he would bother? I mean, if he felt less than mournful, why not just stay quiet?"

"Obviously, because he had to convince someone of his sadness."

I thought about this idea. Who would need convincing? Rose's parents? Her sisters? But why would he need to convince them? And had they known that she had already moved on from Albie? If so, were they *all* acting? It didn't make sense to me. I filled the bowl with water.

"Thanks, François. I'll come back and wash that bowl."

He laughed. "Now who is acting?" he asked.

*

When people began to arrive, we spoke briefly to the firm's partners, who introduced themselves as Angus Peterson and Yvonne Bright. They were visibly impressed with the decorations, the music, the overall vibe we had created. I handed them both a stack of our business cards, and they accepted them with promises to share them around.

The tables began to fill twenty minutes later, and we had finished pouring tea for everyone. François wheeled out the sandwiches and quiches, and we three women made quick work of delivering them to the tables. For a while, then, we enjoyed the sound of appreciative diners: forks clinking on plates, voices murmuring "delicious," and other complimentary words, teaspoons ringing against cups as people added their sugar or cream.

My gaze roved back and forth, checking for unexpected issues. Grandma was on the stage, readying the microphone and adjusting the volume of the Brahms Hungarian Dances we played as dinner music. My gaze caught on two women who had traveled to the bathroom together and who stood now in front of the World Tree tapestry, leaning in to touch the glittering threads and talking in low voices.

I strolled toward them and said, when I reached the hallway, "Beautiful, isn't it? It's an antique, probably Hungarian."

"It's stunning," one of the women said. "I suppose it's one of a kind? I'd love to buy one."

"It is a rare find. But I can refer you to the antique dealer who found it for us. Maybe he can find something similar for you." I reached in the pocket of my apron, where I always kept a couple of Falken's cards. What I pulled out was one of the little funeral poems I had written for the memorial. One of the women read it over my shoulder.

"Sorry—wrong card." I tucked it back in my pocket, but she looked interested.

"You had a memorial for Rose? The girl who taught at Longwood?"

I paused in digging for Falken's card. "Yes. Did you know her?"

She nodded. "My daughter teaches there. Seventh grade."

"Ugh," said the other woman. "Well, bless her."

The first woman laughed. "It's a tricky age, but Kendra loves junior high. She just gets how those kids think."

I tried not to look eager. "Was she a friend of Rose Toth's?"

The woman, tall and slightly heavy with frosted blonde hair, thought about this and shrugged. "They were friendly, but the kind of friendship you have with a colleague. They didn't take it beyond school walls. But they ate lunch together a lot, along with that art teacher and a few other younger faculty members. She said she idolized Rose. That she was beautiful inside and out. That Rose loved nothing more than those children." She looked sad.

The other woman, shorter and dark-haired, was studying me. "Did you know her, this Rose?"

"No. But my family is Hungarian, and so was hers, so we have—people in common."

"I get that," said the blonde woman. "Lithuanian here. Every Lithuanian is excited to meet another Lithuanian. One big family."

The dark-haired woman laughed. "Well, I'm just a hodgepodge of nationalities, and I have no such connection. I'm a bit jealous."

I had found Falken's cards. I retrieved two of them and handed them to the women. "He's kind of magical about finding just the right piece for you. And he loves doing it. Tell him Hana sent you."

"Hana," the dark-haired woman said thoughtfully. "Is that short for anything?"

"No." I smiled.

She moved closer. "And is it true? The rumor I heard that your grandmother is psychic?"

I hesitated. "She's very insightful."

She grinned at me, noting my reticence. "Interesting." I had forgotten that I was chatting with two lawyers. Soon they would be asking me why I was so interested in Rose Toth. I glanced at my watch and made an apologetic face. "Oh, I have to run and get dessert ready."

"Can't wait," said the blonde. "If the main course was any indication, we're in for a gourmet experience."

I nodded and moved past them, past Ördög's evil grin, into the back room, where François was putting things on serving platters.

"Here to wash dishes?" he asked, smirking.

Distracted, I said, "Uh--no. I have to send a quick text."

François started griping about phone use being frowned upon, and I ignored him. I sent a quick message to Bruce Bevington: "I'm picking up Jia today. Any chance we could talk for a minute?"

I imagined I'd have to wait if he were in the midst of teaching, but my phone pinged immediately. "Sure! We can talk in the art room. I'll show you the kids' masterpieces."

I thanked him and put away my phone. Then, with a pointed look at François, I marched to the sink and washed the bowl, then dried it and put it away.

"Oh, the indignant woman!" François said, not at all impressed. "Beware of Haughty Hana."

I moved past him toward the door. "Better Haughty Hana than Fussy François."

The door closed on his expostulations, a mixture of French and English, and I went back out to serve our guests. The partners were at the mic now, thanking everyone for their hard work and urging them to enjoy the repast. "We'll be back later with some firm-related business, but right now, it's party time!"

I passed a table at which people were definitely enjoying themselves. They clapped for the partners and dug into the remaining food. An attractive red-haired woman leaned into the shoulder of the man beside her and whispered something in his ear. His face flushed. Was that embarrassment? Anger? Desire? Both of them wore wedding rings, but I did not sense that they were married to one another. Aside from a waitressing job I had in college, I had never worked anywhere but the tea house. I had never had a male colleague. Was it easy to fall prey to attraction to a co-worker? Was it an inevitable thing? And was Bruce Bevington, one of the few male teachers at his school, inevitably going to receive female attention? Wanted or unwanted?

Grandma put the music back on, and we were treated to Brahms—Hungarian Dance Number 4 in F# Minor. I knew it well, had heard it and all of Brahms's 21 Hungarian Dances and Dvorak's Slavonic Dances. Many of them made me cry, inexplicably, and my mother and grandmother told me that I "had Natalia in me," because my great-grandmother, too, had felt music viscerally. This particular song, to me, sounded like Hungary's history. It started with weeping strings in a minor key, then switched into something more grand, proud, and then it was whipping us away into a sprightly dance. But always, always, it returned to those sad strings, and that melody brought the fat tears to my eyes. They were there now, and I brushed them away.

My grandmother floated up to me on her silent shoes. "You think too much," she said. "Although it's good to see that you feel, as well." She smoothed away one of my tears with a gentle finger. Then her expression changed. "What are you doing today? After this?"

I shrugged. "I have to run some errands, then pick up Jia. Luca has orientation. Then I'm going home and waiting for Erik."

She nodded, her eyes on mine. "Be careful."

"I'm always careful."

Her pupils grew larger, in that spooky way she had. "I should go with you."

"I'll be fine, Grandma. Don't freak me out."

"Miss?" asked a man nearby, holding up his teacup.

Grandma nodded again, two quick dips of her chin, and walked toward the man and his table.

*

Julia Buckley

After work I drove to Runa's, intent on staying only the five minutes it would take me to drop off my grandmother's kiflis and my mother's casserole.

I had texted Runa in advance, and she was expecting me. When I reached her door, though, it was Felix who opened it, looking pale but much healthier, and wearing a Snuggli with Anya inside, facing outward and dangling like a little Christmas ornament, a gold-haired angel ornament that blinked at me and twisted her tiny mouth into something like a smile, which then became a grimace, which then became an audible "berf" in her tiny diaper.

Thyra appeared in the doorway. "Baby fart!" she said, laughing. Felix laughed, too, and put his large hand on Anya's tiny head. I wanted to touch the baby, as well, but my hands were full.

"This is for Runa and Andy, but there's probably enough for all of you Wolves."

Thyra grinned. "Wolves. I like it." She took the heavy bag from me. "You made this, Hana?"

"I'd love to take credit, because it will be delicious, but my mother made the casserole and my grandma made the pastries."

Thyra stopped grinning. "Are these kiflis? Those ones you brought to the hospital when Runa had her operation?"

"Yes. Grandma made them."

"Those are the best cookies in the world."

"Then why do you look like you're about to murder someone?" I asked lightly.

Thyra tilted her head toward Felix. "Because someone is going to try to eat them all. I'm going to go hide some. Come on in, Hana!"

"I can't. I'm just delivering, and now I have to pick up Jia at school."

Felix looked disappointed. "Well, come back. I've barely seen you since I got here. And I've got some news for you and Erik."

"Oh? What is it?"

He shook his head. "I want to tell both of you."

Thyra darted back out, sans food, and patted his belly. "He's pregnant," she joked. "I thought I might be next, but alas, it is Felix."

Felix scowled. "My stomach is flat as a crepe. If I didn't have a tiny baby on me, I would teach you a lesson, little Thyra."

Little Thyra was almost six feet tall; I would have enjoyed watching that sparring match, but Runa's wall clock informed me that it was time to go. I waved to the Wolf siblings. "Say hi to Runa and Andy."

"We will," Felix said. "When they wake up. We're giving them Mommy and Daddy rest time."

"The best gift you could offer." I waved again and made my way back down the hall. Before my elevator doors closed, I heard Anya's silver tones, vocalizing softly. I chose to believe she was saying a gentle farewell.

*

Jia's school looked even more like a fairy tale cottage today because two flowering bushes on either side of the door had burst into bloom, and the scene was picturesque enough to look like CGI.

I reached the throng of parents and guardians, tucking myself into an open spot. I texted Bruce, and soon he appeared at the door. "Miss Keller, can I speak to you for a moment?" he asked in formal teacher tones.

"Oh, sure," I said. People stared; perhaps they wondered if I were the parent of a misbehaving junior high student. In any case, most of the looks I received were sympathetic. I followed Bruce through the doors and into the lobby which faced the main office window. Bruce waved absently at the people behind the counter and moved down a hall to the left of the entrance. At the counter, Edie Pembroke was jotting something in a binder, her face solemn. Behind her, Ursula sat at the desk, expertly putting one call on hold while she answered another. They had waved back at Bruce, but they seemed to have no interest in me. I wondered if every woman in this place enjoyed gazing at the handsome Mr. Bevington, the young and slightly scruffy artist with the soul of a poet.

Despite their seeming lack of interest, I waved at the women, too, and then followed Bruce to his art room, a large sunny space midway down the hall. "Don't you have to marshal a line of littles out to the front?" I asked.

He shook his head. "The schedule changes twice a week. On Mondays and Thursdays I have last period free. Come see what we've been working on."

"Shouldn't I wait in front for Jia?"

He shook his head again, unconcerned. "I told Miss Angie to send her and Iris here. You're picking up Iris too, right?"

I nodded. I had offered Paige the option of staying home, and she had pounced on the idea, thanking me lavishly. "That's right. You thought of everything."

He led me into a large room that smelled like paint and linseed oil and crayons. Huge flower paintings were hung on two of the four walls, and they were good. Great, even. "Are these the eighth grade projects?" I asked.

"Nope. Second grade. Amazing, aren't they? I showed them a special technique that involves color blending and basic shape templates. They really can't go wrong. I took pictures of them all—you can see them on our website." He kept walking to the back of the room, and I followed him.

"These are the junior high projects." He held up a sheaf of line drawings that he had obviously been grading. "Check out the detail. We're working on developing the artist's eye."

I flipped through the pile he handed me and raised my brows. With one or two exceptions, they were impressive pieces of art. "These kids are talented, which means *you* are talented."

"It's all about giving them the right advice. And that has to be personalized to every student."

I was impressed, and I told him so. "Now, I have to see what Jia and Iris have done."

"Yes! Okay, stay here for a minute." He darted to a little anteroom and moved out of my sight. After a minute I called, "Can I come in?"

"Almost done. Okay, now."

I walked a few paces and entered the small room, where a table was covered with stained-glass vases. They were beautiful; but what had the children done? Polished them?

Bruce saw my question and said, "Hang on, let me flip off the light." He did so, and I saw that they were candle holders, and that he had lit the tealights inside them. The effect was absolutely beautiful. "What--?" I said, and a bell rang, surprisingly loud in my uninitiated ear. I waited until it ended, and the hall filled with the sound of chattering children.

Bruce said, "Aren't they great? They're just Mason jars that the moms brought in, and the stained-glass effect is created by tissue paper."

"It is not."

"It totally is!" He was happy, in his element, and I was glad to see that he wasn't tormented all day long.

"I want to make one. Can I make one?"

"Sure, you can. You'll need about half an hour. Can the kids stay?"

"Jia can. I'll text her mom. And Iris's mom. To be honest, I think Paige needs the break."

"Cool. We can see if the adult student manages to do any better than my clever first graders."

"We shall, indeed! How do I start?" I set my purse and keys down on a radiator near the window and rolled up my sleeves.

"Grab a mason jar over there," he pointed to a shelving unit on the back wall, "and some of that decoupage glue. And a brush. Not too wide, but not tiny, either, or we'll be here till midnight."

Ursula appeared at the door just as Jia and Iris bolted in, running to me for their traditional Velcro hugs. Ursula laughed. "Bruce, these are the flyers that you have to pass out in period 1 tomorrow. They'll make an announcement to remind you—it's about picture day."

"Got it," he said.

Ursula set the flyers on a table by the door, still smiling at the girls. Jia had claimed my torso with her skinny wrap-around legs, so Iris hugged me around the knees, and I was in danger of tipping over, like a tree in a storm. "Also, Edie says to please stop in her office before you leave."

"Will do," Bruce said, still gathering supplies. "Her wish is my command."

Ursula lingered. I wondered if she, too, wanted to make a candle. Didn't all adults sometimes feel fascinated by the projects of children? "Would you like to join us? We're making candles."

She shook her head, looking genuinely regretful. "No, I have to finish making some calls. Bruce, how long do you think you'll be? I'm supposed to do the sweep tonight."

"No more than half an hour," he said. "I have an appointment at five."

Ursula nodded and disappeared. I looked at Bruce, distressed. "I don't want to keep you! I thought you had time."

He lowered his voice. "I do. I just want her to tell Edie that, or she'll keep me talking until dinnertime. Which is fine some days, but I'm not in the mood this evening."

"I get it," I said softly. "Okay, girls, get off of me. Your teacher is going to let me do the project you did. Your candles are lovely!"

The girls chattered about how they made them and who they intended to give them to. Children were generous. They wanted to make everything a present, and they were always happy. I thought there might be a connection there.

"Okay," Bruce said. "Let's start --" Another face peered in. I recognized Mr. Partridge, who said, "Bruce, are you staying long? I'd like to lock up."

Bruce avoided his eye. "Ursula said *she's* locking up, so you're good to go."

Partridge hesitated; he had obviously been looking forward to wielding his authority. "Oh. Well, if that's the case, I'll be heading to the theatre. Did I tell you of our new production?"

Bruce tried to look very busy, and he pretended he hadn't heard. "What is it?" I asked.

Partridge turned to me. "*Death of a Salesman*. I lucked out and got the part of Willy Loman. A real honor, truly."

"When are the performances?" I asked.

"Not until May. We have a lot of work to do, a great deal of work." He got out his conductor watch and looked at it. I wondered if the watch even worked. "Well, enjoy," he said vaguely. As he backed out of the room with his bulky frame, I glimpsed Miss Angie walking past, finished with her line duty. She glanced in with her large dark eyes, her mouth an O of surprise, and I waved.

She waved, too, but didn't come in.

"So, are you paying attention?" Bruce asked with exaggerated patience.

"Yes. What should I do?"

He opened a folder and peeked at its contents. "Darn. I need more tissue paper. Can you do me a favor, Hana? I'm going to set up the girls with a special art project --" the girls clapped and jumped with this unexpected treat – "and I need to pour some glue. Can you zip to my art supply room and get tissue paper? It's just across the hall and down one door. It says "Art Office" on the door. There are six steps, and then you are in my art wonderland. First shelf on the left is all paper, and the tissue paper is labeled."

"Wow, organized," I said.

"It's a gift, or a flaw, depending on who you ask."

"Okay, be right back." I jogged out of the room, following the simple instructions that led me to the supply closet and the six cement steps. The space was cavernous and dim, so I peered inside and felt for a light switch.

And suddenly *the misery* flew up inside me like a terrible bird; I had not been able to dispel the darkness, and now a hand, hot on my back, made me gasp in the millisecond before it shoved me forward with great force. I fell, with only time for a short scream, but I thought I heard a wind blowing in my ears, an evil wind that carried the voices of sinners and the mad laughter of Ördög, king of sinful souls. I heard the screaming, too, of those already in his cauldron and tortured by his revolving spoon. The lower world had a musty smell, with an undertone of crayon wax. The floor, like the stairs, was cement, which I saw as it rushed up to meet me.

And then the darkness was complete.

Chapter Eighteen

The Perilous Surreal

I opened my eyes to find that there *was* light, after all, beaming into my face. I squinted against the glare, noting that several figures stood above me. My fanciful brain told me that I was Dorothy, and I had awakened from my dream of Oz to find my family and friends around me.

I snapped into awareness. *The misery* had not left me, and the shadows gathered around me were not my friends.

One of the silhouettes bent down and became Bruce. "Hana, can you talk to me?"

"Yes," I said. I was trying to take stock of my injuries; my mind seemed intact, but my head was aching, and my entire left arm throbbed with pain. "I think I'm hurt," I said.

Bruce's voice, gentle, tried to soothe me. "You fell down the stairs."

Edie Pembroke bent over me, blocking the harsh fluorescence. "I am so very sorry this happened, Hana. I will look into the incident. I fear that our janitorial staff may have mopped there recently, and –"

I shook my head. I knew why I had fallen, but I couldn't

say it here. There were at least five people in the room, and one of them had pushed me. One of them had killed Rose. I felt alone, and frightened. What if they all conspired to kill Rose? Had Bruce sent me here on purpose? Had someone been lying in wait?

I tried to brace myself with my left hand so that I could sit up, but then I yelped with pain. My wrist had no stability; it felt nothing like my wrist, but like a bag of broken things that fired out knives of pain.

"I'd like to call Erik," I said to Bruce.

"Of course," he agreed. "But I think we should call an ambulance --"

"I'd like to call him *now*," I said more firmly. "He'll take care of me."

Bruce nodded meekly and took out his phone. "Tell me the number."

I conveyed the information, and Bruce dialed, then handed the phone to me. Erik's voice in my ear was such a relief I thought I might faint again. "Erik? I'm at Longwood School. I need you to come here right away."

"What's happened?" His voice was clipped, urgent.

I didn't want to tell him that I was sitting in a room with a murderer, so I said, "I fell down some stairs. I'm hurt."

"Oh my God, Hana! I'll be there in ten minutes." The call ended. Erik was a man of action. I handed the phone back to Bruce and said, "He'll be here soon." I offered this news as though it would calm *them* down, the figures who loomed under the light, but it was for myself that I said it.

Then reality struck me another blow. "The girls! Where are the girls?"

"Don't panic," Bruce said, putting a hand on my not-as-painful arm. "They're still coloring. I told them that you slipped and fell, and that we were going to help you up and bring you back to them. Alana, the cleaning lady, is sitting with them. I think she's coloring, too."

I managed a grim smile at this. I went through my mental list of people who could claim the girls while I was otherwise engaged. Luca was busy, and Paige was resting. Mom or Grandma? But they would get too upset. I pointed to Bruce's phone. "I need to call someone else," I said, and I gave him my father's number.

Minutes later Erik appeared at the top of the stairs, glowing with his comforting light. Mrs. Pembroke had gone to let him in and take him to the supply room. The others still lingered. I had determined that the people hanging about included Mr. Partridge, Miss Angie, Ursula from the front desk, a janitor named Tom who assured us that he had not mopped the floor in this hallway. Edie and Bruce were there, as well.

Erik thanked Edie for showing him the way, then said, "If everyone could clear out for a moment, I'd like to get a sense of what happened here."

The group duly trudged out. Erik ran down the stairs and dropped to his knees beside me. "What happened?" he asked.

I shook my head. "First, tell them that none of them can leave," I whispered.

"What?" But he had seen my face, and he already understood what I was saying. "Okay. Just a minute." He climbed up again, and I heard him speaking to Mrs. Pembroke in his official voice. No one was to leave. The building was under lockdown until he said otherwise.

Then he was back. "Where are you hurt? You have a big bump on your forehead." He touched it gingerly. "Did you land on your head?" His tone was fearful.

I had not. I realized that I had put out my hands to break my fall, and that they had taken the brunt of the impact before my head smacked into the cement.

"That may have saved your life," he said, gently examining my hands, my wrists, my arms.

"Ow," I said, with a gush of unexpected tears, as he touched my left wrist.

"Fracture," he said, his face grim. "Let's get you to the hospital."

"No. Not yet. It can wait half an hour or so."

Now he looked indignant. "*Why?*"

"Because I didn't fall, Erik. Someone pushed me. Hard."

"What?" he said again.

"They meant to kill me. And it's one of them—the ones in the room when you got here. They killed Rose. They hit Felix. And they tried to push me to my death."

"And you're sure?" As always, when his rational cop brain came up against my strong instincts, he looked uncertain.

I nodded. "If you press them, and I can be there when you have them one at a time, I think we can work it out. For one thing, I never heard them coming. So, listen to each of them walk. I suppose you can make loud shoes silent if you try, but I think it was someone with soft soles."

"Okay." His eyes went to the door at the top of the stairs. "What else?"

"Well, they all knew I was here. They all went past the room, or came into it, while I was talking with Bruce and the girls. We were going to do an art project." I felt a surge of resentment that I had been unable to create one of those beautiful candles.

"And that's important? Why?"

I tried to determine why. "I think—I got the impression that maybe some of them thought I was with Bruce. Like a romantic interest of his. If jealousy is the motive, then that still aligns with our theory."

"So, we can rule out Mr. Partridge," he said.

"No, not yet. Men can be jealous, too."

Erik looked unconvinced, but he held out his hand. "Can you stand up? Is your right arm unhurt enough for me to grasp it?" He took hold of it with a tentative gesture, then clasped it more tightly. I nodded at him, and he said, "Okay, here we go."

He helped me to my feet. My head hurt slightly, but my legs were surprisingly sturdy. My left wrist was visibly broken. I held my left forearm with my right hand. Both of my palms, I saw, were torn and bloody. A bolt of anger made its way through the cloud of misery. How dare they? How *dare* they?

I took a deep breath. "My dad is coming to claim the girls. He should be here soon."

Erik helped me up the stairs. Edie Pembroke was lurking at the end of the hall; she spiffed toward us on rapid legs, talking the whole time. Nervous, I decided.

"Detective Wolf, I've asked everyone to wait in the Teacher's Lounge. They understand that you wish to ask them some questions. The light switch is difficult to find at the top of the stairs there—we really need to have that looked at." She studied me with that sympathetic, maternal gaze that she used so effectively on the children. It was fairly effective on me, as well, and I found myself hoping for a hug. "How are you, dear?"

"Her wrist is broken," Erik said. His face and voice were uncompromising. Edie grew pale.

The doorbell sounded at the front desk. "That will be my father," I said. "He's coming for the girls."

"Ah! Give me one moment," Edie said, zipping back the way she had come. She returned within the minute with my father, who looked so calm and comforting that I wanted to weep and tuck myself against him.

"I'll let the girls know," Edie said, as Erik explained what had happened.

My father gave me a gentle hug and said, "Are you okay? Emotionally?"

"I will be. You know me, I'm durable."

He chuckled. "Maybe it's time to tap into your Zsa Zsa spirit."

I laughed. When I was little, I had a fierce temper, and my family jokingly called me Zsa Zsa, after the most famous (and infamous) of the Gabor sisters. She had, my mother told me, once slapped a policeman. "Yeah, maybe. Thanks for coming, Dad."

"No problem. I was just leaving school, anyway."

Two tiny girls emerged from the art room, still holding their coloring books. "Uncle Jack!" Jia yelled, and my father was treated to her running leap of a hug, her skinny limbs twined around him.

"Hello, Jia Tortilla!" He kissed her hair and shuffled, encumbered by about fifty pounds of child, to Iris, who slapped him five and showed him her coloring page.

"Outstanding," he said. "So young to be an artist. How would you girls like to ride with me to your palaces?"

"Yes!" said two tiny voices. Then they spared a glance for me, their eyes wide with (mostly genuine) sympathy. "Are you okay, Hana?" Jia asked in her tiny voice.

"Yes. I just have to go to the doctor. I'll see you tomorrow, or soon, in any case."

They accepted this, especially because I had hidden my mangled wrist underneath a flap of my sweater. My father set Jia down and kissed me goodbye, ordering me to call him and my mother when I knew more. Then he led two skipping girls down the hall, and they turned the corner and moved out of sight, but not before I heard Iris, the irrepressible, pipe out, "We should probably all have something to eat."

This made me laugh, and even Erik smiled for a moment

before his eyes rested on the arm I held like a fragile glass bulb. He was angry, and he wanted someone in custody.

Erik went into a junior high classroom where the desks were more likely to fit an adult frame. He asked Mrs. Pembroke to send people in one by one. "We can start with you," he said. His voice was not particularly intimidating, but he wasn't smiling. He had installed me, gingerly, in the teacher's chair. Ms. Angie had appeared briefly with an ice pack, and I rested the ice and my wrist on the wooden surface in front of me. I tried not to notice the growing bruise on my skin, the swollen, misshapen flesh, the strange fissure in the center of my hand.

Erik sat in a student desk and spun a second desk around to face him, as if he were a teacher holding private conferences with students.

Edie perched across from him, nervous yet composed in her principal-of-the-school way. "What information can I give you?" she asked.

"I'll start by giving you some," Erik said. "Hana was pushed down the stairs."

Edie Pembroke's eyes became moons in her face. She looked ready to vomit. "Pushed?" Her gaze flicked to me, and I nodded. "Dear God," she whispered. Then she sat up straighter and said, "This is to do with Rose somehow, isn't it?"

"Very likely," Erik said.

She cleared her throat. "I genuinely can't imagine anyone in this building doing such a thing. Truly. And I can tell you my whereabouts, but I don't have anyone to—corroborate. I was in my office. Ursula was delivering stacks of school picture packets. I cannot account for the whereabouts of the others."

I said, "Ursula said you wanted to speak with Bruce after school. What was that about?"

Edie looked surprised. "He had asked to speak with *me*,

earlier in the day. He wants to add an elective art course to our curriculum. We needed to hash that out, see if it was even possible."

Erik folded his hands. "Do you have any romantic feelings for Bruce Bevington?"

Edie's eyes widened again, and then she laughed. "Romantic feelings? He could be my son!"

"Still."

"No, I don't have romantic feelings for him. Good Lord. I'm a happily married woman, Detective Wolf."

I made a mental note to tell Katie that she was indeed a *Mrs.* Even in my wretched state, I found that nugget of information interesting.

Mrs. Pembroke continued, rather stiffly. "I enjoy his company. He's witty and amusing." She looked from Erik to me, then back to Erik. "He has—I don't know—an artist's way of viewing the world. I find it appealing. It opens my mind, talking with him."

Erik said, "Were you present at the Hungarian Tableau performance where Rose Toth died?"

Stunned by his change of topic, she said weakly, "Uh—no. I was visiting my sister in Rockford."

I nodded. Edie wasn't our person. Without looking at me, Erik knew what I thought, and he agreed. He bowed his head briefly at Edie and said, "Thank you, Ms. Pembroke. If you could send in the next person, that would be helpful."

She stood, and I noticed that her hands were shaking slightly. "And please don't tell anyone what I told you about Hana being pushed."

"No, I won't," she said. And she walked out of the room, most likely trying to resolve several unpleasant realities in her own mind.

Erik turned to me. "Her shoes were quiet." He scratched his chin. "But I don't see her as your assailant."

"Nor do I. She's a Mother Earth sort of person. A nurturer. I don't think she'd harm a fly."

A moment later, Edie appeared again, this time with Mr. Partridge, who was studying his pocket watch with fussy affectation. "I'd like to make this quick," he said. "I have play practice, and I'm already late. My wife will have my head."

Erik gestured to the seat across from him, and Mr. Partridge plopped into it with a "Hmph," sound.

"Mr. Partridge, I don't wish to keep you long. But I do need to tell you that a crime was committed here today, and it was committed by one of the people in the staff room. That number includes you."

His mouth sagged open. "A crime? What sort of crime?" His tone was slightly aggrieved, as though Erik had come here to plant misinformation.

"Hana didn't fall down the stairs, Mr. Partridge." He let the words hang there, and Partridge darted a glance at me.

"You—jumped?" he asked. It was such a ridiculous notion that I laughed out loud, then covered my mouth. As far as I could tell, he was genuinely in the dark, and his first, surprisingly innocent thought had been that I'd indulged in horseplay, by myself, on a dark staircase.

Erik was not amused. "She was pushed, Mr. Partridge. Shoved down the stairs because someone intended her harm."

Partridge peered at Erik through his round glasses, looking like a frightened owl. "Who do you think did it?" he almost whispered.

Again, I wanted to laugh. It was true, Mr. Partridge was an actor, but he couldn't have feigned this level of ignorance. It was utterly authentic. And what motive, really, did he have? To kill Rose, maybe, if he had been secretly in love with her and wanted no other man to have her. Or if Rose had learned something, some corrupt thing that he had done. But why attack Felix? Why attack me?

"Do you get along well with Mr. Bevington?" he asked.

"What—Bruce? Of course. He's come to a couple of my shows. Rita gets on with him, too."

I knew that Bevington was annoyed by Partridge, yet it did suggest a basic friendship if he'd socialized with the man. This hadn't been the week to get a sense of the "normal" Bruce.

"And Rose Toth? Did you get along with her?"

His face fell. "Rose was a wonderful young woman. Kind, gentle. The children loved her. She had only been here one year, but everyone loved her. Yes, I too." He thrust out his chin. "In an entirely acceptable way. I have been—particularly upset by her death. It was unexpected and painful. Very hard for us all."

A thought loomed up in my brain. "Mr. Partridge, I was here the other day, and Ursula was leaving, and you were apologizing to her. Do you remember that? She didn't seem to want to speak to you." Perhaps Partridge had made a pass at her?

"Ursula? Oh—yes. I think she's still put out with me, to be honest. She—we had a birthday party for Jim Prentiss, our P.E. teacher. There was a cake. You know how it is with teachers—we all went for it, and it was gone in no time." His face turned red. "Someone had brought Ursula a piece of cake, and it was sitting on her desk. She had gone off to make an announcement, and I saw it there. I thought I would just steal a little corner of it, and I did. But then, somehow, I was eating it all. No excuse for it—I didn't even think twice. I ate it."

Erik's face was unreadable, but because I knew him, I knew that this time it was he who wanted to laugh. "She was upset with you?"

His face grew redder still. "It's hard to explain. How much teachers and staff look forward to cake. And my wife says that I might have a problem—some kind of sugar addiction. Anyway, Ursula read me the riot act, which I deserved. Then she put on her coat and stalked out. I followed her, trying to apologize, but she was having none of it."

"And the next day?" Erik asked.

"I brought her a piece of cake. From my favorite bakery, actually, and I set it on her desk. A huge piece. She saw it when she came in, and she laughed. She said, 'Okay, you're forgiven.' But there's still a coolness there." He looked both embarrassed and regretful. "Anyway." He turned to me. "I'm very sorry this has happened, and I'll help you in any way I can to determine who did such a thing. Could it have been a student who thought he was joking around?"

What I had felt, in the second before I plunged into space, was not innocence. "No."

He nodded gravely. "What else can I do for you?" he asked, stealing a glance, this time, at a watch on his wrist. Why two watches? I wondered.

Erik said, "That's all for now. If you could send Ursula in, but wait about five minutes."

Partridge nodded and practically jogged out of the room.

Erik turned to me. "Thoughts?"

"Not him."

"No," he agreed. We had learned, a couple of months earlier, that while Erik had no psychic ability, he and I did have a sort of connection that allowed us reliable access to each other's thoughts, and the ability to predict how the other might feel or react in a given situation.

"But the incident with Ursula was interesting. I saw him chase after her, apologizing, and I thought he had somehow knocked her against something because --"

A wave of silence washed through me. I stopped hearing my own voice, the birds outside, the tapping of Erik's pen on his desk. I saw Ursula again, studying her broken nail. It had been bothering her; perhaps it had torn even more. The night before, someone had struck Felix with a fireplace log. My mind went back even farther, to the night that Rose died. I had commented about people leaving before the show even started. A blonde woman had made her way toward the parking lot. But the parking lot would give access to the woods from a different direction.

"Hana?" Erik said.

I stared at him, seeing only his eyes. "When you found Rose, there in the woods. How close was the scene to the parking lot?"

He considered this. "The ambulance parked there, and took her out the same way. It wasn't far. You couldn't quite see the lot, but it wasn't more than a hundred feet."

"There was a woman—a blonde woman—who left early. Do you remember? We joked about it."

Slowly, he nodded his head. "I do."

"Bruce told me that he had dated a few women here before Rose joined the staff. One was Ursula. Another was Miss Angie."

He sat up straight. "Why didn't you--?"

"Because there was a whole list of them. He said that in some cases he was just trying to get to know someone. I didn't have a good sense."

"Okay."

"But thinking back to today: Ursula came by to pass out the flyers about picture day, as Edie said. But she hung around, just sort of looking at us. She said Edie wanted to see Bruce. She asked how long we would be there, because she had to lock up. She lingered. Even after she had no reason."

Erik's green eyes narrowed. "She wanted to know if you two were together."

"Which would make Bruce pretty callous, considering his girlfriend just died."

"Jealousy isn't rational."

"Is that why someone would try to kill a police detective—or someone she thought was him—in order to stop him from finding her? Or maybe to change the focus of the investigation?"

"All of these attacks are utterly reckless. She could have been witnessed on any of the three occasions."

"Falling dominos," I said.

"But do we really know her motive?" Erik asked me.

Ursula appeared in the doorway, offering an uncertain smile. "Am I early?" she asked.

"No, you're fine," Erik said. "If you could close the door behind you, that would be great."

Ursula shut the door, then walked toward us on silent feet.

*

"How are you feeling?" she asked with a sympathetic smile.

"Bad," I said. "I have at least one broken bone."

"Oh, my goodness. After such an unexpected fall! What a crazy thing to happen."

Erik's eyes were steely. "Hana didn't fall. She was pushed."

Ursula's blue eyes widened in an impressive show of innocence. "Oh, my God! That's --" then she pretended to figure it out. "—that's why you're talking to all of us. You think it was one of *us*!" This was a scandalous assumption, her face said.

"Who else?" Erik asked. Then, switching gears, he said, "What is your last name?"

Surprised, she said, "Baxter."

"How long have you worked at Longwood School, Miss Baxter?"

"It's Ms," she offered, unsmiling. "And this is my fifth year."

Erik nodded, jotting this down in his little notebook. My arm was throbbing again, and the pain in my wrist was becoming intense. I teetered on the verge of tears, but I wouldn't have stopped this discussion for anything. Erik said, "And you were previously in a relationship with Bruce Bevington, were you not?"

She laughed, then looked confused. "Bruce? Yeah, we dated for a while. What does that have--?"

"Would you say it was serious?"

She shrugged. "Obviously not."

"When did the relationship end?"

Something twitched in her face. She went for sarcasm. "Sorry, I didn't bring my diary with me." She met Erik's green stare and said, "I'm joking, I don't have a diary. I don't write down the things that happen to me, even when --" she stopped and stared at her long nails.

"Even when they're painful?" Erik said.

She shrugged. "Water under the bridge."

"When did the relationship end?" he persisted.

She sighed. "I don't know. About a year ago."

"And how long had it lasted?"

She shifted in her chair. Suddenly she seemed uncomfortable. "I don't know—about six months."

"Not long after you broke up, he began to date Rose Toth, is that correct?"

Her eyes widened, and she looked directly at him. I saw something change then. A challenge, accepted. "I thought

Rose was dating a guy named Albert. He read a poem at her memorial service."

"No, she and Albie had parted ways, apparently. He had not been with Rose for quite some time."

Her mouth made an O of surprise. "Wow—they really kept that under the radar."

"Did they?" Erik asked. "Because reports suggest that you were jealous."

"Reports? Whose reports? What, is there a spy at Longwood?"

"If there were, would they have found out that you were jealous of Rose Toth? Maybe that you commented to someone about their relationship? Perhaps you said it was inappropriate, or that she wasn't right for him, or that he was a womanizer."

A small flicker in her eyes, nothing else. "I don't know what you're driving at, but you're way off. I know you said someone pushed Hana down the stairs, but it wasn't me. May I leave now?"

"Not quite yet." Erik stared at his notebook, marshaling his thoughts.

I said, "How did you break your nail?"

She looked at me. "What?"

"You have a broken nail. It looks painful—it cracked way down at the bottom, didn't it? I saw you fussing with it when Mr. Partridge was chasing you with his apologies."

"Yeah. He ate my cake." She tried to look casual. "I don't know, I banged it on the file cabinet or something."

"Could you have broken it on the rough surface of a log?" I asked.

That scared her for a minute, but her bravado bounced back into place. "What? You guys are asking the weirdest questions."

Erik swooped in. "Were you jealous of Rose Toth, Miss Baxter?"

She rolled her eyes. "Back to this. No, I was not jealous."

"Did you think that she and Bruce made a good couple?"

"As I told you, I didn't *know* they were a couple. But it sort of makes sense. They both have pretty faces and dreamy attitudes." Her lip curled slightly.

"Are you dating anyone right now, Miss Baxter?"

"Yes."

"And what is his name?"

She shook her head. "I'm not bringing him into this, if you don't mind."

"Did you know Rose Toth was pregnant?"

I almost gasped. This was a rapid-fire interrogation. Even I hadn't expected that question at this point. Ursula had not, either, and the anger appeared before she could cloak it in another emotion.

She took a moment to smooth her face, pretending to be annoyed. "No, I did not know that. I—that is really sad."

"It makes you sad? You would have wanted to see Bruce marry Rose? To see them raise a child together, appear at school events as husband and wife?"

"No!" she said. Then, with a laugh, "No, I don't think that would have happened. Rose was a nice girl, and sooner or later she would have dumped Bruce. He's a bit of a Lothario."

"But you dated him," Erik said.

She shrugged, grinned. "Lotharios have certain impressive skills."

Erik sat back in his chair and folded his arms. "You implied that you were in a committed relationship with him, not that you were just having fun. Were you committed to Bruce?"

She sighed. "Yes. But he wasn't to me—hence my revelation. He is a womanizer. I'm well rid of him."

Erik nodded absently, then picked up his phone and studied it. "Excuse me one moment, this is work," he said, his face apologetic. He tapped in a text message, then waited to see a response. Then he set the phone down and looked back at Ursula Baxter. "So, were you present at the Hungarian Tableau that Rose performed in?"

Again, he had taken her by surprise. "No, not on the evening. Some of us went to the dress rehearsal to support Rose. We all had other plans for Saturday."

"And at the dress rehearsal, where did you sit?"

"There were just a few of us, so we sat in chairs next to the stage area."

"Were you able to see where Rose went when she ran offstage?"

She held out her hands and raised her brows as if to say, "You've got me stumped."

"Rose didn't mention it to you, what happened when she left the stage?"

Her face was carefully blank. "She went off into the woods."

"That's what you did, too. The night of the real show. You were in the bleachers, weren't you? And then you left. You went to the parking lot, right before Rose's performance began."

This threw her. "What? I told you; I was at the dress rehearsal."

"And I was at opening night. The strange thing is that I saw you there." My voice had a frozen sound. Perhaps the ice pack had chilled my blood.

Ursula and I stared at each other. Then she smacked the desk in front of her, loudly and with force. "Listen. I don't know why you guys are giving me the third degree, but I believe I have the right to leave. If you want to accuse me of something, tell it to my lawyer."

She made as if to stand up. I said, "What's that perfume you're wearing?"

She frowned. "Did you guys watch some cop show about partner interrogation? Thought you'd try it out on some defenseless little teachers? Because you're really bad at it. And my perfume cannot possibly have a bearing on anything."

"What's it called?" I asked again in my newly-cold voice. She sighed. "Moonlight."

"Ah. I recognized it when you walked in. It's the scent I smelled right before I was pushed down the stairs."

For a minute, there was silence. Her eyes darted around as she tried to come up with a response.

Erik dove on the moment of vulnerability. "Who told you Rose was pregnant? Did she tell you?"

"No, she didn't. I heard it from Miss Angie."

"Earlier you said you didn't know she was pregnant. But you did?"

"Yes, okay, I did. I felt sorry for her. Knocked up by a guy who wasn't going to stay around."

"He was, though," I said. "Bruce was in love with her. He's still in love with her. He's having trouble imagining life without her. Yesterday I took him to see a painting by Kodaly. It's called True Love, and Kodaly painted it to honor the moment he fell in love." This topic was bugging her, so I dug in. "He said he absolutely understood how Kodaly felt, because that was how he'd felt the moment he saw Rose's face, the moment she came to Longwood for the first time."

She was up in an instant, out of the student desk and flinging it to the side in a cacophonous manifestation of her rage. "He was not in *love* with her!" she cried. "He was in *lust* with her. She was pretty, and she had a curvy body that she dressed to accentuate. Totally unprofessional, the way she bounced around. But he was blind to anything but that face and that figure. There was no love involved, and the idea that she was going to have his b*aby* --" Her fists were clenched tightly at her sides.

"You wanted to have his baby," I suggested softly. "Did he say no?"

Her fury was still at its highest level. "He said he wasn't *ready*. He said we could give it some time and decide in a year or so. But then, he felt we 'weren't the right fit,' mainly because he wanted to fit with Rose, perfect Rose. And they jumped into bed together and he got her pregnant." There were tears on her face now, furious tears that she didn't seem to notice.

"And you killed her," Erik said.

She said nothing, just glared at him.

"Did you hate Rose Toth?"

She looked ready to punch Erik; her fists were still clenched. "Of course I hated her! She took the life that was supposed to be mine! A life for a life, right?"

"Two lives," Erik said. "The child died, too."

She shrugged in a way that suggested the baby had been collateral damage.

I felt sick.

Someone knocked at the door. I looked up to see Greg Benton, who walked into the room without comment, surprising everyone but Erik. Greg stationed himself at the exit, and Erik stood up.

"Ursula Baxter, I am arresting you on the suspicion of the murder of Rose Toth and her unborn child, and the attempted murders of Felix Wolf and Hana Keller." He recited her rights as Greg snapped on the handcuffs. She shook her head in fury and disbelief.

"Even now, it's all about her, Miss Perfect Rose."

"It's all about her because you *killed* her," I said, stunned. Erik sent me a look; I needed to stop talking now. I nodded and remained silent as Greg led her out of the room. Erik said, "I'll be right back. I have to tell the others they can go."

When he returned, I had risen from my chair. I was shaking now, partly from witnessing the interrogation, but mostly because my body was going into shock. "The pain is bad now," I managed.

"I'm so sorry," he said. "I should have taken you to the hospital as soon as I got here."

"No, you shouldn't. Because I needed to get a feel for each person alone." My teeth were chattering, and he bundled me out of the room. Uniformed officers had joined Greg, and Ursula was being marched out of the school.

The last thing I saw was the group of teachers who left the lounge and stared in disbelief as the woman who had run their busy main office for five years, their colleague and friend, was led away.

I took one look at Bruce's face and then could look no more.

"Get me out of here," I whispered.

*

I was in a hospital room, awaiting an orderly who would wheel me to the surgical wing. My wrist was indeed broken in two places, and I needed mending under sedation. I had also torn a tendon in my right arm, so both limbs would be out of commission. I had received a hard blow to the forehead, but the doctor confirmed my assumption that my hands had taken the worst of it. I did not have a concussion, but I did have a splendid bump, he said, like a small egg, and my forehead would sport a brilliant array of colors for the next couple of weeks. Not long after we arrived at the hospital, I told Erik that he should call my family. I had hidden my wrist from my father when he came to the school, and it was time to come clean. Erik lifted his phone and dialed the tea house.. The call was answered by my grandmother, of course. She hadn't needed to be told that something was wrong, and I heard her voice even from my chair in the ER lobby. "What happened?" she demanded.

Erik switched to speaker and I told her the story as briefly as I could. I asked her to relay it to the others. She murmured darkly in Hungarian, then said she should never have left my side.

"I'm okay, *Nagymama,*" I said, my voice affectionate. "You can come and visit me when things settle down."

She said "Ya," and we ended the call.

Half an hour later, when they had settled me in a room, I told Erik, "You need to go to work; there must be a million things to do now that you've arrested her."

Erik sat like a monolith at my side. "Geg has it covered. I'll get there when I get there." He reached out to stroke my hair. "I'm not leaving you."

I didn't argue with this, because it was simply true.

*

After my surgery, I lay groggily in my hospital bed while various family members drifted in and out. Domo decided to play the clown, and thanks to the drugs in my system, I found him very funny. In fact, I could not stop laughing, and a nurse with a stern face suggested that Domo leave my room. Immediately.

Domo looked wounded, but he bent to kiss my cheek and tell me he would be back later. My grandmother arrived alone, assuring me that Grandpa was "doing something at the church" and would visit me later. She was wearing what I had dubbed a "gypsy ring" when I had given it to her as a

Christmas present, and it flashed in the fluorescent light, hypnotizing me. "Your mama and I are putting you on disability leave. I have already filled out the forms for your short-term disability pay."

"Okay," I said.

"Your mama and daddy are coming soon. She is full of nervous energy, packing you a basket of treats. You know her."

I did.

"Now, don't cry," she said, grasping my foot in an unusually tight grip. "You will heal. We will all recover." Her face looked haggard, telling me that they had suffered some fear and anxiety about the state of my health, and the reality that someone had tried to kill me.

"How did you know?" I asked her. "That something was wrong.?"

She met my gaze with her perceptive eyes. She had not let go of my foot. Her hands were warm, and I liked the way they warmed my sole. Now she shrugged. "I heard my mother's voice."

"Natalia?"

Grandma nodded. "She said just one thing: '*Hana*'. And it was urgent, her voice." She adjusted herself in her chair, for something to do, I thought, while she processed the emotion of it. "But even so, it was good to hear her voice." Her eyes sparkled then, most likely with tears. She finally let go of my foot; she looked at me and smiled. "Now, don't cry again. You know she loves you."

I nodded. My family was so weird and wonderful and confounding. My *Hungarian* family, that is. My father's family was as staid and reliably un-psychic as my father himself.

"Grandma," I said.

"Yes, *Hanababa*."

"Do you have any chocolate?"

She did. "From François," she said, materializing a couple of little eclairs from her capacious bag.

It was clear, then, that with friends, and family, and chocolate, and hot Hungarian meals, I would be, in the end, just fine.

Chapter Nineteen

The Obscure Ways of Love

When Erik took me home from the hospital on Tuesday afternoon, I moved tentatively, with one arm in a sling and the other with an elastic support bandage. When we pulled into the little lot of The Driftwood Castle, I saw Teresa Toth emerging from a car. She stood hesitantly by the door of the building, waiting for us to reach her. "Hana," she said, looking with surprise at my trussed limbs. "I'm sorry—I didn't realize that you --" she said, pointing at my cast.

"It's fine. Did you need something from me?" I asked her, my body yearning toward my couch and my cats.

"Just a minute of your time. To tell you a couple things."

"Come on up," I said.

Erik said, "I'll make some coffee." And to me he murmured, "I'll handle the cats."

I nodded in response to both suggestions, and in five minutes I had indeed found my couch, and Antony and Cleopatra had expressed their displeasure at my absence, though I was sure that Paige and Iris had spoiled them. Now the two were eating and occasionally vocalizing sternly to Erik, who stood grinning at them while he prepared the coffee at the counter.

Teresa sat straight in the chair across from me, obviously tense.

"Is this about Rose?" I asked gently.

"Yes. And no. I wanted—I was dishonest with you, and with myself, I guess. And after I read about the arrest --" A flash of her previous anger returned to her eyes – "God, I could kill that woman. Truly. What a horror." Then her eyes filled with tears. "But I don't want to be like her, do I?"

I shook my head. "No."

"So, I'm just trying to process it all. But I wanted to tell you why I was angry with Rose."

"Because she broke up with Albie and started dating Bruce?"

Her eyes, still wet, widened. "Well—yes. I guess you were hanging around with him, right? Bruce Bevington?"

"Yes." I studied her face. "And you should know that he genuinely loved her. He's grieving, for the loss of her and their child."

Her tears flowed again. She wiped at them and said, "I'm glad he loved her. That she had love." She rubbed her hands across her wet cheeks. "God, this doesn't get easier, does it?"

"With time," I suggested.

She sighed. "Anyway, I was angry with Rose, and I took Albie's side, even though he told me it had been a mutual thing, their breakup. I didn't totally believe that. And then, Albie and I just --"

Light dawned. "You became involved with Albie."

Misery filled the eyes that met mine. "Yes. And I was so angry, not with Rose as much as myself, for being a hypocrite and saying things to her, and—everything. And then she *died*." Her expression was haunted.

"And you decided to act as though they were still together. Why?"

She sighed. "Rose had told Albie she would keep her new relationship a secret for a while. Apparently it had been months since she and Albie had ended things, although Lida and I had only found out recently. I guess they had already accepted what I could not, you know? And for some reason, she was nervous about telling Mom and Dad. She knew they loved Albie. She said she and Albie could let people know gradually, in their own time, that they were no longer together. She also didn't want him to feel pressure or embarrassment. That was Rose." Tears glided down her cheeks again, an endless rain.

I was still confused. "You kept up the charade, even at the memorial. Why?"

"Because we both felt so guilty. I had made a mess of things, and Albie had been sort of hiding in a dead relationship, and then we lost her, and we both realized what we had lost. The grief was real. The sentiments were real."

"Of course they were," I said.

She let out a mighty sigh, weary and sad, and then slapped the knees of her blue jeans. "Well, I just felt I owed you an explanation. I've already come clean to my parents and Lida. They were nice about it." More tears, more wiping at her cheeks. Her anger was dissipating as her sadness finally emerged. "And they were glad to hear about Albie and me. They already think of him as a son."

I had not met Mrs. Toth, but Mr. Toth had struck me as a gentle man, a man who loved his family and would cling to the daughters—and adopted son—that he had left. "That's great, Teresa. Really. I hope you'll let Bruce grieve with you, as well. He could use your support."

She nodded gravely. "I've sent a text, asking if we could

talk. He agreed. After he and I meet, I'll ask if he'll come to a family dinner. We'll take baby steps, but I want to welcome him in. The man who would have been her husband and our in-law."

"Those are healthy steps. Have you told Maria?"

She laughed, a tiny sound. "This morning, as a matter of fact, when I bought milk. I told her just the basics, but we agreed to talk later. I only wish --" She broke down then, weeping into her hands. I wanted to hug her, but I was still feeling delicate and encumbered by my cast.

Erik, as always, knew what I needed. He brought in our coffee, set it down on the table, sat beside Teresa, and took her into his arms.

*

When the package arrived, days later, at three in the afternoon, I was trembling with anticipation. What was it about William Kodaly, and his legacy of art, that touched me so deeply? I called Domo immediately. "It's here. You paid for most of it, so you should be here to open it with me. When do you get off work?"

Domo said, "Looks pretty dead around here. I'll leave now."

"Can you just *do* that?" I asked in disbelief.

"Sure. Besides, I'm bored here. And I really want to see the painting."

He arrived less than an hour later, and the two of us gloated over the parcel like conspirators. I handed him a box cutter (why do you *have* this, Hana?) and he carefully cut away the packaging. Inside the box was all sorts of protective plastic, and Domo said, "Did we get ripped off, Hana? Is there nothing in here at all?"

"Be glad it's been carefully wrapped. It's treasure," I said.

I was inexplicably nervous, my heart beating loudly in my ears and my free hand tapping against my side.

"Stop being weird," Domo ordered.

"I'm excited. Shut up."

He pulled back a final layer of soft tissue paper, and there was our mother's face.

"Oh my God," Domo said. He took a startled step back, as though birds had flown out of the box.

I knelt in front of the painting. I had never seen it in person; instead, I had viewed a photograph projected on a screen, back in October when Erik and I had watched a tribute to Kodaly. The photograph had not even begun to do this painting justice. Kodaly had been a master of light, and he had painted Magdalena Horvath Keller in the garden behind her house. The focus was on her eyes, those beautiful blue eyes that had smiled into my face since the day of my birth. He had matched the color of her eyes to the hue of the sky behind her, and somehow, the echoing shade created a magical effect, as though my mother were a creature of the air, a being not quite human, but definitely beautiful. In his vision, the sunlight touched her golden hair and made it sparkle. Best of all, he had captured her expression so perfectly that I felt that my mother herself was lying there, forever young, perpetually smiling out of those azure eyes that had once and forever captivated my father. "Wow," I said.

"That's unbelievable! I know you go on about how talented this guy was, but that's like some kind of other-worldly stuff." I knew he was genuinely moved, but couldn't find the words.

"He captured her essence. That's Mom."

"He did." He squatted down and put a brotherly arm around me. "It's really beautiful, Hana. Thanks for letting me be a part of this present. I can't wait to see Dad's face."

"And Mom's! She always downplays the whole thing—that she had a sitting with him, that he painted her picture, that Dad couldn't afford it and that was that. But I think it hurt her to see it go. She cared about Will Kodaly, and she was flattered when he asked to paint her portrait. And now 'Magdalena's Eyes' is coming home!"

In an unexpected gesture, my brother pulled me into a careful hug and said, "Yay!"

A moment later he warned me that if I told anyone he had said the word "yay," there would be severe consequences.

*

My father's birthday party took place in my childhood home, a beloved place with large rooms and wide windows, situated on a shady street in the south of Riverwood. It was always a pleasure to go back, to peek into my childhood room (now an office) and to sit with my childhood cat, General, on my lap. He purred in an eternal and comforting way, and I felt that I had everything—home in the past and home in the present—and could not ask for more.

My father strolled in, holding a beer and sporting a Jia-shaped tumor on his hip. The child was made of Velcro. "Your mother said we can't eat cake until we open presents," he said good-naturedly. "So, I guess I'll have to sit down and receive gifts, difficult as that may be."

"Yes, we need to open presents," Jia said, her dark eyes wide and serious. Her silky black hair was tied back with a big blue bow that matched her pretty blue dress, and Luca had found white tights with little blue flowers on them. Luca, too, was going for an enchanting effect, and Jia was a sweet little canvas for her artistry.

My father sat down in a chair large enough for Jia to tuck in against him. My mother brought him a little stack of gifts.

"These are from me, and that one is from Mama and Papa."
The room, filled to capacity, went relatively quiet.

My father asked Jia if she would be in charge of bows and
ribbons; he may as well have dubbed her the Princess of
Childhood, so honored did she look. He handed her the first
bow, which she put immediately into her hair. He opened the
package, which contained a history book (no surprises there—
he got history books all the time) which was some sort of
"definitive" tome about World War II.

"Oh, good," said Domo. "So, we can forget the information in the other million books about World War II?"

My mother smirked at him, and my father unwrapped
several presents: a Riverwood High School Faculty sweatshirt, a
picture of General in an elegant frame (my father was secretly
devoted to General), a bag of coffee beans from his favorite
local shop, and (from my grandparents) a giant bag of paprika
imported from Hungary. In addition, Luca and Jia had given
him chocolates and a sweatshirt with Jia's handprints on it (Jia
got a big hug for that). There was an Ulveflokk sweater from
Runa and Thyra, a Columbia coffee mug from Andy, and a
very nice pair of Trekker running shoes from Felix. Erik's
parents, who were working, sent their regards and a generous
gift certificate to their store. My father looked at Domo and
me and said, "How is it that you two make friends and I get
presents?" Everyone laughed.

My father was genuinely moved by the thoughtfulness of
the gifts, and he said so.

I felt as nervous as someone about to go on stage at
Madison Square Garden, and Domo was bursting at the
seams. "Don't you wonder what your children got you?" he
bellowed.

Everyone looked at him with casual curiosity. "I'd like to

think you got him *something*," said my mother, who was pointedly looking around for a wrapped gift.

Domo made a grand gesture toward the door. "Erik!" he cried.

Erik came in with an impressively large present which I had wrapped in some "Great Artists" paper I found online.

My father raised his eyebrows and said, "You didn't already design my coffin, did you?"

More laughs. Domo said, "No, but thanks for the idea for next year."

My father tore gently at the paper. He wasn't a package devourer; he was a package savourer. Jia took the paper in an almost ceremonial fashion, and my father knelt in front of the box where it now lay on the floor. "You've got me intrigued," he said in a mild voice.

And then he pulled back the final bit of paper.

There were some gasps from onlookers; my mother let out a little scream of surprise, and my grandmother looked extremely gratified, and slightly wise, as though she had known what was in the box. Perhaps she had.

But our eyes were on my father, who had not looked away from the painting of the woman he loved. I thought of Kodaly's 'True Love' painting in Runa's bedroom. The moment of falling in love . . . .

Domo couldn't stand the suspense. "Do you like it?"

My father seemed to remember in that instant that he was in a room full of people. He looked up at us, full of awe.

And then my sweet and gentle father began to cry.

*

Later, with the painting propped on the mantel while my parents debated where it should be hung, my father confided something my mother had never known. He had visited the man who bought the painting. "I explained that I was Maggie's husband, and I really wanted the piece. And would he sell it to me?"

My mother looked thunderstruck. "We couldn't have afforded six thousand dollars back then!" she said.

He shrugged apologetically. "I was going to put it on a credit card."

My mother and my grandmother gasped, as though he'd confessed to a kidnapping. "Credit card?" my mother said hoarsely.

He looked sheepish. "I loved it. And I didn't want some other man looking at you every day."

My mother went to sit beside him, and she kissed him in a way that I'd never seen them kiss.

Domo opened his mouth to say something obnoxious, but I pointed at him, adding a threatening look, and Margie put a finger over his lips.

My mother said, "I love it, too. And I love you for wanting it so much."

They sat together, gazing at the painting. "He had a gift," my father said. "Because he captured exactly what I saw on the day that I met her. The way her eyes seemed to glow."

Domo held up his hand, and I high-fived it. "Dad," I said. "That's from Domo and me, but also from Erik and Margie."

My father said, "I am grateful to you all."

Jia wandered in, acting the part of 'innocent child' while sporting a blue smear of frosting on her lip. We all started laughing, and my father said, "I believe we promised cake after the presents."

My mother gave him one more kiss, and then she jumped up to prepare cups of coffee and slices of cake. "Come and blow out your candles, Jack!" she said in a merry voice.

"I know what Dad is wishing for," said Domo in a voice dripping with innuendo.

"You have a one-track mind," I said in a low voice. "And I doubt he has to wish hard for that particular fantasy to come true."

My parents, I thought, as I studied all the faces around the table—smiling, laughing, chattering in happy tones—had modeled love for me since my childhood. How wonderful they were. How pleased I was to have found a way to give them a gift that they deserved. In essence, the gift of one another.

Luca had picked up Jia to explain why she could not have a third piece of cake. Margie and Domo were laughing into each other's faces over some little joke. Runa and Andy stood proudly in front of my grandmother, who held little Anya like a queen embracing a beloved subject. She was whispering into the baby's ear, and Anya's little face--to everyone's vast entertainment—looked interested.

Felix had brought Maria with him. "We never did get our date," Maria said. "So, he invited me to this event. A lot of people for a first date, but I get the whole family thing." I had never seen Maria in a dress, and she looked stunning. She had straightened her dark hair into a silky sheet, and hr dark eyes were lined with an attractive violet color. Her dress, a simple apricot linen, emphasized her trim figure. Felix kept darting glances at her, as though he feared she would run away.

Later, when everyone was full of cake and coffee and we all lounged in the living room, staring at the painting that drew all eyes, Felix cleared his throat. "Listen, I already told this to Mom and Dad today, but I figured I'd tell you, since I have you all in one room, Wolfs and Kellers."

Surely, he hadn't gotten engaged? He and Maria had just met. Or was it a medical thing? Oh, God, had he suffered a setback?

"My company is opening a Chicago branch," he said. "And I've taken a job as manager of the new facility." Voices rose in happy response, and there was a smattering of applause.

Erik's smile was heartbreaking. A little brother, longing to be back with his hero. "So—you're moving back?"

Felix grinned. "I am. And just in time, now that I have a niece who told me I'm her favorite uncle."

Erik laughed. "Not a chance, pal. My girlfriend *delivered* her. I'm taking some of the credit for that."

Felix held up his hands. "Okay, okay. I'm not going up against Hana and her clan. But it will be good to be home."

Thyra stood up, pulled him into a bug,, and gave him a kiss on the cheek. "The Wolfs together again," she said. Then she looked at me, grinned, and said, "The *Wolves.*"

My grandmother was next to enter what had apparently become "the announcement area" of the living room. She still held Anya, whose tiny face remained serene in Grandma's embrace. "So," Grandma said with a theatrical sigh. "Bálinka has delivered her kittens." She sent a stern glance around the room. "Who wants a cat?"

Chapter Twenty

Legacies

Two weeks after the party, I sat with Bruce Bevington in my apartment. We were drinking iced tea and he was showing me, at long last, how to make my tissue paper candle. He had brought some samples, made by him, all of which were actual works of art. He hadn't generated predictable stained-glass patterns with the tiny shreds of varicoloured tissue; instead, he had created a design with them, a mosaic, and each candle had its own theme: butterflies, autumn leaves, sky, sea, and sand, I aspired to make mine like Bruce's, but decided to start with a random pattern, using color blends that I liked.

We had talked about light and happy things, anything but Rose or Ursula, until he finally said, "I'm okay, you know. I can talk about it. I kind of want to, because maybe you have some details I don't, given who your boyfriend is."

I dipped my brush in decoupage glue and began to feather the paper onto the glass. "He doesn't really talk about his cases," I said, but of course I did know some elements of the case, of Ursula's arrest and subsequent incarceration. "I do know she's pleading not guilty."

"Don't they all," Bruce said, his eyes weary. "I still can't believe it of her. Ursula! She's –she was—a normal person. A nice person. She was great with the kids, friendly to the staff. I would have thought she and Rose were friends."

I thought of the days, back in September, when I had acted irrationally because I had a crush on Erik Wolf. I glanced at my kitchen counter, in front of which we had first kissed each other, hungrily, inexplicably, and I blushed. "Love—or what we think is love—can mess up our heads. But it's love that goes wrong, a twisted love, that makes a person homicidal."

"I guess." He sipped his tea and looked around him at my kitchen. "This is a nice little room. And it smells good, like something hearty."

"I made beef *gulyás* last night," I said.

He pointed at my bandage. "With that on your arm?"

"The right arm is usable now, as you've seen with my skillful artwork," I joked. "Although I can't wait to have the left one back in action."

He nodded. We sat quietly for a while, and then he said, "So—why did she do it? And why did she hurt Erik's brother, and you?" His curiosity came from a deep well of hurt; I felt that. He had cared for Ursula, trusted her, believed that she wished him no harm.

"Erik said that her motives were all related. She wanted to remove Rose from your life so that she, Ursula, could try to work her way back into it. She believed you were meant to be together."

He shook his head, saying nothing.

"She saw Felix at Fair Share Foods, just coincidentally, and thought he was Erik. She had seen Erik when he came to the school to ask questions. She had also heard Mr. Toth say, at the memorial, that Erik had a great reputation and would find the person responsible. And of course she had seen Erik there, despite his attempt to keep a low profile. She acted on impulse: eliminate Erik, reduce the chance of exposure."

"Or not."

"Yeah. I don't think Ursula was playing with a full deck once she was bent on murder. Anyway, when she saw us together, she was furious because she thought you'd moved on already, to me, and that she'd lost her chance to be with you. Unless she took action."

"God. I don't know what to think. I'm devastated about Rose, but it's not anger I feel for Ursula. I kind of—pity her. She's pathetic. Are they going to make sure she doesn't have, like, some kind of psychosis, or a brain tumor pressing on her center of reason?"

"I don't know. Maybe her defense attorney will do that. I would actually be relieved if they found some physical explanation. At least that would make a kind of sense."

He nodded. "I like to think that Rose was very happy when she died. They did tell me that she was unconscious from the time she fell, and when the other blows came. So she never suffered .. .." He breathed out heavily, a sigh that said he was starting to accept. "But she was so excited about the show, about the audience response, and she loved that costume. She said when she turned on all the lights it made her feel genuinely powerful, like an actual goddess, and when she ran down the path, she felt ethereal."

A beat of silence. We looked at each other, and I saw that he was thinking something very similar to my own thoughts. "Kodaly," I said.

"Yes! The fairy, bright and beautiful, skimming down the path, feeling jubilant and free. He would have wanted to paint that, wouldn't he?"

I nodded. "He loved stories, human stories. That was how he came to paint Henrik's reunion with his mother."

"He's basically the reason the case was solved." His face grew thoughtful. "If you and I hadn't talked about Kodaly, and I hadn't come to your place with François, we never would have become friendly. We never would have found those connections." He squinted an apology. "And you wouldn't have been hurt."

"Almost healed," I said lightly.

He said, "I went to a therapist to talk about Rose, and about the baby."

"That's great. A healthy choice."

"It helped." He pointed at my candle. "That looks good now. You can leave it to dry. Once the glue dries, the colors will emerge and you can pop in a candle."

I nodded, pushing the candle to the center of the table. "What did he or she say?"

"He said that it's all right to grieve, but that I shouldn't bog myself down trying to picture things that might have been, or to torture myself with images of what might have happened that night. He said that what I *can* know is that the child and mother were together, curled into one another in love, and that neither died alone."

My eyes filled with tears.

"Yeah," Bruce said, noting my response. "But that idea helped me a lot. It gives me something relatively positive to take out of the horror. He suggested that although I had suffered a tragic loss, I could keep them both close to me, tucked into a chamber of my heart. That idea has sustained me." He smiled. Beneath his hurt, I could feel the rough and painful stitches that would begin to heal him. "The experience showed me that I do want someone to love, and I want children, at some future time. I will always view Rose and the baby as a first wife, a first child. And I talk to them. That helps, too."

"He sounds wise, too, this therapist. What thoughtful counsel. Like a comfort blanket for your soul."

"Truly. I kind of use his words as a mantra. The repetition of that mantra brought me closer to peace. Not there yet, but closer."

"I'm glad, Bruce." I cleared my throat. "Listen, Erik and I are moving to a larger unit in this building. We'll be throwing a housewarming party some time over the summer. I'll be sure to send you an invite."

"Thanks! I hope François will be there. He's hilarious."

"He will. And several other people that I'd like you to meet." I was thinking of all my friends, but also of our lovely florist, Rania. I had sensed that the two of them would have chemistry. My grandmother knew things like that; it was why she had encouraged me to date Erik, despite his last name (and her dislike of wolves for superstitious reasons). Perhaps by summer Bruce would feel peaceful enough to open his heart to new experiences.

Bruce was standing now and looking at his phone. "I should go. I want to check in with Rose's family, make sure they're all right. We've bonded a bit over this loss. And Albert has told them all the truth, which was good of him. He kind of had to, because now he's dating their other daughter."

"Teresa. Yes, she told me."

He shook his head. "Life is weird, Hana. And people are weird. But I'm still grateful for the beautiful parts of life."

"You're an artist. You'll always have an eye for beauty."

"And a soul for it."

I gave him a hug in the apartment hallway, and he moved toward the stairway. When I shut the door behind me again, I was thinking about Kodaly, and what Bruce had said about his involvement in the solving of the crime. One way or another, Kodaly had been a part of both murders which had occurred after his own death, nearly four months apart. Something in his paintings spoke to me, to others, and gave us insights we might not otherwise have had.

Was Will Kodaly's psychic ability something that he was able to translate to canvas? Had he imbued his beautiful paintings with a wisdom that could be "read" by those insightful enough to translate the message? He had suggested, while he was alive, that he had a sort of link to my family; other people, though, felt the magic he had left in his art. Runa, François, Bruce, my father and mother. Kodaly's one true love, and his son. What an amazing way to be immortal— through art, which transcended all—and what a beautiful way to connect with the living.

I stared at the street scene on my wall: Keszthely, Hungary. A brilliant blue sky full of pain and poetry; a colorful street of tilting houses and bustling people; a horse in a distant field; a dirt road edged with summer grasses, dotted with purple and white wildflowers. *Beauty is truth, truth beauty.*

The cats strolled up and bonked their heads into my legs. I bent to scratch their ears. "You guys are getting kind of fat," I said.

They ignored my rude comment, purring with loud contentment, and I laughed.

*

On the last day of April, my cast was removed, and I treated myself to some shopping in downtown Riverwood. I stopped in at Stones by Sparkle and greeted its proprietor. "Hana," she said. "How good to see you." There was something amused in her expression; I studied her for a moment before dismissing my rather paranoid assumption that she was laughing at me.

She walked around the store with me, showing me new baubles and shiny things that she had purchased for her spring line. Everything glinted attractively in the light. There were little children's bracelets with birthstones embedded into small silver hearts. I selected them for Iris and Jia (Amethyst and Topaz, respectively).

There were lovely silver rings with engravings like "love," "forever," and "family." I picked one up, struck by its simplicity. "You can get the inside engraved. The name of the person you love."

The first image that popped into my head was Andy Bell, saying "My daughter," to anyone who would listen. "Do you engrave them here?"

"Yup. I have an engraver in the back. Same font as you see there."

I had always been a creature of spontaneity, especially when it came to shopping. I handed her the love ring and said, "Can you engrave "Anya" inside? It's for a man; do you think this would fit?"

"It's adjustable," she assured me. "Just write down the spelling so that I get it right. Oh—you found my mother and child necklaces."

I had. On very thin, glittering gold chains hung a gold silhouette of a woman embracing a little child. In the center was a red, glittering heart that the two shared. I sighed. Runa, Andy, and Thyra all had more money than I did. So why did I always want to buy gifts for them?

Sparkle smiled her sympathy. "Hard to resist giving gifts, isn't it?"

"Yes, somehow. Okay, I'll take two of these. One for the mother, one for the aunt. They're twins. And the baby will belong to both of them, I'm sure."

Sparkle laughed and went off to engrave Andy's ring. "Just browse for a while—this won't take long."

I drifted up and down the aisles, looking at the various precious gems, the rings and necklaces that shimmered and sparkled, alluring in an inexplicable way.

Sparkle returned and showed me the ring. I knew, in a moment of smug confidence, that Andy would love it. I nodded and paid for all of my items. "Thanks so much, Sparkle. I'll see you around."

"All righty then," she said cheerfully.

When I left her store, I made my way to the florist. I wanted to treat myself to a vase of flowers, now that I could arrange them with both hands. Rania was there, seemingly unaware of her own lush beauty in a room of lovely blooms. She led me around the shop, showing me some new acquisitions. All the flowers were bright and fresh, from spring tulips to pungent lilies. Erik suggested that I was a traditionalist, and I proved him right when I said, "I think I'll choose roses." The Wolf sisters might find this mundane. They would probably order some exotic plant I'd never heard of for their spring tables. Katie would get the lilies, and Paige would probably go for varicoloured tulips. But my mother and my grandmother would share my instinct—they would get roses. I chose six creamy white roses and six raspberry pink, and she whipped them into a vibrant bouquet. "Rania," I said. "My boyfriend and I are going to have a housewarming party soon—we're buying a condo together—and I really think you'd hit it off with one of the guys who will be there. Would you like to come by?"

Her eyes widened with interest and what seemed to be excitement. "When? Tonight?"

I laughed. "No, in a few weeks. We're closing tomorrow, and then we need time to move in."

She picked up one of her business cards and jotted something on the back. "There's my cell. Text me the information—it sounds like fun."

I left soon after that, grinning. Perhaps I could start a new career as a matchmaker. Everyone was looking for love . . . my phone buzzed, and I saw a text from my mother. *We hung the painting!*

I replied that I was out in the car, and I would be stopping by. I was more than curious to see what they had chosen as the best spot for "Magdalena's Eyes." I reached my car and stowed my bouquet and my bag of jewelry in the back. My parents' house was about ten minutes away, and I drove sedately, enjoying the sunny day and the spring breeze that smelled of soil. I flexed my hands on the steering wheel, working through the stiffness.

I pulled up in front of their place minutes later, and my phone buzzed again. Erik, not texting, but calling.

"Hi," I said brightly.

"Hey, Babe." He sounded a bit distracted and out of breath. "Listen, we have to meet with Jon again tonight at the condo."

"What? But we gave him everything he needed, and he said we were all set a week ago!"

He sighed in my ear. Poor Erik had been handling most of the Real Estate issues while I convalesced, and I knew it had been an extra burden on top of his busy job. "I know. He says it won't take long. He says he'll meet us there at seven."

"Okay." I shrugged, even though he couldn't see me.

"I might be a little bit late, so can you dart up there at seven and just let him know I'll be there ASAP?"

This did not sound promising. "Well, *will* you be?"

"Scout's Honor. I already told my captain that I had an appointment I couldn't miss. Plus, for the promise of food,

Greg will do just about anything, like covering for me if I'm not finished with my paperwork."

I laughed. "All right. But don't make me have tons of awkward conversation with Ion."

That amused him. "I won't. How's the wrist? I can't wait to see it again. That cast was covering up a perfectly good erogenous zone."

"It's uncovered now, Lover." He chuckled in my ear, and a feather of desire tickled my interior. "And it's fine. A little stiff, so I'm flexing it a lot."

"Take it easy. I'll see you tonight, okay?"

"Jon, seven o'clock in the penthouse."

"Right. Later, then."

I ended the call smiling, as I always did when Erik was on the other end. I must have sat there with a dumb expression for longer than I thought, because a knock at the window had me jumping back into reality and recognizing my father's friendly face. I opened the window a crack and said, "Hey, Dad!"

"Hey." He grinned at me, a devilish twinkle in his eye. "Am I interrupting? You seemed to be doing some day-dreaming."

"Yes, okay. Haha. I'm getting out now."

I gave him a big hug right there on the street, and then we strolled to the front door together. "So, you're pretty happy with the painting where you've hung it?"

My father's face still held some of the euphoria that had lingered beyond his birthday party. "I'm thrilled with the painting in general, and we both think we've found the perfect spot."

Inside, my mother hovered, smiling in anticipation of their revelation. My gaze swept over the living room, but there was still a dried flower wreath above their fireplace mantel, and a large screen tv took up too much of the wall contiguous to the hearth.

"Okay, so where is it?" A sudden thought had me blushing. "You didn't hang it—in your bedroom, did you?"

My parents laughed. "Oh, Hana, you look fourteen again," my mother said.

Fourteen had been an awkward year.

"We thought about hanging it there," my father said. "But in the bedroom, I want to look in your mother's actual eyes."

That was a beautiful sentiment, but they made me uncomfortable, beaming at me while they talked about their bedroom. Maybe I *was* fourteen again. "Okay, anyway. Lead on."

We walked down a little hall, past my father's office, and to the "sun room," which had once been Domo's bedroom. It sat on the eastern side of the building, and had always gotten the most sun. Now it held a window full of potted plants, a cozy loveseat, a wooden table with two chairs, and a bookcase that covered an entire wall. The wall across from the loveseat had once held a framed poster of Budapest and the Danube that my mother had purchased at some Hungarian event. Now the poster was gone, and "Magdalena's Eyes" was the only adornment.

In the midday light, the painting nearly glowed. The image of my mother was different somehow; she still sat in the garden, but now it was Eden and she was radiant with joy. Her eyes dominated the painting the wall, the room. Beauty came alive in them.

"Wow," I said. "Perfect,"

My father put an arm around me. "Mom and I like to sit here on the little couch and read our books, and glance up at the painting whenever we wish."

"It's wonderful."

"We won't let the light hit it all the time. We don't want it to fade," my father assured me.

"I don't think he used paints that would fade easily. He was about quality, and longevity."

My parents nodded; their faces eager.

"Has Domo seen it?"

"He's coming by tonight," my mother said. "He and Margie. You can feel free to come back then --"

"No, I can't. I have a Real Estate thing."

"Sounds boring," she said, reading my face. "But you must be so excited about the new place."

"I am," I admitted. "And will be crazy with excitement once we finish the closing and they hand us our keys. I couldn't pack too much before, but look!"

I held up my wrist, and both of my parents shouted at once. My mother said, "Oh my goodness, you're cast free!" at the same time that my father said, "How could we forget?"

They both hugged me, and I enjoyed their warmth and attention for a while.

I guessed that a fair amount of my psyche was, in fact, fourteen again.

*

At six-fifty-five I closed the door of my dear little apartment and climbed the stairs to the floor above—the penthouse floor—where Erik and I would be living. The stairway door led to a little hallway, at the end of which was the apartment door. Jon had left it open a crack, so I pushed it inward and entered the large living area. There was no illumination in the main room, but a kitchen light shone at the end of the space, so I turned in that direction. "Hello!" I called. "Jon?" I heard a murmuring voice which told me that Jon was on the phone.

He was almost always on the phone. Fine, then—let him talk until Erik got here.

I moved farther into the room. Even in the dimness I could appreciate the polished shine of the wood floors, the lofty height of the timbered ceiling. It was such a beautiful space. A table sat in the middle of the room. Oh, no! Did we have to sign things? Wouldn't we do all that at the closing? Tiny lights flickered on the table. Candles! This was interesting. I grinned. Jon was going for something dramatic, celebrating our closing with us. And here I had thought he was just a dry businessman.

I walked to the table and bent down to see the four objects around which the candles glowed. They were framed photographs. I peered at the first one: it was a wedding picture. My heart lurched in surprise: it was my great-grandmother in the picture, along with her young husband. They had a short marriage, resulting in the birth of Juliana, my grandmother. She never met her father, who died in the Hungarian uprising of 1956. I had never seen this picture before. Had Erik given this to Jon? But where would Erik have gotten it?

"Jon?" I called. The voice told me that the call continued, and I heard the phrase 'earnest money'. The next picture was also a wedding portrait: the union of my grandmother and grandfather. The two of them held hands, beaming at the camera. The overall impression was one of relief. They had relaxed into a marriage to each other, something they had known as their destiny. When my grandmother first saw my grandfather, she said he looked like "a man walking out of a sunrise."

The third frame held my own parents' wedding picture. There were Magdalena's eyes again, but also Jack's beautiful smile. I thought that they were as happy now, if not happier, than they had been on that day.

The final frame was empty. Was this a puzzle? Was there some sort of home buyers' tradition that I didn't know about?

The voice had stopped. Darn it, Erik wasn't here yet. At least I had my first conversational topic for Jon: what the heck *is* all this?

I heard a rustling on my left, and I swung toward the sound, startled. No one stood beside me, but someone was there, speaking my name. . . .

Erik Wolf knelt on the polished wood floor, holding a velvet box. Inside was a ring that seemed to encompass the sun, the stars, the moon, the green of his eyes, the gold of his aura.

"Hana," he said again. "I want our picture to fill the fourth frame. I want to be a part of the tradition of Horvath women, and I want to be the man who loves you forever."

My eyes had filled at the first sight of him kneeling there, and now tears ran down my face unchecked. One tear fell on Erik's hand. "Hana Natalia Keller," he said, his own eyes glinting with unshed tears. "Will you marry me?"

I laughed, wiping at my wet face. "Yes, yes, if you'll marry me back!" I dropped to my knees and embraced him, and then we kissed each other. I couldn't seem to hold him close enough; he understood, and smiled while I pawed and grasped at him. Then I hesitated. "What about Jon?"

Erik laughed. "Jon isn't here. I lied to you to trick you into marriage."

I shook my head. "But I heard a voice --"

"That was Felix."

Felix appeared from the hallway adjoining the kitchen and bowed theatrically. "Congratulations, you two. Erik, I let everyone know."

"What?" I said, panic rising. "Who is everyone?"

Erik was briefly solemn. "I meant what I said. I want to marry you, and I want to be a part of your family. So, we should all celebrate together. Are you going to put on this ring?"

Dazed, I held out my left hand, and he slid the ring on my finger. It was beautiful. A large diamond nestled into a setting dotted with sapphires. "Ohhh," I breathed.

"Sparkle told me that April birthstone is the diamond. That seems fitting for an April engagement, too."

"Sparkle! I *thought* she was smirking at me!"

"She was very helpful. She said you would like this."

"I love it. I love *you*." I pulled his head toward me and kissed him, and Felix whisked past us to answer a pounding at the door.

Erik murmured against my mouth, "I was dying to ask you. But I wanted to wait until the cast was off so that I could slide the ring on your finger."

I managed to give him one more giant kiss before they came tumbling in like people emerging from a clown car: Andy, Runa, and Anya (now a Christmas ornament on Andy's chest instead of Felix's). Thyra and her boyfriend Rolf. My mother and father, Domo and Margie, my grandmother and grandfather. Paige, Paul, and their daughters; Aunt Luca and Jia. Katie and Eduardo, Marta and Magnus Wolf.

The lights went on, and people milled around, admiring the space, poking into the rooms, studying my ring. Jon had given Erik the key for this event, but had warned that no food or drink could be consumed in the apartment until after closing, so when everyone had received the grand tour and, in some cases, had taken pictures of us, of the table full of framed memories, of the crowd assembled, we went down a flight and crammed into my place, where François had put a blue cloth on my dining table, and at its center had placed a pale blue frosted froth of an engagement cake that was a work of art.

"François," I breathed. "It's glorious."

"Oui," he said, lighting the candles.

*

I managed to steal some moments to deliver my own gifts. Andy was first. I pulled him and the dangling Anya into a corner. Anya had fallen asleep, and was drooling slightly, but remained the loveliest baby I'd ever seen. Andy took the ring, and I pointed out the inscription. "Your left hand shows you love Runa. I thought your right hand could show your love for Anya."

Andy cried. He was a wonderful man, and a sensitive one. Runa came over, starting to make some joke about me having an affair with her husband, until she saw Andy's tears. "What is it?" she asked stiffly.

Andy showed her the ring. She looked at me in pleased surprise, and I handed her the necklace. "To commemorate your bond with your daughter."

Runa cried. Andy put an arm around her, and Thyra came over, ready to make a sarcastic comment. She stopped dead, and said, "What's going on here?"

I handed her the aunt necklace. "In honor of your devotion to Anya."

Thyra looked furious; then I realized that it was because she was trying to hold back tears. Then Thyra cried.

I laughed at the three of them and sad, "Look at all of you! Turned to mush because of a sweet little baby."

"Thank you, Hana." Andy kissed my cheek, and I felt Anya's soft hair touch the bottom of my chin. "We're always thanking you, aren't we?"

I shook my head. "Gestures of love, that's all."

I left them to compare their gifts and dote on the sleeping baby. I found Jia and Iris and pulled them to one side, as well. I showed them the bracelets and explained birthstones. They were interested and eager, and they asked me to help them put on the jewelry. "Now you match," I said.

Neither of them cried.

Paige appeared and admired the bracelets, then asked the girls if they had forgotten to say something to me.

"Is there a matching necklace?" Iris asked, with the honest desire of a child.

"Not just now," I said.

Then both girls thanked me very prettily and pranced into my bedroom to try to catch the cats.

An arm went around my shoulder, and I turned, smiling, to the tall blond man beside me. "No more fooling me now, Felix," I said. "I've got your scent, and I'll know when you're coming."

"Oh, darn!" he said. "I was hoping to get an offer of some Hana love."

Some people nearby laughed at his joke. Surely the whole world knew it by now. "Seriously, though, Hana. I'm glad you'll be my sister. And I'm glad you said yes to Erik. If you hadn't, I think he would have jumped from the penthouse roof."

I smiled. "That was never a danger. But thanks. I'm glad you're moving back to town and I can get to know you better."

Erik arrived with two pieces of François's cake. "Have some before the crowd devours it," he said. "Those little girls are on their seconds already. François is surprisingly lenient in the face of cuteness."

I took the cake and smiled at my new fiancé. I scanned the crowded room. Everyone was chatting happily, laughing, enjoying. Big loud Domo had for some reason lifted my mother off the ground, and she shouted, "Domo! Domo!" in a stern voice. My father came to rescue her, poking his son in the arm and saying something quiet that made Domo set her instantly on the ground. Good ol' Jack Keller. Now he and my mom would go home and sit on their love seat and stare at an artist's vision of her. They would hold hands and enjoy the quiet love that had always been theirs.

My grandmother appeared beside me, nodding.

"Hi, Grandma."

"You remember, when he mooned over you at the tea house, and you pretended not to see?"

"No, that never happened."

She laughed her mysterious laugh. "It did, and I had to encourage you to ask him out. You were so stubborn, Hana."

I turned to her, indignant. "As I recall, you were horrified by him because his name was Wolf."

"Only at first. I knew what was to come, in one sense."

I sighed. "I guess you probably did." I reached out and gave her a sudden fierce hug. "Thank you for pushing me in his direction."

Her embrace was equally fierce, loving, protective. "My Haniska," she said.

Felix strode up to us; like his sisters, he had little use for other people's personal space, and he didn't seem to notice that we were having a private moment. "Hey, Hana," he said. "Hey, Juliana." To my surprise he slipped a casual arm around my grandmother, and to my further surprise, she smiled.

Felix held out his phone. "I thought you'd like to see the photos I took of Erik prostrating himself at your feet. He said girls like those things."

I took the phone. "They also like not being called girls." My eyes dropped to the screen, where Erik and I, nicely candlelit and surprisingly close up – "I zoomed in!"—looked young and beautiful, our expressions earnest. My face was surprised, but happy. My hand had lifted to my heart, and he held out his box like a talisman that would protect us both. I scrolled through a few more similar pictures, and saw that in the final one we were embracing. Wordless, I handed the phone to my grandmother, who flicked through them with quick fingers.

"Very good, Felix. Good for the family album, to join Domo's proposal to Margie."

My grandfather materialized at my grandmother's side, and their hands linked. The gesture was as natural as breathing, and I don't think either of them consciously realized they had done it. He said something low in her ear, and then they were both hugging me and saying they had to go. Felix bent to kiss my grandma's cheek. When had they become such good friends?

I learned later that she had visited him in the hospital, and they'd had a big old chat. My grandmother never ceased to amaze me.

Felix and his siblings left not long after that. The Wolves came to embrace Erik and me, and we all chuckled at Anya, who was still sleeping and also making tiny baby snores.

Then they all drifted out, my friends and family, Katie warning me that we *would* have dinner soon, Paige holding a wide-awake Iris and Paul holding a Daisy who was so tired that she looked confused.

Finally, Erik and I flopped on the couch in a now-silent room, eating the last of the cake and listening to the cats who purred beside us.

"Thank you," I said. "It was perfect." I turned to him. *"You* are perfect."

"No." He smiled. "But perfect for you."

I nodded, then touched his face with a tender hand..

242

"And how did you happen to decide on today? Was it just because I got my cast off?"

"Yes and no. I didn't want us to move into that new place without putting that ring on your finger. I wanted you to see that my love is the permanent kind. And I wanted to know that you loved me back that way."

"I do." I lifted my ring and admired it in the lamplight. "This is truly beautiful. I won't want to wear it when I make dough and wash dishes and stuff like that."

His eyes closed. "Rings can be cleaned."

I snuggled against him, still admiring the ring as it glinted in the light, the way its many facets kept changing as it twinkled. It made me think of the complexities of my life: many friends, many family members, many events, many thoughts, many memories. Many moments.

"Haniska," Erik said.

"Yes?"

"How do you say *I Love You* in Hungarian?"

I licked some frosting from my finger. "*Szeretlek*. Why?"

"Because I love you in every language. But I should be able to say it in at least two. The ones that are important to you."

"*Szeretlek*," I whispered again.

And we sat together, for the last time like that, in the home where we had fallen in love. Outside, an April gust buffeted the window with its strenuous farewells. But Erik and I, tucked together and flanked by warm, rumbly cats, were contented and ready for whatever May would bring.

For just an instant, I thought I heard my great-grandmother Natalia's voice, happy and doting.

The voice said, "Blessings, Hana."

The End

About the Author

Julia Buckley is a Chicago-area mystery writer. She has written four series with Penguin/Random House and several stand-alone mysteries. She is half Hungarian, and her own grandmother called her "Juliska." She lives with her husband, Jeff Buckley, a Black Lab named Digby, and four spoiled cats named Daphne, Peach, Ash, and Panther.

If you liked this mystery, check out the other **Hungarian Tea House** mysteries:

Death in a Budapest Butterfly
Death of a Wandering Wolf
Death on the Night of Lost Lizards

Or check out her other series:

The Writer's Apprentice

A Dark and Stormy Murder
Death in Dark Blue
A Dark and Twisting Path
Death Waits in the Dark
Death With a Dark Red Rose
A Dark and Silent Night (e-book novella)
Death Through a Dark Green Glass
A Dark and Starlit Sea (coming soon)

Dinner and a Murder (The Castle Series)

Death in Castle Dark
Castle Deadly, Castle Deep
(Book Three Coming This Year!)

The Undercover Dish

The Big Chili
Cheddar Off Dead
Pudding Up With Murder
A Fatal Fettucine

Made in the USA
Las Vegas, NV
24 May 2025

22641514R00152